CONFESSIONS O

The ride ended before the portals of a large mansion in a quiet street and shortly thereafter I was ushered into my new home. It was a place of quiet elegance soft plush carpets and tapestried walls. I gazed about in wonder. There was nothing visible to the eye to mark these circumspectly luxurious premises as an atelier of prostitution, but I was soon to learn that things are not always as they seem, and that within these sedate walls dramas of licentiousness such as I had never seen were of nightly occurrence.

And thus did I cross the threshold of a new life, and the doors of the past closed behind me.

CONFESSIONS OF AN ENGLISH MAID

&

THE AMATORY EXPERIENCES OF A SURGEON

Anonymous

NEXUS

Published in 1986 by
Nexus Books
Sekforde House
175–179 St. John Street
London, EC1V 4LL

Reprinted 1988
Reprinted 1989

Phototypeset by Input Typesetting Ltd, London
Printed in Great Britain by
Cox & Wyman Ltd, Reading

ISBN 0 352 31788 4

CONFESSIONS
OF AN ENGLISH MAID

CHAPTER ONE

During the course of the years in which I have been more or less closely associated with other prostitutes, I have frequently listened to explanations as to just what this one or that owed her degradation; the particular villainy to which she attributed her advent into a life of shame. The usual story is one of seduction by a lover under the inevitable extenuating circumstance of 'before I really knew anything,' with the occasional variation, 'he put something in my drink, and when I came to . . . ' or, 'he was stronger than I was and I couldn't do anything.' In these glib stories, in which none but the inconsequential details vary, the man is always to blame and the girl is never a willing accomplice. She is always, by artifice, force or deception, and subsequent abandonment, the victim of some man's depravity.

I confess that I have listened to these tales and even witnessed a few tears of self-pity, with a certain amount of scepticism. In thinking back over my own life I can find nothing which would serve as a valid excuse to shift upon somebody else the responsibility of my own condition, nor can I, in justice accuse any man of having instigated my moral degradation, although the number of those who have taken advantage of my voluntary delinquency is legion. True, were I to hyprocritically search for some contributing factor with which to justify myself in my own mind or in the minds of others, I might place some blame upon the environment under which I was raised as a child, yet, a conscientious analysis of my subsequent life leads me to no other conclusions than that had these conditions been entirely normal I would still, just as water seeks its level, have drifted into a life analogous to that in which you find me.

I do not believe that character is made by environment or training. I am something of a fatalist and it is my conviction that the seeds of goodness or badness, kindness or malevolence, virtue or viciousness, are implanted in the soul right from the beginning, and while some slight modifications either for better or for worse may be possible under varying circumstances, the net result will not be greatly changed.

In my childhood days I knew two brothers, sons of affluent parents highly respected in the community. These two boys were raised under the most favourable home and moral environment possible to imagine. The elder, always the personification of honour and circumspection, occupies a position of trust high in the affairs of the nation. The younger child of the same parents, raised under exactly the same conditions and influences, early in life manifested all the characteristics of an irresponsible nature and is today being sought for his participation in a robbery which culminated in murder. I know of other such instances.

I was eight and Rene, my foster brother, ten when mutual curiosity about each other's little sexual attributes first began to take the form of childish efforts to unravel Nature's mysteries. These efforts, which at first did not pass much beyond the observational stage, with an occasional touching and fingering, were inspired more by curiosity than sexual promptings; nevertheless, we sensed more elements of forbidden fruit and exercised considerable caution in hiding

6

ourselves when the impulse was upon us to gratify our curiosity.

Under the roof of our home was an attic which was used as a sort of storeroom for discarded furniture and other odds and ends. Rene and I converted it into a species of playhouse. Access to this attic was gained by a steep and narrow stairway enclosed between dark walls, and our parents rarely climbed these stairs, and would have given us ample warning by their footsteps had it occurred to them to do so; we felt reasonably secure, and always repaired to this obscure hideaway when the mood to do something naughty was upon us.

Mamma Agnes was not my real mother. My own mother had died when I was four years old. With the practical philosophy of a widower left with a small child on his hands, Papa lost no time in acquiring a new wife, and in less than six months I had a mamma and a stepbrother two years older than myself.

I lay neither censure nor praise at the feet of Mamma Agnes. She was kind to me in an indifferent way and I believe she cared as much for me as she did for her own child, Rene. She was simply not the maternal type, and though she accepted the material obligations which our presence represented uncomplainingly and kept us clean and well fed, there existed an almost complete absence of anything in the nature of moral or spiritual upbringing. We were punished occasionally, but only when our misbehaviour constituted an annoyance to others.

Rene and I slept in the same bed but when I was about ten I remember hearing Papa tell Mamma Agnes that we were too big to be sleeping together. Mamma Agnes made some protest which I didn't understand, but the next night a bed was arranged for Rene in another room and thereafter we slept apart. I missed

7

feeling Rene's warm little body close to mine in the night and wanted to know why we were not to sleep together anymore. Mamma Agnes made an evasive explanation. 'It isn't nice for boys and girls to sleep together,' was the tactless reply which only served to kindle the restless fires of curiosity. During the next year or two some light, still of an obscure nature, was thrown on the subject by other children who were not averse to sharing their knowledge with us.

I was not supposed to see Rene's dickey, and he likewise was not supposed to see my cunny. This was the sum and substance, apparently, of the incomprehensible order of things which had abruptly terminated our bedfellowship. And immediately we both began to feel the itch to see what we were not supposed to see, and to which we had paid but scant attention when the opportunity had been freely at hand and unforbidden.

The juvenile soul thirsts for knowledge—of a certain kind. What was the real basis of all this sly mystery about little boys' dickies and little girls' cunnies? 'A boy puts his dickey in a girls cunny,' said one. 'That's the way you get babies, only you can't have a baby until you're married.' 'When you rub your cunny it gives you a nice feeling,' said another.

In the security of our attic hideaway Rene and I diligently sought the answer to the mystery. We dragged an ancient mattress from behind an accumulation of wrecked furniture and laid it out on the floor. I straddled out on this mattress with my legs apart while Rene looked and fingered until his curiosity was temporarily satisfied and I was compensated by being permitted to look at and squeeze his little dickey. It was a source of never-ending wonder to watch it go through its erotic evolutions, expanding, swelling, hardening, until it projected stiffly and rigidly

8

forward. I tried to see whether, by holding it tightly in my fist, I could prevent it from getting big, but in my grasp it seemed to grow even faster, easily displacing my clenched fingers and causing me curious, shivery sensations.

This playing, looking and fingering were pleasant, but there was something lacking, something sweet, something elusive which we sensed was close at hand but which still eluded us.

Picture to yourself a group of twenty happy, care-free youngsters of both sexes, their strident little voices ringing out in careless abandon as they pursue their innocent amusements, converting a refuse-strewn lot into an enchanted fairyland. Even the bloated loafers and derelicts of the street who cast a casual glance at the little innocents must not fail to feel a twinge of sentimentality.

> London Bridge is falling down,
> Falling down, falling down,
> London Bridge is falling down,
> My fair lay-dee.

But, hark! There is more to the song. The shriller masculine voices take the ascendancy, and little girls are heard only in a confusion of laughter and giggling.

> Madge and Jerry are having a suck,
> Having a suck, having a suck,
> Madge and Jerry are having a suck,
> My fair lay-dee.
> After the suck they'll have a fuck,
> Oh, what luck, oh, what luck.
> After the suck, they'll have a fuck,
> My fair lay-dee.

Out of a house whose open windows are in close proximity to the merrymakers bursts an old Irish woman, brandishing a broom, her wrinkled face suffused with rage.

'Git out o'here ye narsty little spalpeens or I'll swab yer dirty, stinkin' mouths fer ye, blarsted little imps o'Satan!' she screams as twenty pair of feet fly in twenty different directions under the menace of the broom in the hands of the scandalized old beldame.

When I was about fifteen a neighbourhood scandal was bruited about among the residents of the vicinity. Down the street, in the big house on the corner, lived a retired sea captain and his rather large family. They were rated as well-to-do and employed a maid-servant, a cute little thing whose trim, silk-clad legs, black uniform and lace-edged apron I had always secretly envied.

Among the younger children of his household was a boy named Leonard and a girl named Maisie. Leonard was about the same age as Rene, but was undersized and wore glasses which gave his wizened countenance a peculiarly owlish aspect. Maisie was very pretty. She was two years older than I. Both these children were precocious. It was said that Maisie would show her cunny to any boy who wanted to see it and Leonard bragged that he fucked the maidservant whenever he felt like it. There was some doubt as to the veracity of this, but the doubt was dispelled abruptly when the maidservant suddenly disappeared and the older children of the household whispered into the ears of their special confidants that she had been summarily dismissed after having been caught in the very act of sucking Leonard's dickey while supposed to be supervising his bath.

'She had it right in her mouth when Mamma caught her!' they whispered impressively.

Rene pressed Leonard for details when the opportunity later presented itself, and listened to an entirely frank exposition of the affair, which he then communicated to me.

The liaison with the maidservant had been started several months previously by the versatile little maid herself. Each night, on tucking him into bed, she had been in the habit of putting her hand under the covers to see whether he had a hard-on. Inasmuch as such was almost invariably the case, and the condition not being favourable in her opinion to sound sleep, her remedy was to reduce the rigidity by means of a hand message to make it 'lie down and go to sleep.'

One night she told Leonard that her efforts to make him sleepy were having a contrary effect on her and that she couldn't go to sleep for hours after having put him to sleep. There was a way both could have their sleeplessness cured. She would slip into his room later that night after everybody was in bed and explain it to him. She squeezed his dickey to make sure it was in its usual state of erection but refrained from taking the customary measures to make it lie down.

When all was quiet in the household she slipped into his room like a little ghost in her white nightgown, threw the covers back and lay down by him. Taking his dickey in one hand she worked it until it was in its maximum state of rigidity. With the other she guided his fingers between her legs and with various motions and whispered instructions showed him how to reciprocate the massage.

'Her cunny has hair all around it.' confided Leonard.

After a while she stopped the rubbing and told him to get on top of her. When he was in the proper position she started his dickey in the right direction and, poppo! It went, inside, just like that.

At this juncture in the recital, Rene interrupted to clear up a confusing point. Had Leonard's dickey gone clear in, or had it just sort of rubbed along her cunny?

Emphatically, it had gone in, entirely and completely, not a bit stayed outside. He was sure and specific on this point. It was dark that time, but they had done it subsequently in the daytime when he could even look down and see it while it was going in and out, and it absolutely went clear in.

The story of Leonard's relation with the maid-servant progressed from frigging to fucking and finally to the last act, in which the unexpected entry of his mother into the bathroom while he was enjoying, and not for the first time, the delights of being sucked off by the versatile maid had brought an end to the fun.

Now the maid was gone and he was obliged to massage his dickey for himself at night in order to make it lie down and go to sleep.

The sucking part was rather incomprehensible to Rene and me. We were still rank novices in the arts of love and had much to learn. It was a cause of preoccupation to us that we hadn't been able to approximate anything like the success Leonard and the maidservant had achieved. Rene's dickey simply couldn't find its way in. We knew in theory that it should, and we had both peered and looked and fingered in an effort to find a hole big enough. There didn't seem to be any, or if there was, it was closed up very tightly.

With the candidness of youth Rene confided the difficulty to Leonard and Leonard promptly offered to show him how to do it. I never objected to anything Rene proposed, and submitted myself obediently to the demonstration. Leonard knew no more about maidenheads than Rene but he had the confidence which comes with experience and when I took off my panties and lay down on the mattress he placed himself between my knees and got his dickey which, despite his slighter stature, was fully as big as Rene's, against my cunny. He gave a lunge, and a shriek escaped my lips which, had there been anyone else in the house at the time, would have brought an investigation. His dickey had gone in all right, but the sensation I experienced was far from being conducive to further experimentation. After the first shriek of pain I began to cry, the tears rolled down my cheeks and I struggled to release myself.

Panic-stricken at the unexpected results, Leonard jerked away from me and his dickey came out stained with a reddish fluid and a few drops trickled down the inside of my thighs. Leonard was so frightened that he fled from the scene, leaving Rene and me alone.

The pain was only momentary and as it died away I stopped crying, but gazed with fright at the spots of blood which stained the white flesh between my thighs. Rene dabbed at them nervously with his handkerchief, and when no more appeared some of our assurance returned, but I was aggrieved because of the stab of pain I had suffered. When I stood up a feeling of soreness in my sexual parts was very pronounced. Fortunately, Mamma Agnes made no embarrassing inquiries when she found me in bed at an hour much earlier than my accustomed one, and by the following day the soreness had mostly passed away.

Thus I lost my maidenhead with pleasure neither to myself nor to my violator.

Having my hymen punched out in so disagreeable a manner without knowing exactly what had happened except that it was something decidedly unpleasant resulted in a reluctance on my part to lend myself to further exploitations which lasted for some weeks and might have endured longer had not my emotions been stimulated anew by a curious incident.

While rummaging through a pile of trash, old newspapers and discarded magazines which had been swept out of a long-vacant house nearby, Rene found a little green-covered book which, on being opened, disclosed to his startled eyes a picture which confirmed the basic theory of love. It was a rather neatly executed sketch showing a beautiful young lady reclining upon a grassy mound under a tree. Her dresses were drawn up, she had no panties on, and above the edge of her disordered and half-open bodice peeped a pair of bubbies of most astonishing proportions.

Between her thighs, half-lying, half-kneeling, with one of her silk clad legs thrown over his hips, was a young boy. From his middle projected a dickey which penetrated and was lost to sight for half its length in her cunny, the protruding lips of which were plainly indicated just below a profusion of curly black hair.

As soon as he recovered from the shock this picture caused him, Rene streaked for home and excitedly signalled for me to follow him to the attic. Breathlessly we gazed at the picture, then turned our attention to the text which accompanied it. As we devoured the printed pages I became aware of that moist, swollen, itchy feeling in my cunny. The desire to experience anew the delicious sensations the tip of Rene's dickey had afforded me began to surge through me and grow more and more insistent as we slowly digested the revelations contained in the booklet and which were phrased quite within our powers of comprehension.

The title which graced the story was: 'The Passionate Governess, or Hubert's First Fuck.' Before that book finally left our possession we had read it so many times either of us could have recited it word for word by memory.

It was about a beautiful young governess in a wealthy home who entered into amorous adventures with one of her charges. Hubert, a boy of sixteen. After a number of tantalizing episodes, in one of which she catches Hubert peeking through the keyhole and masturbating himself while she is bathing, she decided to gratify his curiosity and save him from the vice of masturbation by letting him have sexual intercourse with her.

The scene chosen for the sweet lesson in love is a beautiful sylvan glade reached by crossing a lake in a rowboat. As the pretty governess sits in the prow of the boat with Hubert at the oars facing her, she carelessly permits her skirts to become so elevated above her knees that Hubert is afforded a delightful opportunity to peek between her legs and get teasing glimpses of the charms only half concealed under the frilly lace of her panties. Under the stimulation of this enticing sight he is in a suitable condition for his initiation in the rites of love.

After exciting preliminaries in which passionate kisses, caresses and fondling of each other's sexual parts are indulged in, and during which Hubert's curiosity regarding the more intimate aspects of feminine anatomy is completely satisfied, the real initiation takes place as shown in the illustration, and Hubert learns that the delights attendant to plunging his dickey into the mossy glen between a pretty girl's legs are far superior to those he had formerly experienced in masturbation.

It was a story with a moral, as you will have observed, intended to discourage young people from practicing self-abuse.

When we had finished the last page I felt moist and

15

sticky and it seemed to me that my panties were wet. Rene's trousers were jutted out in front in a way which showed what effect the story had had on him.

He looked at me, and I looked at him.

'Shall we?' he whispered.

'Yes!' I answered, all recollection of the pain I had suffered the last time this attic had been used for purposes of fornication completely obliterated.

While Rene was unfastening his trousers I kicked off my panties and lay down on the soft mattress. My emotions had been greatly excited by the vivid little story and the first touches of Rene's dickey against the moist flesh of my cunny were indescribably sweet. For a few moments I lay there languidly thrilling to the soft friction and pressure as the tip of his dickey roved about over the sensitive area like a person groping for a door in the dark. But suddenly I stiffened in alarm for I distinctly felt the constriction which accompanied an actual penetration and which brought back to my consciousness what had happened before.

With muscles tensed in readiness to free myself with the first indication of pain I held my breath and waited. But there was no pain. To the contrary, the sensations I felt as Rene's dickey slipped further into the tight little hole were more agreeable than anything I had yet experienced.

I moaned, not with pain this time, but with delight, and the next moment, actuated by those natural instincts which need no previous experience nor teacher to guide, we were both frantically heaving our bottoms up and down in an effort to taste without delay the supreme delight of which the intoxicating thrills now tantalizing us were but the forerunners.

It comes but once in a lifetime, that indescribable, celestial glow which suffuses the souls and blends the bodies of lovers in unforgettable rapture, the first perfect sexual union of two beings who feel toward each other the tender passion of youth unmarred as yet by maturity's grosser complexities, and I affirm that those who have not tasted the fruit of love under these conditions have missed what is probably life's sweetest experience.

Rene and I had finally succeeded in unlocking the door which had hitherto obstructed our progress and with the unlocking, the latent germs of sensuousness, undoubtedly implanted in my very soul, sprang rapidly to full bloom. My ardour exceeded his, and it was I who now suggested and even begged frequent visits to the dusty attic where, with my panties off and my dress up or entirely removed, I writhed and suspired ecstatically in response to his vigorous thrusts. And, after a delicious orgasm had rewarded our efforts, I sighed inwardly with regret at the inevitable transformation his cock underwent, dropping slowly but surely downward, its virile rigidity degenerating into a flaccid inertia which incapacitated it from further immediate use.

CHAPTER TWO

We now had plenty of time to be alone. Mamma
Agnes was working with the result that we had several
hours at our disposal between the time school was
over and the hour at which she returned.

One day while we were standing on the pavement
in front of the house Leonard appeared. Leonard,
being entirely in Rene's confidence, had been
appraised of the new state of affairs. He had intimated
that he would like to try it again with me, which
intimation I had listened to with no great enthusiasm,
not through chaste reluctance, but because of the still
lingering recollection of what had happened the first
time.

I was still in ignorance of the exact physical facts
and blamed him for the pain I had suffered. After
some desultory conversation the enterprising Leonard
suggested that the three of us proceed to the attic and
have a hoochy dance. If you are familiar with juvenile
parlance you may know that a hoochy dance is a
simple but interesting form of entertainment in which
the participants take off their clothes or 'get naked'
as they express it, and either with hands joined or
independently, will jump and cavort in a circle in a
sort of primitive dance.

The element of attraction in this otherwise inspired
diversion being that the boys can look at the girl's
cunny and the girl can look at the boys' dickies. 'And
. . .' continued Leonard, after contributing this

suggestion for a pleasant manner in which to pass the afternoon '. . . afterwards, you can fuck Jessie and I'll look, and then I'll fuck her and you can look.'

As for me I was entirely agreeable to the first part of the programme, and open to acceptance on the latter. It was Rene who interposed the logical objection that three of us weren't enough to properly stage a hoochy dance and we set to speculating as to the possibility of getting additional recruits. A hurried inventory of acceptable prospects only brought to light that this one was not at home, that one was sick, and another being 'kept in' as a disciplinary measure, etc. It seemed there was little hope of rounding out the party on short notice and as a last recourse, Leonard rather apologetically suggested that maybe we'd be satisfied with Maisie.

This was a thought. Maisie had never participated in any of our doings, nevertheless, Maisie had earned quite a reputation of her own and Leonard made no secret of the fact that before his ideas had been broadened by the vanished maidservant he had often diddled his sister. He looked on hopefully while Rene studied the suggestion.

'Can you find her?' queried Rene.

'Sure I can, if you'll wait for me!' responded Leonard.

'Well, all right, then. Hurry up!'

In less than five minutes Leonard was back with Maisie in tow. She was a beautiful little thing and her eyes were shining with elation at the idea of being permitted to participate in our secrets.

'Now we're going to have a hoochy dance in our attic,' explained Rene, addressing her. 'If we let you come, you won't tell, will you?'

'No, no! I won't tell, ever!' she exclaimed

vehemently. 'I'm not a tattletale, am I, Lenny?' she added, turning to her brother for corroboration.

'No, she won't tell. She knows bloody well we'll knock her block off if she does!' responded Leonard with menacing emphasis.

Up to the attic we trooped and with much giggling and laughter began to undress. True to the usual formula of feminine hypocrisy, Masie and I both made a great show of being concerned about the boys seeing us before we were 'ready' and chided them hysterically for peeking while we were undressing.

This incitation had its natural effect upon the two boys and when we finally faced them, every stitch of clothing removed from our white bodies, their cocks were standing out in stiff and rigid excitation.

We dragged the mattress to one side and, joining hands, began our hoochy dance, which consisted of nothing more complicated than swinging around in a circle and jumping up and down to the accompaniment of some ribald verses which we repeated over and over while the feminine eyes of the contiguity were fixed on jiggling dickies which bounced up and down with the violent movements of their owners, and the masculine ones on fat-lipped cunnies.

When we had finally exhausted our acrobatic and musical repertoire we sat down, breathless, to rest and devise further exploits. Leonard wanted to fuck me while Rene and Maisie looked on, and then have the arrangement reversed with him and me the spectators while Rene fucked Maisie.

I protested that it hurt with him and expressed a preference to do it with Rene. My protest was partly actuated by something akin to jealousy. Somehow, I didn't exactly relish the idea of Rene fucking Maisie. But Rene intervened, and his word was law. It wouldn't hurt me now if I did it with Leonard. I was used to it now.

And so, with Leonard crouched on one side and I on the other, both watching with wide eyes, my foster brother Rene straddled Maisie's naked body, got his cock into a crevice which fitted around it like a tight little ring of flesh and, without a mishap or indication of discomfort on her part, fucked her until he had an orgasm.

Maisie never stirred or made a sound. She just lay there quietly, looking up into his face with her big, wondering eyes until he had finished and then calmly wriggled out from under him, sat up and murmured:

'Now it's our turn to watch!'

'Didn't it make you feel nice, Maisie?' I asked in some astonishment at her placidity. 'When Rene and I do it, I just tremble all over, it makes me feel so good!'

'Sure, it makes me feel nice, I like to do it!' affirmed Maisie, but it was apparent that she had not yet experienced a real orgasm, even though Leonard had long since removed her maidenhead.

With some inward misgivings I submitted to Leonard's ministrations and, of course, quickly discovered that my fears were groundless, for his dickey was in almost before I knew it, and this time without causing me any pain. Not counting Leonard's previous attempt, this was the first time I had been really fucked by any boy except Rene and, despite my affection for him, the novelty of a new cock had its emotional reaction and very quickly brought my quivering organism to that delicious borderland wherein for a few seconds the senses vibrate in ecstatic anticipation before definitely rendering their delicious offering. Another wiggle or two served to precipitate the ejaculation.

21

A few days later, on the way home from school, a boy named Bryan sidled up to me and rather timidly asked me if I would do it with him.

Bryan was a boy I would have described as nice. He always dressed very neatly, had a pleasing personality and agreeable features. To say that I was not surprised at the overture would be an exaggeration, yet I was not displeased. If I had any doubts as to precisely what he meant by 'do it' with him, the doubt was dispelled with one look into his flushed fact and averted eyes and the uneasy, furtive glances he cast about as though to assure himself that there was no one else within hearing. Nevertheless, to delay an answer until I could gather my confused thoughts, I murmured innocently:

'Do what with you?'

'Aw, you know what I mean, Jessie!

'No, I don't!'

'Something nice . . . like you did with Lenny Connors!'

His reference to Leonard caused me a slight chill of apprehension, but did not entirely prejudice me against him. He continued to coax, and I, beginning to enjoy the thrill of being begged for something with such humility, neither definitely denied nor promised my complacency.

'Where could we go to do it?' I asked evasively.

His answer to this revealed the fact that he was well informed regarding my private life and affairs.

'Couldn't we go up to your attic before your mamma comes home?' he suggested hopefully.

This was something Rene would have to be consulted on, so I evaded a direct answer by saying I'd tell him the next day, and with that I skipped off.

'Bryan wants to do it with me. Shall I let him?' I asked Rene.

22

'Bryan? Bryan who?'

'Bryan Thompson, that boy that lives over on Little Goose Neck Road.'

Rene considered the matter for a moment and deciding apparently that it was of insufficient importance to trouble his head over, disclaimed responsibility with an indifferent shrug.

'Oh, I don't know. Do what you want. What do I care?'

'He knows about Leonard and me. I bet Maisie. . . .'

'You'd better do it with him so he won't tell. I've got to go now and see a chap. Goodbye.'

And so it came about that Bryan's name was added to my now growing list of youthful paramours. He was bigger than Rene or Leonard, and had a growth of dark, crisp hair on his pubic regions. He hurt me a little, but he was careful and despite the slightly painful distension I soon began to feel the warm, sensuous tremors which precede orgasm. His slow, cautious thrusts brought my organism to a pitch of excitation such as I had not yet experienced, and when the climax came I almost fainted with the intensity of the ecstasy. Afterwards, he showed me where my fingernails had actually cut into his flesh while I was hugging him in the crisis. He was a very gentlemanly fellow and thanked me in the most courteous and serious manner imaginable for having let him do it to me. In addition, he made me glow happily by telling me that I had the prettiest legs of any girl he had ever seen. Bryan had the makings of a real courtier.

Before long my popularity was spreading and new suitors for my favours were appearing almost magically. Sometimes even young men I did not know accosted me in the streets, some humbly and supplicatingly, and others quite impertinently.

Instead of being alarmed at this situation I took it as a flattering indication of my popularity. And, inevitably, I discovered that the soft nest between my legs, upon which grew a filmy growth of silky hair, could be made to hatch financial rewards as well as genetic pleasures.

That some horrible fate did not overtake me as the result of my complacency with utter strangers is only proof of the old, old theory that guardian angels look after the safety of the young, sometimes, at least.

Once I made an appointment with a man to meet him at a certain corner after dark, expecting to be taken to a room. He led me into an alley of such sinister and abandoned aspects that I did indeed become alarmed and refused to go any further. For a while he tried to persuade me with flattering words and promises of generous compensation, but the more he talked, the more uneasy I became, and finally, cursing me viciously, he turned away and quickly disappeared.

One night a young man of genteel but delicate physical features accosted me in terms so respectful and courteous that I listened to his insinuations and consented to accompany him to his room which, though far from pretentious, was neatly and comfortably furnished.

I had long since discovered that men's first thoughts were to see me naked as quickly as possible; they seemed literally burning to gorge their eyes with the spectacle of my nudity, so as soon as I was in the privacy of a room I always undressed down to my hose and slippers without waiting to be asked.

No sooner was the door closed behind us in this instance that I started to take off my clothes. But the young man stopped me with a gesture.

'No, no!' he exclaimed, 'don't undress!'

24

I paused uncertainly.

'I've got to take off my clothes . . . my panties anyway . . . don't you want to see me naked?'

'No, no! Don't take off anything! I'll tell you what to do, don't do anything except just what I tell you. You'll get your money.

'But . . . but what do you want me to do?'

'I'll show you. Just sit down and wait. I'll be back in a minute.'

I sat down in the chair he indicated and he disappeared into an adjoining room, closing the door behind him. I heard him moving about, and five minutes later he appeared again, stark naked. He was rather thin, but his skin was white and clean. His cock, entirely indifferent to the proximity of a feminine spectator, hung down inert and listless.

Crossing the room he unlocked a cabinet and took from it a bundle of thin, pliant switches. Selecting one of these he extended it toward me and murmured in a voice which was both low and supplicating:

'Take this switch and whip me as hard as you can.'

I gazed at him mute with stupefaction.

'Come!' he urged, putting the switch in my hand.

'You're joking!' I managed to exclaim. 'What do you want me to whip you for?'

'Oh, don't waste time asking questions! Do as I ask and you'll get your money!'

I saw that he was in earnest and, thinking that I had to deal with a crazy man whom it would be best to humour, dazedly got to my feet clutching the switch which he had placed in my hand.

'Whip me as hard as you can!' he whispered huskily, indicating the cheeks of his bottom with a gesture.

Fearfully, I drew back the slender birch and brought it forward against his flesh with a smart thwack.

'Harder!' he said, 'as hard as you can!'

I repeated the blow, with greater force.

'Keep on! Don't stop! Don't be afraid!'

In obedience to this exhortation I struck him several more blows in succession.

'That's the way . . . only harder!' he exclaimed.

Again I drew the birch back and this time it fairly whistled through the air as it rained stinging cuts over his thighs and buttocks. In its wake livid crisscross lines began to appear on the white flesh. As I saw these marks developing under my blows a curious sensation began creeping up through my own body. A sort of fury took possession of me and instead of feeling sorry for the pain I was inflicting I felt an urge to increase his torment. My face was hot and my heart beat violently. I clenched my teeth and put all the strength I possessed behind the swishing birch.

He stood there rigidly, his eyes glassy, distended, an ecstatic expression on his face. And then I noticed something else. His cock, which had at first been hanging lifelessly down, was coming into a slow erection. It was expanding in size and jerking convulsively at short intervals and with each jerk it lifted itself upward a little higher.

I watched it with fascinated eyes and as it slowly assumed its maximum of rigidity and erection the first shiver of something akin to lewd voluptuousness kindled within me. I comprehended that in some manner there was a relation between the whipping I was inflicting on him and my own obscure, erotic reaction, and I tried to increase the severity of my blows.

'Enough!' he gasped suddenly, and snatching the whip from me he flung it across the room. 'Now! Frig me quick!' And he seized my hand and placed it upon his cock.

I was now in a state in which I would have welcomed a reciprocal caress, even masturbation, but I dared not disobey him. Supporting his testicles with one hand I pumped his cock frenziedly with the other and before I had made a dozen passes his seminal fluid was spurting from my fist in copious jets.

For this service, my first experience in the realms of abnormal sexual practices, the young man presented me with ten shillings and I went home marvelling, not only at his curious eccentricity, but at the peculiar sensations I myself had experienced while occupied with the weird business.

My moral status was now pretty well established in the neighbourhood in which I had lived since infancy. The echoes from shrewish tongues to the effect that 'something should be done' had reached my ears on more than one occasion. I had not been able to conceal my occasional financial affluence from Mamma Agnes who had taken note of mysteriously acquired bits of finery and articles of personal adornment which could not be readily accounted for. Her comments, at first veiled, became more cynical as time went on. Her well-founded suspicions were justified when, returning one afternoon at an hour much earlier than the usual one, she opened a door which Rene and I, grown careless with respect to elementary precautions, had left unlocked.

When we first saw her she was swaying tipsily in the open door. Tipsy, yes, but not too tipsy to realize the significance of the picture which confronted her. I, my breasts still heaving under the stimulation of an orgasm just effected, lying on the bed with my panties off and the rest of my clothing in guilty disarray, and Rene, his pants unbuttoned in front and his still rigid cock projecting therefrom as he reached for a towel to wipe it off in the precise moment in which the movement of the door attracted our attention.

There was a dull minute of silence; silence frozen and absolute except for the imperturbable ticking of the small china clock on the dresser. Raising her hands in front of her with the palms outward in a gesture of renunciation, Mamma Agnes murmured thickly:

'I war-r-shh me hands of the pair of ye!'

And she closed the door upon us, leaving Rene and me to stare at each other in blank dismay.

'Sis! Why didn't you latch the door?' exclaimed Rene when the sound of her footsteps had died away.

'Why didn't you?' I countered weakly.

From this time on Mamma Agnes maintained a stoney indifference toward me, speaking only when unavoidable, and then with caustic brevity.

One Saturday morning about a month later, as I was returning to the house after having spent the afternoon with a girl friend, a young man passed me in the street. His glance, as it appraisingly flitted over my face and body, conveyed the message I had learned to recognize and in a brief moment of passing I was able to observe that in addition to a handsome appearance, he was more than commonly well-dressed. The immaculate linen and modish cut of his clothes, together with an expensive topcoat, suggested money, of which at that moment I had none, and I had seen in a store that very day a pair of high-heeled slippers of irresistible appeal.

I slowed my steps and paused before a shop window. I was not mistaken in my anticipations, for he was quickly at my side, murmuring seductive blandishments in my car.

Up to a certain point my knowledge of what transpired subsequently is quite clear, but beyond that only incoherent and fragmentary recollection remains.

There was a long ride in a cab which took us into a distant section of the city unfamiliar to me, a luxurious residence into which we were received by a uniformed domestic who bowed servilely to each curt order from the young man who accompanied me. I had made a conquest this time which far outshone any previous adventure. All this stands out vividly in my memory, together with the beautiful and costly furnishings of the rooms to which I was conducted, the rich, red wine I drank from a sparkling crystal goblet and which sent the blood coursing through my veins, filling me with a delicious languor as I sat naked on my companion's knees while his hands and lips caressed my body, lips which tugged and sucked at the little nipples of my breasts causing them to puff up excitedly and send delicious radiations vibrating through me, soft, well-kept hands with delicate fingers whose exquisite titillations between my yielding legs evoked other delicious ecstasies.

Another goblet of ruby-red wine, two, maybe three, and the recollection begins to dim, with only an occasional flash reacting upon my memory; a bed, wonderfully soft and warm and yielding, silken covers which caressed my naked body like the touch of feathers, oblivion, and then a return to semiconsciousness and an indifferent realization of the fact that I was being fucked, another period of darkness and again the awareness of a warm, throbbing cock stirring inside my body.

And so on, throughout what seemed interminable hours, I alternated between moments of lucidity and long periods of oblivion. Whether it was one fuck which lasted all night, or a dozen repeated at intervals I do not know. I had never been drunk before, and it was more like some incoherent dream than a reality.

When I awoke I could not at first remember the

circumstances which accounted for my presence in such unfamiliar surroundings. I sat up among the disordered coverings and looked about. I was alone. My clothes were draped over a settee where I had placed them on disrobing the previous night. I was entirely naked and had a splitting headache, the explanation of which was apparent in the form of empty bottles and wine-stained goblets on a small taboret near the bed.

As my glance roved about the room it encountered a clock sustained in the uplifted arms of a porcelain shepherdess, and I saw with a start that it was past the hour of eleven. I had never been absent from home all night before.

In this moment there was a rap at the door and hardly had I time to snatch a sheet up over my bubbies than it opened and a servant, the same one who had admitted us the previous evening, entered, bearing a tray with a pot of tea, some buttered toast and marmalade.

'The marster's horders, Miss, to serve you breakfast, and get a cab for you when you're ready.'

With the sheet still clutched over my breasts I watched him as he drew up a small table which, pivoting on an iron base, swung directly over my lap as I sat there in bed. After placing the tray on the table he indicated a silver bell.

'You may ring that, Miss, after you're dressed, when you're ready to go.'

I sipped the tea and nibbled at the toast after he had gone, immersed in uneasy meditations which the situation naturally inspired. When I had eaten as much as I could with an appetite impaired by a throbbing headache, I slipped out of bed and began to dress.

When I picked up my stocking I felt some lumpy article inside of it. With the thought that a garter had gotten inside I ran my hand down within the silken sheath but instead of a garter I retrieved a crumpled five pound note. I smoothed it out and gazed at it incredulously. I had never possessed that much money at one time in my entire life. And yet, when I picked up the second stocking there was another note of the same denomination in that one also.

Ten pounds! A veritable fortune.

I forgot both my headache and the uneasiness as to what the consequences of my all-night absence might be. I hurried through my dressing, tarried but a moment in the beautiful bathroom, and rang the bell.

The domestic appeared immediately and led me downstairs and out to the street where a cab, already summoned, was waiting. In answer to the driver's query, I mentioned a corner a few blocks from where I lived, and when we reached this destination I got out and walked the rest of the way.

Mamma Agnes listened to my unconvincing story of having spent the night in the home of a girl friend in frigid silence, except for an observation to the effect that she only hoped the girl hadn't given me a dose of clap or perhaps put me in a family way.

I was not discreet enough to hide the harvest of this adventure and my sudden acquisition of riches, flaunted in the form of resplendent new dresses, silk hose, modish slippers, a new hat and other articles of adornment, in the face of envious and resentful females of the neighbourhood, brought a reprisal.

Upon information gratuitously submitted by a committee of righteous ladies I was taken into custody as a delinquent minor, and as a result of the investigation which transpired, I was first subjected to a physical examination of a most embarrassing nature, and then committed to a reformatory for wayward girls, destined to remain there until I became of age.

CHAPTER THREE

Three drab and dreary years I passed in this institution, submerged in an atmosphere of repression and humiliation which was fairly soul suffocating.

My complete lack of adaptability to the manual work assigned to new arrivals made me the special target of persecution by the female warders. My delicate physique and small hands and tiny, pointed fingers, so patently incapable of performing scullery work, laundering, and floor scrubbing with any degree of efficiency seemed to kindle their resentment.

Quick enough to show fight at first to these manifest injustices, I soon learned that, right or wrong, I was always on the losing end and that the slightest indication of insubordination brought punishment of a heartbreaking nature to say nothing of the loss of certain prerogatives and so called privileges which were greatly prized in this barren place and which were accorded only to those who accepted their fate with the proper show of humility and servility.

The first two or three months were a perfect nightmare of horror. Let me make myself clear, the sufferings were more mental than physical, for there was little or no actual physical brutality. Corporal punishment, though authorized for incorrigibles, was rarely resorted to. I do not think there were more than half a dozen whippings inflicted on girls during the entire period I was in the institution. These whippings though, when they were administered, were something not to be forgotten.

In addition to the humiliation of being forced to lie face down across a massive table with her panties removed, the blows inflicted on the victim's naked bottom were of such severity as to cause her to shriek with anguish. Five or six or seven times during my incarceration my face blanched at the sound of those shrill cries, intermingled with the dull slap, slap, slap of heavy leather against naked flesh.

However, time reconciles us to any misfortune and we become hardened to the inevitable.

As this institution admitted only minors educational facilities were provided with four hours of classes daily, except Saturdays and Sundays. I discovered that in study there was a surcease from the deadly monotony. I had never been very studious; in fact, during the year preceeding my commitment my interest in learning had waned almost to the vanishing point.

Now, however, I found that time devoted to study passed very quickly. It was something like a mental narcotic which kept one's thoughts from useless repining. My application impressed the teachers and matrons favourably, and gradually they became friendly and treated me with greater consideration. And, if it be true that every cloud has its silver lining, the silver lining in this one was that I received my education which I would otherwise never have possessed.

I passed the probation period and was relieved from further scullery work. It would be carried on by new unfortunates, two or three of whom appeared each week.

We slept in dormitories or wards, each ward a long room with from twenty or thirty narrow iron beds in a row. These wards were locked at night, and a matron slept in each one, locked in with her charges. In addition, there was always a night superintendent on duty, who could be called in any emergency.

At nine o'clock each night all lights excepting a dim one near the ward matron's bed were turned out and no conversation was permitted between girls after that hour. Our movements during the day, except in school or work hours, were fairly unrestricted within the confines of the building and grounds, but at seven o'clock we entered our respective wards and were allowed to talk, read, and attend to our toilet necessities. At nine we had to be in bed and cease all conversation. As it was impossible to fall asleep immediately, the hour which followed was probably the most disagreeable of the deadly routine. By ten o'clock most of us had found peace in slumber.

But there was a variation to this feature to which we always looked forward. The ward matrons were rotated weekly between dormitories. And, as is sometimes the case in correctional institutions, there are occasional kindly hearted individuals who, instead of exercising the last ounce of their authority to make life as miserable as possible for their unfortunate charges, are disposed to mitigate their wretchedness when possible to do so at no great cost.

A certain matron who slept in our ward one week in every five condoned whispered conversations after nine o'clock, even though it was against the rules. Another, also with us one week in every five, was a very sound sleeper and snored so loudly we were never in doubt as to when she was asleep. So, during the weeks when either of these two matrons were on duty we were fairly safe in exchanging whispered conversations as late as we wished. When the snoring matron was on duty we told naughty stories or exchanged venal confidences.

Occupying the bed on my left side, with a space of about four feet between us, was a girl named Hester. She was but a few months older than I, but much more so in experience. She was taller than I and very pretty. Her hair, which almost reached to her knees when unbound, was that beautiful shade of auburn which just misses being black by the narrowest margin. She had been very nice to me from the start and had given me much kind and useful advice. She was philosophical in her attitude and possessed of an extremely likeable personality. Nearly all the girls in this reformatory owed their commitment to delinquencies of a sexual nature. Hester had been taken out of a house of prostitution.

She questioned me as to how much money I had been accustomed to get for the bestowal of my favours and when I told her, ruefully, that though my last and fatal adventure had brought me ten pounds, I had rarely received over ten shillings, frequently far less, and sometimes nothing at all, she exclaimed.

'Why, you little fool! With your form and baby face you could earn fifteen or twenty pounds a week. In the place I was last I got a pound every time I did it beside what the madam got, and lots of times I got more than that! Why, you were just a little charity chippy!'

One night, taking advantage of the snoring matron's somnolence, we whispered stories and experiences until eleven o'clock. The ward lights were out at this hour, but the shaded lamp near the matron's bed gave just enough light to break the darkness. Hester suddenly kicked off the bed coverings and, stretching her legs out lasciviously, exclaimed.

'Oh, Lord! For a good stiff cock!'

I murmured some sympathetic rejoinder as, lying on my side facing her, I observed her pretty round legs dimly visible in the half darkness.

'Don't you ever get that way, Jessie? Sometimes I want to fuck so darn bad I nearly go crazy!'

'Who wouldn't, locked up in this miserable place month after month?' I answered gloomily.

She sighed, and after a moment of silence, whispered:

'Did you ever kiss the baby in the boat, Jessie?'

'Did I ever what?'

'Kiss the baby . . . suck another woman.'

'No!'

'I never did, either. But there are girls here that do. I sucked a guy's cock once. I didn't like it much, but if I had one now I could eat it alive.' She giggled faintly.

'Well, I don't know what you're going to do. Go hungry, I guess.'

'I darned well know what I'm going to do. It's better than nothing!' she exclaimed, and arching her legs she placed a hand over her cunny and began to rub it vigorously.

From around us came the sound of suppressed giggles, sighs, and the movements of other listeners as they stirred uneasily in their own narrow beds.

I watched the rapid movement of her hand, dimly visible in the partial darkness. And when, with a groan of satisfaction, the movements ceased, my own hand edged down between my legs and under discreet cover sought to quench in like form the fires her frank words and franker actions had aroused.

What she had said about girls who did certain things was true. To be caught in another girl's bed or in any other compromising circumstance indicating that something of this kind was going on was one of the things that girls could be whipped for, and two or three of the whippings which took place while I was there were for exactly this cause.

Nevertheless, something of this kind was going on most of the time without the matron knowing about it. Sometimes the girls would take a chance in the night-time while the ward matron was asleep and get two in a bed, but this was very dangerous because the switch which controlled the lights was right near the matron's hand, and she could flood the room with light instantly should she hear any suspicious sound.

There was a safer way. In each ward there was a linen-room where clean sheets, pillowcases, towels, and extra blankets were kept. It was a very small room, mostly filled with shelves, but there was a little extra space. The doors to these closets, were kept locked, but the keys were in the possession of linen room girls, or trusties, assigned to distribute towels, sheets, pillowcases, etc., as needed in their respective wards.

If satisfactory arrangements could be made with a linen room girl, the door would be left unlocked, and when two lovers had slipped inside unobserved by matrons, she would lock the door, leaving them inside for half an hour or so, and when the coast was clear, let them out and lock the door again.

Some weeks before my entry in the reformatory, there had been a linen room rendezvous of this kind in another ward and the lovers had been caught. It came about through a peculiar accident. A matron, coming down the long corridor between wards, saw a girl she wished to speak to entering a certain ward. She followed her, but when she got inside the ward the girl she had seen was not visible, which mystified her, and with good reason. The girl she was following and a companion were already locked inside the linen closet. Seeing the linen room girl standing nearby, the matron asked her if such and such a girl had not come in a few moments before.

'No, ma'm,' was the reply. 'She isn't in here. She must be out in the yard, or downstairs.'

'But I'm positive I saw her come in here not half a minute ago!'

'It must have been someone else, ma'am!' answered the frightened girl.

'Someone else? There's no one else in here but you! What's going on here, anyway?'

The puzzled matron glanced around the empty dormitory. Her eyes fell on the door to the linen room. She went to it and tried it. The door was locked.

'Give me the key to this door,' she requested.

'I . . . ah, I've lost it, ma'am!' stammered the poor girl.

'Give me that key!'

Inside the linen room two trembling lovebirds were listening to the ominous conversation. Naturally, when the matron opened the door and found not only one girl but two, she grasped the situation and both the lovers and the linen room girl were strapped over the table in the superintendent's office and whipped on their bare bottoms.

For a while after this a watch was kept on the linen rooms, but the vigilance gradually relaxed and now they were being used again with considerable frequency.

There was Heloise, whom everyone called Frenchy, who would suck another girl off for any trifling payment. And several others who were known or suspected of similar complacencies.

Hester, who had become my special pal and confident, used to joke with me in her dry, half

38

comical, half serious way, as we sat on the edges of our beds at night before lights out.

'Darn you, Jessie, you give me a hard-on every time I see you undressed. I believe I'll sneak into your bed some night and give you a good fucking.'

'I don't think you've got what's needed!' I replied, snickering.

'Well, I could gamahuche you, anyway. Do you think you'd like that?'

'Gosh, I don't know. Two different fellows I went with did it to me that way. I don't know how it would be with a girl.'

'Must give one a funny sensation to have another girl do that to you. There are women who pay for it that way. And maybe you don't believe it, but there are even some that will pay you just for letting them do that to you, without you doing a thing. Some people have the funniest ideas.'

I told her about the fellow who had paid me to whip him.

'That's nothing,' she replied, 'there are lots of men like that. The ones you have to be careful about are the ones that want to whip *you*. Some of them go crazy and whip you so hard the blood comes. They don't care how much they hurt you.'

'Why, I wouldn't let them whip me!' I exclaimed, horrified.

'Well, when you're in a sporting house you have to do everything and pretend to like it. Those fellows who do funny things are generally the best spenders. They're always springing something new on you, too,' she continued, 'the best paying regular I had was one of the funny kind; you'd never guess what I had to do with him.'

'Tell me, Hester!' I begged.

She began to giggle.

39

'Well, there really wasn't much to it, but it was so . . . so . . . crazy, I nearly went into hysterics the first few times, until I got used to it. He'd lie down on the bed and make me get on my knees, straddling him, right over his face. Then I had to jack myself off with my fingers, and just when I started to cream, put my cunny down on his mouth. And will you believe it, right then he'd start to squirt without my even touching his cock, and the stuff would fly all over my bare back.'

'My heavens!' I breathed.

'I couldn't sleep last night,' she continued, changing the subject. 'I laid awake the longest time, just imagining things, and thinking what I'd like to have the first night after I get out of here.'

'I can guess,' I said dryly, 'a stiff cock.'

'No; five of them, all at the same time.'

'Five? At one time?'

'Yes, one in my cunny, one in my mouth, one in my bottom, and . . .' she burst into laughter, '. . . one in each hand!'

'Hester, you're the limit!' I exploded.

'I get so darn tired of jacking myself off I've half a mind to go in the linen room with Frenchy. She's crazy about that new shoulder scarf I have, and it's no good to me in here, anyway.'

'Why don't you?' I suggested. 'You can tell me all about it afterwards. But be careful! I'd faint if I ever heard you getting the strap.'

'Maybe I will. There isn't any danger. They don't watch the linen rooms much. Besides, I thought of a dandy way to fix things so they couldn't catch us. I saw Amy and that new girl she chums around with sneaking out of the linen room in ward five this afternoon. I had a suspicion that's what Amy was up to when she started being so nice to that little kid.'

'Jessie! Jessie!' I heard someone calling softly as I was sitting on a bench in the exercise yard reading the next afternoon. I glanced up, and saw Hester hurrying toward me. 'Frenchy and I are going in the linen room. You come up and stand in the corridor where you can watch the stairs! If any of the matrons come, you signal the linen room girl before they get upstairs, and she'll have time to get us out before they reach the dormitory!'

'All right!' I agreed, rising to follow her.

This was a very practical plan. The ward was far enough from the top of the stairway to allow ample time for them to get out of the linen room should the girl on watch in the doorway receive a signal from me. The only risk they ran was that of being abruptly interrupted in their affair.

I followed Hester up to the corridor and stationed myself where I could watch the stairs and at the same time be seen by the linen room girl in the doorway of the dormitory who, in the event that I suddenly started to walk toward her, would quickly warn Hester and Frenchy.

But there were no interruptions. I stood there twenty or twenty-five minutes, watching the stairs and picturing in my mind what was taking place within the linen room. The girl finally disappeared from the entrance and I knew she had gone to unlock the door.

A few moments later Hester and Frenchy appeared in the corridor. There was nothing in Frenchy's calm demeanour to indicate anything unusual, but Hester's face was scarlet and she was holding her handkerchief over it. Frenchy sauntered coolly into another dormitory and Hester went on downstairs with me and out into the yard.

'Well . . . ?' I invited, after waiting for her to say something. 'How was it?'

'Oh, Jessie! It . . . I . . . she . . . wait till I get my breath . . .' and she began to laugh hysterically. When she recovered her composure and her face had resumed its natural hue, she said: 'I can't talk about it yet; I'll tell you tonight. Look: my hands are still shaking, I'm so nervous!'

'Oh, all right,' I answered disgustedly, 'but I don't see what you have to be nervous about now.'

'It's the reaction. Don't be sore; I'll tell you all about it tonight, honey!'

And, that night, sitting close together on the edge of my bed before lights out, at my insistent urging, Hester told me in whispers what there was to tell.

'Well, we got inside, and as soon as we heard the door lock we turned on the light and took our panties off and hid them under some sheets on a shelf so in case we had to come out quickly we could just leave them there and get them later. Then we put a blanket on the floor and I laid down on it. Frenchy wanted to do 69 but I told her I didn't want to do it that way because I couldn't get my nerve up to do that to a girl. So she said all right, she'd just do it to me. It was the funniest thing, Jessie, all last night and today, while I was thinking about it. I felt hot, but no sooner did I get inside that room with her than my passion all left me. I felt like telling her I had changed my mind and letting her keep the scarf anyway. But then I thought, what a silly thing to do after going to so much bother, and why not let her go through with it. When she pulled my dress up I started to giggle, I couldn't help it, I felt so funny, not passionate, just silly. Well, she squeezed in between my legs, and stuck her tongue right up inside. When I felt it go in I wanted to push her away, but I didn't and after she put it in and out a while, she began to lick me all around down there, and then she started to suck my

42

bottom. I thought I'd go crazy, really. I couldn't stop laughing. It didn't make me feel passionate, but the sensation started to come anyway, and sure enough, she did make me cream something fierce. If she'd have stopped then it wouldn't have been so bad, but she stuck to me like a little leech and it set my nerves on edge so, I felt like scratching her. I almost had to yell at her to make her let go. She wanted to know when I'd let her do it again, I told her 'someday' but I don't think I ever will. It isn't so hot. I don't see how some girls can go batty over that kind of stuff.'

CHAPTER FOUR

The time dragged on. With the exception of such little momentary distractions as those I have described, there was little to break the monotony. During the first year and a half I received occasional visits from Mamma Agnes, and sometimes from Rene. How I would have enjoyed an hour or two with him in privacy, but such was not to be, for visiting was confined to the reception room and there was always a matron present to see that no contraband gifts were passed to inmates. Even the letters written to us were opened and read before being placed in our hands. Often, letters written to girls by male friends were destroyed without being seen by those to whom they were addressed.

Through some artful manoeuvre, a seventeen-year-old girl in our ward named Georgette succeeded in getting some little pictures of men and women doing everything imaginable. They were not drawings like the one in the little book Rene had found, but real photographs.

Georgette had these pictures about two weeks when apparently some word of their presence, either accidentally or through malicious tattling, reached the ears of the superintendent.

Accompanied by two matrons she entered our ward one night just after lock-up, and proceeded to search it thoroughly. One of the matrons found the little packet of pictures under Georgette's mattress and we knew it was the pictures they were looking for because they stopped searching as soon as they found them.

They took poor Georgette out, downstairs to the superintendent's office. As soon as they had gone a profound silence fell over the ward. Nobody said anything. We were all waiting with strained nerves to hear certain sounds which would cause some of us to tremble, others to murmur curses, and others to giggle with callow indifference or maybe hysterical nervousness.

Moment by moment we waited but the expected sounds did not materialize. The minutes dragged on, ten, fifteen, twenty, a half an hour. Maybe they were not going to whip Georgette after all. But suddenly the tense silence was broken by a distant but sharply audible thwack. It was followed by another, and another, and with the third blow an agonized scream reached our ears. Four, five, six, seven, eight, nine, ten. Mechanically we counted the strokes as the blood-chilling cadence of strap and shrieks rent the air. With the tenth stroke it stopped, and those of us who were inspired with sentiments of pity and sympathy breathed a sigh of relief.

Five minutes elapsed, and to our surprise, the woeful dirge with its horrid slap, slap, slap accompaniment began again. From one up to ten it again ran its ominous course. This was something unusual; we recalled of no previous instance in which the punishment had been inflicted twice-in succession.

At the tenth blow, as before, came silence. Unconsciously I had clenched my hands so tightly that they were numb with the pressure. I glanced at Hester. She was sitting on the edge of her bed, her chin cupped in her hands, gazing morosely downward. After the second whipping there was a long period of silence. Momentarily we expected to see Georgette

45

being brought back into the dormitory, and were fairly paralysed with horror when the dolorous refrain commenced anew. Even the face of Mrs Barrows, our ward matron, was pale as she sat at the little desk near her bed, nervously twisting a pencil in her fingers.

'If they whip me like that I'll come back here and kill them if I never do another thing in life!' whispered Hester.

A few minutes after the echos of the tenth and last blow of the triple inquisition had died away we heard the door of the superintendent's office open, and the sound of slow steps on the stairs and in the corridor followed. Finally, there was Georgette, sobbing huskily and supported by the arms of the two matrons. Mrs Barrows unlocked the door and helped Georgette to her bed.

Kindly hands undressed her and laid her face down on her cot. When her bottom was uncovered we gasped with horror. It was a mass of purple welts, each welt puffed up and swollen terribly. Even Mrs Barrows expressed surprise as she hastened to get a jar of cold cream with which to allay the inflammation.

'Why did they whip you three times, Georgette?' we whispered in sympathetic wonder.

'They were trying to make me tell how I got the pictures,' answered Georgette, her voice broken with intermittent sobs

'Did you tell them?'

'No!'

All things must end and the time of my release was near at hand. Mamma Agnes was dead. She had passed away during the second year of my imprisonment, and Rene had shortly thereafter come to bid me good-bye. He was going to Canada, and would send me money to join him when I was free, he said. For a while my thoughts were brightened with his

46

hope. But his letters, coming at first with regularity and sometimes containing small sums of money, gradually became less frequent and were less definite in tone with regard to our original plans. They finally ceased altogether and the walls of oblivion closed about my brother Rene.

It was destined, seemingly, that the day of my liberation would find me homeless, the last tie which linked me to my former life cut off, and with no provision for the future. It was in this extremity that Hester, whose freedom was due several months in advance of mine, and who had confided to me that a place was arranged for and awaiting her in the atelier of a certain Madame Lafronde, suggested that I also place myself at the disposition of this lady in whom she had the utmost confidence.

She painted a glowing picture of the comfortable life and financial rewards to be enjoyed in the high-class establishment operated by this Madame Lafronde. It catered to a very select clientele recruited among the gentility and nobility. She was certain that Madame Lafronde would welcome me with open arms and so eloquent was she that I did not long hesitate in accepting her offer to intercede for me.

Before Hester passed through the big front doors to freedom it had been arranged that I was to have a visitor, ostensibly an aunt, who would call on me a few days before my own release was due. This aunt would be no other than Madame Lafronde herself, and the purpose of her visit would be to decide whether I was an acceptable candidate for her atelier.

The tight pressure of Hester's hand, and the soft kiss she left on my cheek as she bid me farewell filled my eyes with tears. I had come to regard her with great affection, and her absence would weigh heavily on my heart.

'Don't cry, Jessie darling,' she whispered, 'we'll soon be together again. I won't forget you. Remember now, when Madame Lafronde comes, call her Aunt Mary, and act as though you knew her or else. . . .'

Further conversation was interrupted by a matron, and with a last hug and kiss we separated.

The four months which followed were the longest and dreariest of all the long months I spent in the reformatory. The fact that a new life was close at hand actually seemed to regard the passage of time rather than hurry it.

But there were moments of happiness occasioned by the arrival of little packages containing candies, cakes and other gifts of a nature permitted by the regulations. There were also letters which, despite their discreet wording and the mysterious signature 'your loving cousin, Frances,' conveyed to me their messages of cheer and the certainty that Hester had indeed not forgotten me. And, true to her promise, a week before my liberty was to be restored, I was called to the reception room to receive a visitor.

As I entered, my surprised gaze fell upon the only occupant, aside from the ever alert and watchful matron on duty, an elderly lady of most respectable, even pious aspect, gowned in sombre black silk. So contrary was her appearance to that of the visitor I expected that I hesitated, momentarily, forgetting Hester's parting admonition as I gazed on the grandmotherly picture. As I stood hesitantly, she arose from her chair, and coming toward me with outstretched arms, exclaimed.

'Jessie, my darling child!'

The sharp eyes of the matron were on me.

'Hello, Aunt Mary,' I murmured as I mechanically returned her embrace.

And so, under these curious circumstances, the

Madame of a house of prostitution interviewed a prospective inmate. Her eyes roved incessantly over my body as we carried on our aimless conversation, designed to fool the matron who sat idly watching us. I felt from the first that I had found favour with my visitor, and her comments as to how I had changed for the better since she 'last saw' me and how nice I looked, and how happy she was sure I would be when she took me to live with her now that my dear, dear mama had passed away, gave me the clue to my future and assured me that for the time being at least, it was assured. 'Cousin Francis' was eagerly awaiting my homecoming, she said, and sent me her most affectionate regards.

Before leaving, she advised the superintendent that she would be at the institution the morning of my release to see me safely home. I went back to my ward in a regular daze, my thoughts in a confused whirl. It was very difficult to imagine that nice old lady in the role of mistress of a house of prostitution.

The long awaited day arrived at last.

At nine o'clock I was summoned to the superintendent's office and the usual formalities related to the discharge of inmates were fulfilled.

'Your aunt said that she would call for you at ten o'clock, Jessie. You may go to your dormitory and pack your things,' she said kindly, after concluding the customary harangue on the folly of a life of sin and the rewards of virtue.

As I spread my few effects upon the narrow cot in the dormitory, preparatory to wrapping them up in a bundle, a small group of friends and companions gathered around, some to bid me an envious farewell and others to extract promises from me to send them this or that from the outside.

The hour sped by and almost before I realized it I

was going down the long stairway which led to the outer offices and freedom.

My benefactress was waiting in the superintendent's office and greeted me with a motherly embrace in keeping with our reserved relationship. The superintendent conducted us to the outer door and as it closed behind us I paused to glance back, hardly able to believe that my freedom was an actual fact. As I did so, Madame Lafronde shook my arm.

'Come on, girl! This damn place gives me the willies!' she exclaimed as she hurried me down the steps to the street. She signalled a taxi and within a few moments the institution which had been my home for nearly three years receded in the distance and became at last only a disagreeable memory.

Within the taxi, Madame Lafronde relaxed, and leaning back against the cushions she extracted a packet of cigarettes from her purse. After proffering me a cigarette which, unaccustomed to their use, I declined, she lit one and puffed away abstractedly.

The taxi, in accordance with her indications, after travelling a dozen blocks, slowed up and came to a stop. But we had not reached our ultimate destination. A few steps away, waiting near the kerb, was a large black limousine. As we approached it on foot, a chauffeur sprang out and opened the rear compartment and to my surprise and delight, Hester stepped out and flung her arms about me. She was beautifully gowned and her face was radiant with sincere joy at seeing me. I had always thought Hester pretty, but I was hardly prepared for the change a splendid wardrobe wrought in her appearance.

We did not tarry long and soon, ensconced in the luxurious privacy of the big car, were again winding rapidly through the streets, Hester and I babbling excitedly while Lafronde placidly blew long streamers of smoke through her nostrils, interrupting us occasionally with some questions or observation.

'Let's see your legs, my dear.'

I giggled nervously as she coolly raised my skirts and eyed my legs appraisingly.

'Um-m, very good, my dear, very nice legs, indeed. I was afraid Hester might have exaggerated a little . . . and how about your bubbies, let's see what they're like . . .' and an inquisitive and bejewelled hand passed over my chest and after a brief exploration was withdrawn. 'Ah, yes, very nice legs and very nice bubbies. A fortune in them, my dear, if you are wise.'

The ride ended before the portals of a large mansion in a quiet street and shortly thereafter I was ushered into my new home. It was a place of quiet elegance, soft plush carpets and tapestried walls. I gazed about in wonder. There was nothing visible to the eye to mark these circumspectly luxurious premises as an atelier of prostitution, but I was soon to learn that things are not always as they seem, and that within these sedate walls dramas of licentiousness such as I had never seen were of nightly occurrence.

And thus did I cross the threshold of a new life, and the doors of the past closed behind me.

CHAPTER FIVE

A small but furnished alcove with a tiled bath in connection was waiting for me, and after I had examined it Madame Lafronde left Hester and me together, saying that she would have a talk with me later in the afternoon.

A maid appeared with a luncheon tray and as I ate, plying Hester with questions between bites, I learned that Madame Lafronde's 'family' comprised eight other girls in addition to Hester and myself. I would meet them later, they did not get up until after twelve, which accounted for the silence and absence of movement I had already noted.

When Madame Lafronde returned, her first request was that I strip myself entirely so that she could examine my body. I did so with some embarrassment, for though I had often enough exposed myself to boys and men, the impersonal, appraising eyes of this strange old lady filled me with a nervous dread that I might be found wanting in some essential.

I was small of stature and feared that the absence of clothing might accentuate the possible defect. However, to my vast relief, she gave every evidence of satisfaction and nodded her head approvingly as I turned around and around in obedience to her indications. When I had replaced my clothing she shot question after question at me, until every phase of my early and subsequent sexual life had been revealed. To her questions I endeavoured to give frank and truthful answers, regardless of the embarrassment which some of them evoked.

'Now, my dear,' she said, when the interrogating had been concluded, 'I want you to know that we're all one big, happy family here. There must be no jealousy or friction or petty animosities between girls. Our gentlemen are very nice, but men are men, and a pretty, new face always distracts their attention from older ones. I have a plan in mind which fits you as though you were made for it. If you handle it rightly you'll be helping the others girls as well as yourself, and instead of being jealous of you they'll all have reason to be grateful. We're all here to make money and as it must come from the gentlemen our aim is to get them to spend it and then come back and spend some more. Never forget that.'

And Madame Lafronde explained the unique role I was to play, a role which to a more mature mind than mine would have at once revealed the astuteness and subtlety of the guiding genius behind this lucrative business and which accounted for its success, measured in terms of gold. Madame Lafronde was nobody's fool.

In brief, she proposed to dangle my youthful prettiness before the jaded eyes of the clientele as a sort of visual aperitif, much as water was placed before the thirsting Tantalus, in view, but just beyond reach, the psychological effect of which would be to so whet their passions that they would in the end, perforce, satisfy themselves with such feminine fruit as was within their reach.

I was to tantalize masculine passion while leaving to others the duty of satisfying them. This with respect to the regular 'parlour' clientele. Exceptions would be made privately with certain special patrons who were always able and disposed to pay well for favouritism.

Things were not as they had been before the war, explained Madame Lafronde. Even this profitable business had suffered from the falling economic barometer, and too many of the gentlemen who dropped in were inclined to pass the evening sociably in the parlour. Of course, between liquors consumed, tips to the girls, and various other sources of minor revenues, their presence was desirable, but the real profits of the business were garnered in the bedrooms, not in the parlour. It was a case of a bird in a bedroom being worth five in the parlour.

As a sort of stimulant designed to inspire blasé gentlemen with an irresistible urge to make use of the bedroom service, I was to be rigged up in an enticingly juvenile fashion and paraded constantly before their eyes in a semi-nude state. Various pretexts and artifices would ostensibly account for my presence and movements. I would carry a tray of cigars and cigarettes, serve drinks, and be available for general services and accommodations with but one single-exception. I would joke and chat with patrons, tell a naughty story now and then, even permit them to fondle me within certain limits, but, because of my youth (I was to pretend to be only fifteen years old!) my services were not to be expected in a professional capacity.

I gasped at hearing that I was to play the part of a fifteen-year-old, but Madame Lafronde insisted that it would not be difficult in view of my small body and the fact that certain artifices in costume, hairdressing and other details would be employed to help out the illusion.

The first step was to call in a barber who trimmed my hair so that it hung just below my ears. It was naturally wavy, and when the work was finished it was quite apparent that Madame Lafronde had not erred in assuming that short curls would lend a peculiarly childish effect to my face. I gazed in the mirror with genuine surprise at the transfiguration.

When the barber had gone Madame Lafronde ordered me to undress again, and after taking certain measurements left the room to return later with several garments and a box which on being opened revealed a safety razor, soap and brush.

'We could have let the barber do this, too,' she commented dryly, indicating the razor, 'but maybe you'd rather do it yourself.'

'Do what?' I asked, looking at the razor in perplexity.

'Shave the pretty little curls off your peek-a-boo,' she answered, with a gesture toward the dark shadow which was visible through the texture of my single garment.

'What!' I expostulated. 'Why . . . even girls fifteen years old have. . . !'

'Shave it off,' she interrupted. 'If you don't know how, I'll do it for you.'

'I can, I can!' I reponded hastily. 'I've shaved the hair under my arms lots of times . . . only . . .' and I glanced around in confusion for, in addition to Madame Lafronde and Hester, several girls had appeared and were standing in the door watching me curiously.

'Go over by the window with your back to us and stand up, or sit down, whichever you wish, if you're afraid someone will see your love trap. You'll get over that before you've been here long.'

Without further protest I took the shaving equipment, turned my back on the smiling assembly and sitting on the edge of a chair with my legs apart I lathered and soaped the hair and shaved it off the best I could. I had to go over the ground several times before the last prickly stubs were finally removed, and when I stood up, much embarrassed, to let Madame Lafronde view the results she expressed her approval and suggested that I dust the denuded flesh with talcum powder.

The absence of the hair from its accustomed place caused me to feel peculiarly naked, and I turned my gaze downward. The two sides of my cunny stood out prominently like fat little hills, the crease between them tightly closed as I stood with my legs pressed together.

I was now to don black hose of sheerest silk and a pair of tiny slippers with exaggerated high Spanish heels. Around my legs, just above the knees, fitted narrow scarlet garters, each adorned with a little silk rosette. Next came an exquisite brocade coat or jacket of black velvet into which was worked fantastic designs in gold thread.

'What about my bubbies?' I asked, as Madame Lafronde handed me the garment. 'Will I have to cut them off, too?'

A gust of laughter followed and I slipped on the loose-fitting coat. It terminated at a point about halfway down my thighs, leaving a few inches of naked flesh between its lower edge and the tops of my hose. Fastening just below the breasts with three braided loops, it covered my stomach all right, but from there down the folds hung loose and a naked, hairless cunny would be exposed with any careless movement.

The last item of this bizarre costume was a tall, military style cap of astrakhan, fitted with a small brim of shiny black leather and a strap which passed under my chin. Madame Lafronde adjusted the cap on my head at a rakish angle and stood back to view the effect.

I glanced at my reflection in the wardrobe mirror.

Without undue conceit I realized that I presented a chic picture, one which undoubtedly fulfilled Madame Lafronde's expectations, as was attested to by the satisfied gleam in her shrewd old eyes, by Hester's enthusiastic felicitations, and by the half-admiring, half-envious looks of the other girls who were watching silently.

From beneath the edge of the black astrakhan cap my hair hung loose in short, crisp curls. The low bodice of the brocade jacket teasingly revealed the upper halves of my breasts, while its wide and ample sleeves displayed my arms to good advantage with every movement. The jacket itself, fitting snugly around my waist, flared out sufficiently to show my hips to good advantage. Further down, the sheen of glossy silk with the brief variation in colour provided by the scarlet garters gave just the right touch to my legs, and the high-heeled slippers completed the exotic ensemble.

The rest of the afternoon and evening Madame Lafronde devoted to coaching and instructing me. The doors were open to visitors at nine o'clock, but it was never until after eleven or twelve that gentlemen returning from their clubs or other nocturnal entertainment began to drop in in any considerable number, and from then on patrons came and went, singly or in small groups, some to linger briefly, others to pass an hour or two, or to remain all night.

I made my debut at eleven o'clock. With inward nervousness at first, but with growing confidence as I observed the electrical effect my entry made upon the half-dozen gentlemen who were lounging about the salon in various attitudes of interest or indifference to the wiles of the feminine sirens about them. As I crossed the room with my tray of cigars and cigarettes and matches supported by a strap over my shoulders the hum of conversation ceased as if by magic and every eye was on me.

I approached a tall, well-dressed gentleman who was sitting on a sofa with a girl on either side of him, and proffered my wares in a timid voice. His startled gaze took in the picture before him and lingered a moment on my legs. Shaking himself free from the arms of his companions, he sat up.

'My dear, I never smoked a cigar in my life, but I'll take all you have, if you go with them!'

This was Madame Lafronde's cue. Entering the room from a side door where she had been waiting, she said:

'Dear gentlemen, I want to present a new member of our family to you. This is Jessie. Jessie is here under peculiar circumstances. She is an orphan and, strictly speaking, not old enough to be here in a professional capacity. Though as you see, she is nicely developed, she is in fact only fifteen years old and I am sheltering her here only because of her orphaned condition. She is to make her living selling you cigars and cigarettes, gentlemen, and serving you in all other possible ways . . . except one.'

Madame Lafronde paused.

'In other words,' interrupted a tall, thin young man with a tiny moustache who was indifferently stroking the silk-clad legs of a damsel on his lap, 'she can be only a sister to us. I knew she was too good to be true the moment she came into this room.'

A burst of laughter followed and Madame Lafronde, smiling, answered:

'A sister . . . well . . . maybe just a bit more than a sister, gentlemen, but not too much more!'

From across the room Hester beckoned to me.

'This is my friend Mr Hayden, Jessie. He wants to know you,' she said, indicating her companion.

I acknowledged the introduction.

'Bring us two Scotch and sodas, will you, honey?' added Hester.

Mr Hayden spoke to me pleasantly and took a packet of cigarettes from my tray, courteously declining the change I tendered him. As I turned to execute Hester's order, the man I had first addressed detained me.

'Wait a moment, Sister. I've decided to take up smoking.'

I might add that the nickname 'Sister' was unanimously adopted and clung to me during the time I was in Madame Lafronde's house.'

The gentleman took a handful of cigars and reached toward his pocket. As he did so, his eyes drifted down below the edge of the tray.

'Hold on! I'm making a tactical error!' he exclaimed, replacing all the cigars but one. 'I see right now that cigars should be purchased one by one. You may bring me another when you come back!'

Nothing else was needed to start the ball of my popularity rolling and soon the salon was echoing with hilarity and laughter as all called for cigars and cigarettes at once, each trying to keep me standing in front of him as long as possible.

If this kept up there would be substantial returns on the tobacco concession, for half the profits were to be mine, according to Madame Lafronde's promise, and this in addition to whatever was given to me in the nature of tips or gratuities. Flushed and happy, I ran from one to another, replying to jokes and quips in a half-innocent, half-cynical manner, calculated to fit the role of a fifteen-year-old ingenue.

As the evening wore on new arrivals appeared and I was instantly the first object of their attention. Before long the pockets of my brocade jacket were heavy with silver, I had replenished my tobacco stock several times and received several generous tips for bringing in liquor, and in addition, a gentleman had given me four shillings for being permitted to feel my bubbies, 'just in a brotherly way', as he expressed it.

What the effect of my presence was on the regular revenues of the house I could not judge, for though there was a constant movement of couples in and out of bedrooms I had no way to knowing whether this was a normal or an increased activity.

With the advancing hours the movement gradually diminished and by four o'clock the last guest had departed. The door was locked, the girls ate a light luncheon and prepared to retire. It was then that Madame Lafronde informed me that the bedroom service had showed a decided increase, which increase she was fair enough to attribute to my presence.

She was well satisfied and I surely had reason to be, for when the money was counted up and the tobacco sales checked there remained for me the sum of two pounds and eight shillings, which was duly credited to me and would be at my disposition on request.

I was tired out; I had hardly slept the previous night, yet such was my excitement that I did not feel sleepy and preferred to gossip with Hester for an hour in my room. I had a hundred questions to ask. I wanted to know about the nice-looking, gentlemanly Mr Hayden, and learned that he was one of Hester's regular and most favoured friends.

He had been much interested in me, and Hester had unselfishly confided to him that I might reservedly be at his disposition on some later occasion, to which he had gallantly responded that in such an event he would insist on having the two of us together. How good Hester was, I thought, to be willing to share this nice man with me and maybe risk my supplanting her in his affections. He had appealed to me greatly, and there had been several others whom I would not have been averse to doing something with.

'You made a tremendous sensation, darling,' said Hester. 'You could have a dozen roomcalls. I heard what everybody said. But Lafronde is right. The other girls would have been ready to scratch your eyes out. There's nothing makes them so mad as to have a new girl take their regulars away from them. Did you notice that fellow who went with me? He comes here very three or four nights. I guess every girl here has had him, but now he always takes me. He's got lots of money and he's kind of nice, but, gee, he never has a hard-on and it takes about half an hour of work to give him a stand. Sometimes I even have to put the buzzer on him, but tonight, oh, baby, it was as stiff as a poker. I jollied him about it and told him I bet it was thinking about you instead of me. 'My word,' he said, 'you're a deucedly clevah mind reader. That little tart did have a most extraordinary effect on me. Wonder what the chawnces would be to secure her company for an hour or two? I think that's all bally rot about her virginal estate, don't you know!' I told him to talk to Madame Lafronde and maybe it could be arranged. That's two of my regulars that have fallen for you already, but I'm not jealous. You can have Bumpy if you want him. It takes too long to make his cock stand up.'

I laughed.

'What did you mean, putting the buzzer on him?'

'The juice, the electric massage machine.' Don't you know what an electric massage machine is?'

'Of course I do. They use them for facials. But how . . . what. . . ?'

'Facials! Oh baby, you don't know the half. Wait . . . you're tired out. . . . I'll fix your bath water for

61

you and after you're bathed I'll give you a massage that will make you sleep like an infant.'

Hester ran into the bathroom and turned on the water. Then she went to her room and came back with an entrancing little pink silk nightgown, face cream, perfume, and a large leather-covered box.

While I lay splashing lazily in the tub, soaking in the pleasant warmth of the foamy, scented water, she laid out the nightgowns and opened the box to show the apparatus it contained and which was, in effect, an electric vibratory massage machine fitted with a long cord for attachment to an electricity outlet. There were several assorted pieces in the box and from these Hester selected one fitted with rubber lips which turned out in the form of a small cup.

When I had gotten out of the tub and dried myself I lay down naked on the bed. Hester dipped her fingers in the jar of cream and passed them lightly over my face, neck, breasts and limbs.

I thought suddenly of the peculiar aspect the shaving had given me in a certain place and flipped a corner of the sheet over it. Without a word Hester flipped it back and her hands were between my thighs, softly spreading the cold cream over them and down my legs.

'You're awful good to go to so much trouble for me, Hester,' I murmured.

'It's nothing. You can do as much for me sometime,' she replied.

When she had finished anointing my body she connected the massage machine. It began to hum and the next instant the rubber cup was buzzing over my forehead, cheeks and neck. My flesh thrilled to the refreshing stimulation and I lay still, enjoying it to the full. Gradually the rubber moved down over my chest, between my breasts, then up over one of them right

62

on the nipple. I came out of any languid rest with a bound. That bubbling, vibrating cup over the nipple of my breast was awakening sensations quite remote to those of mere physical refreshment.

Both my nipples stiffened up, the sensitive area around them puffed out and radiations of sexual excitation began to flow through my body. Laughing hystericaly, I sat up and pushed the tantalizing device away.

'Be still, will you? Lie back down!' expostulated Hester, giving me a shove which tumbled me back over the pillows.

'But, Hester! That thing . . . it's positively distracting! Don't put it on my bubbies again . . . I can't stand it!'

Hester smiled.

'You'll think it's distracting before I finish with you. Keep quiet or you'll wake the girls in the next room.'

Down over my stomach, in widening circles, around and around, and then back and forth moved the diabolical apparatus guided by Hester's hand. I had a premonition now of what was coming, and as it slowly but surely crept downward until it reached the upper part of the rounded elevation of my cunny, I clenched my fists and held my breasts.

No sooner was it close enough to impart its infernal vibration to my clitoris than tremors of sexual agitation began to shake my body. It was simply irresistible. I could not have forestalled its action by any conceivable exercise of willpower.

But I did not try. The fulminating intensity of the sensations which now had me in their grip nullified any will or desire to thwart them. I threw my head back, closed my eyes, and surrendered supinely. My legs parted shamelessly beneath the insinuating

63

pressure of Hester's fingers, and the humming, buzzing cup slid between them. Up and down it moved, three, four, maybe half a dozen times, pressing lightly against the flesh.

My orgasm, wrought up to the final pitch of excitation and unable to withstand the infernal provocation longer, yielded, and in a second I was gasping in the throes of sexual ecstasy.

When I recovered my breath, and in part my composure, I exclaimed:

'Hester! You . . . you . . . I could murder you! Fooling me with that thing!'

'Make you sleep good, honey, and keep you from having naughty dreams,' she answered complacently, and she disconnected the device and restored it to its container.

'Does that work on men like that, too?'

'Yes; we use it on them sometimes to give them a stand when they either can't get one or are too slow.'

'Well,' I commented. 'I'll say it gave me a stand I wasn't expecting.'

She giggled, tucked the covers around me, kissed me on the cheek, and turned out the lights.

'Sleep tight, honey. I'll wake you in the afternoon.'

She departed, leaving me alone to drowsily review the stupendous transition which twenty-four hours had wrought in my life. Last night, a hard, narrow cot in the drab and comfortless ward of a reformatory. Tonight, the soft luxury of a beautiful bed with the seductive caress of silk and fine linen about my body and all around me the material evidences of a life of ease, gaiety, and luxury. Gradually my thoughts became hazy and I drifted off into a pleasant, dreamless slumber from which I did not awaken until nine or ten hours later.

CHAPTER SIX

A week slipped by quickly, each night a pleasant
repetition, without any notable variations, of the one
I have described. This was time enough to assure
Madame Lafronde that the experiment was a success.
The continued approval with which my seminude
appearance was received by patrons, together with
certain other indications, was proof that I really constituted an attraction which was imparting a new popularity to the resort.

But it was not Madame Lafronde's intention to limit
my activities to exhibitional purposes. She was already
being importuned by gentlemen whose interest in me
was not to be resigned to mere optical satisfaction
and the subtle old procuress was but biding the time
necessary for these gentlemen's inflamed fancies to get
the best of their financial perspectives. I was being
reserved for the sensual delectation of a half-dozen or
so of her most exacting and best-paying customers. To
the rest, including the general run of parlour guests, I
was to remain only a visual aphrodisiac.

Into the ample pockets of my brocade jacket these
more or less credulous victims of my enticements and
beguilings poured their silver, eagerly taking advantage of such opportunities as I permitted them to
fondle me tentatively or superficially, bought my
cigars and cigarettes, tipped me generously for every
trifling service, sighed, and generally visited a
bedroom with one of my companions where, doubt-

less, evoking visions of my naked legs and other presumed charms, they ravished me by proxy.

Of the patrons I subsequently served in a more intimate fashion, five developed into 'steadies,' that is, became exclusively mine, and came with more or less regularity. A sixth, no other than the gentlemanly Mr Hayden, kept his promise to Hester and either by virtue of genuine affection for her or actuated by a kindly sentiment to avoid wounded feelings, insisted upon having both of us with him at the same time and maintained an attitude of strict impartiality.

I think Hester's generous spirit would not have resented a surrender of her priority to me, but though Mr Hayden was one of the nicest men I ever met, I was glad that his instincts of gallantry saved me from being placed in the light of having distracted his attention from one who was beyond doubt my best and sincerest friend. I have never found another such.

Patrons like Mr Hayden, unfortunately always in a minority, were the bright and redeeming features of a life otherwise vicious and degrading. They were the ones who, regardless of a girl's lost social status, always treated her with respectful consideration. Generous in recompensing the efforts which were made to please them, they never exacted arduous or debasing services, nor were they addicted to unnatural vices which went beyond the pale of those sexual practices ordinarily considered acceptable and legitimate.

To my lot fell the patronage of a Mr Heeley, a gentleman of this desirable category though with the minor disadvantage of being much older and less attractive physically than Mr Hayden. There was a Mr Thomas, middle-aged and wealthy, who had garnered his fortune in Ceylon and who always had some interesting story to tell. There was Mr Castle and Mr Wainwright, both of whom were addicted to eccentricities of a peculiar and disagreeable nature. At first I protested to Madame Lafronde that these two gentlemen were personages *non grata* with me and insinuated that I would not be loathe to dispense with their attentions. It was unequivocally impressed upon me that my inclinations were quite secondary to those of wealthy patrons. 'Do whatever they want within the limits of endurance. Satisfy their whims, fancies, even their aberrations if possible as long as they are willing to pay accordingly. Humour them, please them, get the money and keep them coming back as long as you can!' This was the unwritten law in the world of prostitution.

Mr Hayden was, I think, about thirty years old. I could easily have become really infatuated with this pleasant-spoken, educated, and cultured gentleman. We never knew exactly who he was with reference to his place in the outside world, nor even indeed that his name was really Hayden, for it was not unusual that gentelemen frequenting such places of entertainment as that provided by Madame Lafronde prudently concealed their identies under fictitious names. Nevertheless, there was no doubt that he was of the real gentility.

I liked him very much and I think the affection was reciprocated to an even greater extent than was ever manifested, but he was of that conscientious, kind-hearted type, disposed to go out of the way even at personal inconvenience to avoid causing pain to others and he knew that Hester adored him.

To Mr Hayden fell the honour, if such it might be styled, of initiating me into the real service of which I was now a recruit. My absence from the salon accounted for the numerous inquiries with the old alibi 'a bad time of the month, don't you know.'

Hester and I and Mr Hayden enjoyed a little dinner by ourselves and thereafter repaired to Hester's room where we disported ourselves lightheatedly for an hour, romping and tumbling over the bed in good-natured abandon as the wine we had imbibed warmed our blood and attuned our receptive senses to lecherous ideas.

Mr Hayden was a healthy, vigorous young man, a splendid example of physical perfection. The sight of his clean-cut, well-kept body, and the magnificently rigid and well-formed member which was disclosed when he undressed sent the blood surging through my veins. I did not know by what procedure he intended to make use of two women at the same time, but imagined that he would probably take us in turn, maybe changing from one to the other at intervals.

I waited expectantly for Hester to take the initiative. Inside, I was fairly burning up. Though I had bathed most carefully but a short while before, my cunny was wet with anticipation, my clitoris swollen and pulsing. In excuse of this ardour was the fact that I had not been with a man for three long years and during this sterile period there had been no outlet for my passions except the one provided by my own nimble fingers, an occasional wet dream and, as I have related, the orgasm effected by Hester's so-called massage.

We lay down on the bed on either side of our male companion, Hester and I both naked except for our slips, hose and shoes, which we intended to leave on until done with our play and ready for sleep. Mr Hayden caressed us impartially for a while, passing his hands over our breasts, fingering the nipples until they stood up stiffly, and finally a hand drifted down over each of the two cunnies. The contact of his warm hand as it lay over mine with one of the fingers pressed lightly within the cleft produced in me an effect which was almost sufficient to put my orgastic mechanism into immediate action. I literally had to 'clench' my nerves and strain my willpower to keep from coming. Had he let his finger linger there a bit longer, or had he imparted the slightest friction, my efforts to restrain orgasm would have failed then and there.

But he removed it after a short interval without apparently having observed my delicate condition, and straightening out on his back he drew Hester across his body where, by urging her forward bit by bit, he eventually got her straddled across his chest with her knees doubled beneath her on either side of him. Her dark auburn curls were right at his chin and it required no great imagination to devine that her cunny was going to be licked French fashion.

'If he does that to her before my eyes I'll cream despite anything I can do to hold it back. I know I shall!' I thought to myself.

In the light of experience throughout subsequent years I confess this: that the sight of another woman being Frenched by a man, or a woman Frenching a man, reacts upon me more violently than any other spectacle of a lewd nature. My senses are excited to a frenzy at the sight of this act, and if I let myself go I can have an orgasm without even touching myself, but simply through the impulse conveyed to the genital system through the trajectory of the eye.

Having accommodated Hester comfortably on his strong chest, Mr Hayden reached over and took me by the arm, manifesting by his motions that I was to seat myself across his middle, impaled upon the turgid emblem of masculinity, behind Hester. Obeying his wordless indications I crouched over him, passing my arm around Hester and clasping her plump bubbies in my hand. Then, gently, breathlessly, I sank down until I felt the entire length of that glorious member throbbing within the living sheath I was providing for it.

But, alas, to my consternation, barely had I perceived the contact of his crisp hair on my naked cunny than my emotions, overriding all powers of resistance, as though deriding my futile efforts to hold them in abeyance, rebelling incontinently, loosed themselves and in a second I was gasping, writhing and suspiring in a regular paroxysm of passionate ecstasy.

As the reverberations gradually died away and my thoughts took on a semblance of coherency, I was filled with mortification. What would Mr Hayden think of such amazing lubricity and precipitation? Hester, surprised at first, had twisted around, and now burst into laughter.

'What happened?' she gasped.

'I don't know! I did it . . . I couldn't help it!' I answered, shamefaced.

Mr Hayden was also laughing.

'You're a fast worker, Sister,' he said, his sides shaking, and realizing that I was momentarily, at least, exhausted by the orgasm, he added compassionately: 'Better get off and rest a moment while Hester and I catch up with you!'

I discharged myself and threw my still trembling body on the bed beside them. With his hands against Hester's knees Mr Hayden pushed her backward to take the place I had vacated and a moment later his cock slid in between her legs. Crouching over him, supporting herself on her hands, Hester worked gently up and down on the glistening shaft, alternating from time to time, with a twisting, rolling movement of her hips as she sank down upon his member, completely hiding it from view.

As I watched this sensuous play the tide of my own passions began to gather anew. Yielding to sudden impulse I inserted my hand between Hester's thigh and got my fingers around the base of the white column which was transfixing her. With each of her downward lunges my hand was compressed between the two bodies, and each time it was compressed my own clitoris throbbed in sympathy.

Hester began to moan softly. A delicate colour crept into her pretty cheeks, and her movements became more vigorous. As I perceived the more powerful pressure of her moist cunny crushing down upon my fist, and the strong, regular pulsations in the hard flesh about which my fingers were clenched, the fires of reawakened lust again glazed within me. My sexual potency was back in full force.

In this opportune moment Mr Hayden murmured something to Hester. Instantly she ceded the post of honour, slipped forward, and again crouched over his face. A second later I was on the throne she had vacated, and with my arms embracing her from behind, was quivering in response to the throbbing of the rigid shaft which penetrated me and filled me with its soul-stirring warmth.

To the accompaniment of Hester's low moans as a vigorous and active tongue teased her organism into expression I gasped out my own ecstasy and clung to her, half-fainting, while jet after jet of the hot balsam of life flung itself against my womb.

I was no longer a novice. I had graduated from the chippy stage of harlotry and was a full-fledged practitioner of the oldest profession. I was now a professional prostitute.

Mr Hayden came regularly, adhering faithfully to his programme of impartiality, and his visits were interludes in which both Hester and I forgot the sordid, commercialized circumstances under which we were prostituting our bodies and enjoyed ourselves like healthy, robust young animals.

CHAPTER SEVEN

The next patron to whom my companionship was pledged by the astute Madame Lafronde was Mr Heely. Mr Heely had been until now what was termed an occasional parlour visitor. He drank little and had never taken a girl upstairs, but he was very liberal with gratuities and it was suspected that he was more than well-to-do. He was a man somewhat between fifty-five and sixty, very courtly and dignified, a gentleman of the old school.

Until my advent in the bordello he had, on the occasion of his rather infrequent visits, confined himself to sitting quietly in a corner, a silent onlooker as a rule, sipping an occasional peculiar combination of liquor which was mixed in accordance with his own instructions. Sometimes he would engage a girl in conversation and after he had departed the subject of the conversation would be reported with considerable amusement. The nice old gentleman could find nothing more interesting to discuss with a half-naked girl than politics, economics and postwar social problems!

Nevertheless, the rewards which were falling to girls who were alert enough to accord him courteous hearing were sufficiently generous to have attracted Madame Lafronde's unerring eye, and she had him tabulated for future attention.

Now I had observed a more than casual interest in Mr Heely's attitude toward me in the course of my

73

ambulations about the salon, and had perceived the covert squeeze he always gave my hand as he pressed a liberal tip into it after selecting the single cigar he invariably tucked away in his pocket. Consequently, it was with no great surprise that on being called downstairs early one evening to the little private room which Madame Lafronde reserved for confidential business, I found Mr Heely with her and learned that I was the subject of the interview.

'Dear Mr Heely has taken a fancy to you, child. If it were anyone but him, I would positively not consider the matter for a moment. But Mr Heely is an honourable gentleman, my child. He knows your . . . ah . . . untarnished condition, my dear, and he will be quite contented to . . . ah . . . enjoy your companionship without encroaching on your . . . ah . . . virginal integrity. In fact, my dear. Mr Heely doesn't care for the sophisticated type, and it was exactly your . . . ah . . . so apparent maidenly innocence which intrigued his . . . ah . . . admiration. Hereafter, my dear, you will be at liberty to receive Mr Heely any evening he wishes to call on you. You may let him select one night each week.'

Mr Heely bowed courteously.

'But I hope my attentions will not be distasteful to Miss Jessie,' he interposed gently. 'Perhaps we should consult her first before coming to any definite understanding. I assure her, and you also, Madame, that I will be most considerate in my demands, and will endeavour to reward each of you in a suitable manner for your kindness. Do you think you could care for me as a good friend!' he added anxiously, turning to me.

Madame Lafronde's peculiar words had filled me with amazement. I did not know what to make of the conversation. Mr Heely was watching me with an intent, almost supplicating look on his face. I glanced uncertainly at Madame Lafronde. As I did so, the lid of her left eye descended slowly. Her face was solemn, impassive.

'Yes, Sir,' I answered, 'I'm sure I could care for you. Very much indeed, Sir.'

The alliance was pledged over three tiny glasses of wine and it was agreed that the following evening I was to be at Mr Heely's disposition and thereafter the same night each week.

As soon as the interview was concluded I rushed upstairs to find Hester. Into her attentive ear I poured the details of the mysterious contract. My mystification was so genuine that she nearly burst with laughter.

'But what does he want with me, what does he expect me to do?' I begged.

'The old fool has taken it for gospel truth that you're only fifteen years old and that you've never had a cock in you,' she answered finally, wiping her eyes. 'He'll be a regular gold mine. I had one like that once. He preached religion to me and sucked me off between sermons. I'll bet all you'll have to do with that man will be to let him go down on you. Those old fellows always want to do that. You'll have to pretend it's the first time, act ashamed, take on, cry about it afterwards a little and, baby, will he fill your stocking with bank notes!'

How different people were in real life to what they seemed, I reflected, as the picture which Hester's words evoked passed before my mind's eye. That dignified, cultured, respectable, elderly gentleman going down on me! It was too bizarre, too preposterous. It didn't seem possible.

Hester broke in on the train of thoughts which were passing through my head.

'Really, darling, you're lucky. Imagine having something like that supposed Italian count wished on you.'

'I heard Lafronde tell Rhoda she could chase him if he got too rough with her.'

This count, real or alleged, constituted something of a house scandal. He had the whipping mania, and though Rhoda submitted to him voluntarily, the pain he inflicted on her caused her to shriek in a way which alarmed everyone within hearing.

'I think she's half in love with the crazy brute. Do you know what he does to her? He puts her across his knees just like a baby, and whips her on the bare bottom with one of her slippers. He keeps her bottom black and blue.'

'What in the world does he do it for? What possible pleasure can he possibly get from hurting her?'

'Oh, what do any of them do funny things for? It gives him a hard-on, I suppose. Imagine having a man whip you like that and then wanting to fuck you afterwards.'

Madame Lafronde opened the door and came in.

'You'll have to get up early tomorrow morning and go shopping with me,' she said. 'Mr Heely has given some very specific instructions about your wearing apparel. Your present mode of dress is not in keeping with his ideas as to what nice girls should wear. And . . .' she continued dryly, glancing at a pencilled list in her hand, 'he has provided the funds necesssary to renovate your wardrobe.'

As a result of the shopping expedition which was duly effected the following day, I found myself in possession of some new clothes which, though of the finest and most expensive material, were so incongruously at variance with the ambience in which they were to be worn that I could only look at them with amazement.

There were three black silk dresses with cream-coloured lace cuffs and bodices, all of the same general type, but varying in minor details of style and trimming. They were very beautiful, but of a style suitable for extremely young misses, and reached barely to my knees. Underwear there was in profusion, but instead of the slithery, diaphanous tinted silk. I would have selected, it was of the finest English linen and cambric; slips, petticoats, and panties with little bands of lace around their edges, and all snow-white. There were two pair of little, round-toed, low-heeled patent leather pumps, and a long narrow box filled with black silk hose.

As we unpacked the purchases Madame Lafronde said:

'Ah, yes, I nearly forgot to tell you, my dear, that your new gentleman has a special abhorrence of rouge, lipstick and face powder. He prefers nature in the raw. So you may abstain from employing your usual artifices on the occasion of his visits.'

I nodded my head in assent. My mind was still floundering in a maze of contradictory whys and wherefores.

'Can you tell me, please, just what that man expects of me?'

'My girl, I haven't the slightest idea. But I don't doubt he'll treat you kindly. Men of his age often have very curious whims and ideas. My experience is that it's profitable to cater to them. Use your brains; find what pleases him, and act accordingly. If the screwy old fool thinks he has found a fifteen-year-old innocent running around naked in a whorehouse don't destroy his illusion. It will pay dividends. But remember this: he made the proposition himself that he would respect your alleged purity and right now he intends to live up to it. But if he runs true to form, before very long he'll be itching to get his pecker between your legs. And after he's fucked you two or three times it will be good-bye Mr Heely. Now I'm only speaking in the light of experience. There are exceptions to every rule, and he might be one of them. So use your brains, girl, use your brains. This is your chance to show what you can do.'

At eight o'clock I bathed preparatory to dressing for the evening. One of the pretty little black frocks was laid out on the bed waiting for me, together with the childish underwear, the silk hose and the patent leather pumps.

Having a little time to spare I decided to get out a jar of depilatory cream I had bought the day with the idea of using it in preference to a razor. To my great satisfaction it removed the hair thoroughly and easily without leaving the suggestion of a stubble which, try as I might, I had not been able to eliminate entirely with a safety razor.

The pubic mound and the sides of my cunny felt as smooth and velvety to the touch as a baby's skin. According to the information which accompanied the preparation, hair would not reappear for some time as it was destroyed clear down to the roots. This would be a great convenience, as the task of shaving frequently was growing irksome.

When Mr Heely appeared promptly at the specified hour of ten, I was all ready for him, waiting demurely in my room, dressed in a little girl's silk frock which barely reached my knees, my hair neatly combed back and tied with a ribbon, and my face sedately free of any artificial colouring or embellishment. There had been much giggling and laughter when earlier in the evening I had paraded this ensemble before the eyes of my companions. Even Madame Lafronde had laughed.

In one hand Mr Heely carried a large bouquet of beautiful hothouse flowers, in the other a square package containing a box of delicious candied fruit confections. I thanked him for his gifts, took his hat and coat, and arranged the flowers on my little table.

What should I say to him? What should I do? The thoughts buzzed in my head as I toyed with the flowers to gain time to decide, and ended by doing nothing except sitting down before him to wait for him to begin a conversation.

Considering our previous speculations and Hester's suppositions the visit simmered down to what constituted almost ludicrous simplicity and naiveté. Mr Heely did absolutely nothing more than sit in my room and talk, for the most part on generalized subjects, departing from those orthodox themes only now and then to pass compliments upon my appearance and conduct in his dignified, courtly way. He manifested pleasure at the good taste with which my wardrobe had been selected, and seemed to feel that I was now dressed in a seemly and befitting manner. He stayed for about two hours.

When he arose to go, he took my hand and pressed a kiss lightly upon the back of it. As he lowered it a folded bank note was resting in my palm. I did not want to look at it in his presence, so did not know until after he had gone the value of it. Before bidding me good-night he said:

'May I have the pleasure of calling upon you again next Friday, my dear?'

'Certainly, Mr Heely, I'll be very happy to have you,' I replied.

Not until the door had closed behind him did I straighten out the folded piece of currency. Before my surprised sight was a five-pound note. I could hardly believe my eyes. Surely the good old man was out of his mind.

Straightaway I rushed to find Madame Lafronde, laid the money before her and told her exactly what had transpired. She listened, smiling cynically, and pushed it back toward me.

'It's yours, girl. I've already had mine. Take it if you want to spend it. If you don't I'll put it away for you.'

'All of it?' I gasped.

'Certainly. Now just use your head, girl, and there'll be plenty more where that comes from. I'll get my share, and you may keep all you get from him. Wait a moment . . .' she called, as I turned to leave after thanking her, 'here's some more advice for you. Don't brag about your good fortune to the other girls. Keep it to yourself. That old green-eyed monster is always lurking around, waiting for a chance to make trouble. Don't tell others things that will make them envy you.'

How deeply these words struck home could only be guessed by one familiar with the circumstances of my past disgrace which had come about under the very conditions against which she was now warning me. Then and there I resolved to keep such good fortune as might come my way carefully hidden from envious eyes in the future.

As far as Mr Heely was concerned, I ceased for the moment to bother my head with trying to fathom his purposes. If he was willing to pay me five pounds for dressing up like a doll and listening to him for a couple of hours I had no reason for complaint. Both Hester and Madame Lafronde were of the opinion that he would eventually want to do something besides talk, and in this way they were right in a sense, but his

80

conduct never degenerated into anything of an obnoxious nature.

Indeed, his ingenuousness was almost pathetic, and I often felt a twinge of conscience at the imposition which was being practised upon him. But I salved it with the thought that it would be more painful to him to be disillusioned than to be deceived. He derived a certain happiness from the strange association, and it doubtless filled some lonely space in his heart.

On his second visit he asked permission to sit on a cushion at my feet, a request which was of course granted, although for the moment I was mystified. A bit later the circumstance of the extremely short dress flashed over me and the suspicion which it engendered was verified when I observed an occasional covert glance being directed between my legs.

From this time on I was more careless as to how I sat, but even in this the kindly old gentleman had frustrated his own wishes by having provided me with panties which were so substantially made as to constitute an effectual barrier to the eye.

Slowly but progressively his familiarities advanced as the visits continued. The sitting on a cushion before my knees reminded me of Hester's predictions. It brought his face conveniently close, and I wondered . . . but nothing came of it. Later, he came to seating me on his lap. This provided me with an opportunity to satisfy my curiosity on another point which I had not been able to determine.

Masculine wearing apparel of present times is deficient in one particular. It is prone to reveal in a rather frank manner a certain physical condition to which men are at times subject, one which does not, on such occasions, escape the observant feminine eye. I had never noticed this condition in Mr Heely, a circumstance which intrigued my curiosity.

Furthermore, his continued liberality was beginning to inspire me, with a desire to show my gratitude in some form. It stood to reason there was something he wanted, some inner wish which perhaps he himself had not fully defined, or else was too timid and reticent to express.

And so, partly to satisfy my own curiosity, and partly actuated by a really unselfish wish to give him something in return for his generosity, I decided to encourage him a little more actively, even though this was contrary to Madame Lafronde's counsel.

It was very difficult to convince myself that he was taking this farcical 'make-believe-lady' comedy seriously. How could he possibly think I was chaste and innocent, living as I was in a house of prostitution and associating with harlots? It hardly seemed possible that a man of his age and experience could be so credulous.

Surely he was, like myself, just pretending, and finding in the pretence some peculiar psychic compensation beyond my comprehension. Surely he must know in his heart that it was all sham and fraud.

I had observed that his gaze was frequently on my legs. There are men to whom the feminine leg is almost a fetish. Also, I had not forgotten the floor-sitting inclinations. The next time he came after I had made my resolution I sat on his lap, and as he talked I worked and fumbled through the texture of my dress at my garter which I had purposely tightened until it compressed my leg unduly.

'Mr Heely,' I murmured plaintively, 'I wonder if you could fix my garter for me. The buckle is so stiff I can't loosen it and the garter is almost cutting my leg in two.' So saying, I drew my skirt up in the most casual manner, exposing the garter, the top of my hose and a tiny bit of flesh above. 'Look,' I continued, 'it's making a regular ring around my leg!' I pulled the garter toward my knee and turned down the upper part of my hose. There was a purple indentation around the leg.

Mr Heely was instantly all compassion.

'My dear little girl,' he exclaimed, 'why didn't you speak of it before? Why, this thing is so tight it's cutting off the blood circulation. We must open the buckle and lengthen the elastic.'

As he spoke, his fingers tenderly caressed the puckered flesh. He slipped the garter down over my knee and off my leg. It took him but a moment to pry open the buckle and lengthen the band, whereupon he replaced the garter and smoothed my hose back into place.

'How about the other one? Is it tight? Perhaps we'd better fix it, too.'

'I wish you would,' I replied. 'It hurts my fingers to open those buckles.'

My other leg was laid bare above the knee and the second garter received his attention. He spent several minutes rubbing the flesh to restore the impeded circulation, adjusted the garter and put my dress down over my knees.

'You're so kind to me, Mr Heely, I fear I shall never be able to repay you.'

'Why, Jessie, dear,' he answered, obviously pleased, 'just being near you is quite payment enough. I have lived a very lonely life, my dear, and these are happy hours for me. I only wish they were half as pleasant for you as they are for me.'

What could I do with a man so ingenuous and innocent that he refused to rise to such bait? It was not sufficient that I sit on his lap and let him play with my garters. Either he was the world's prize simpleton or he didn't, in truth, want anything from me. I decided to make a bolder effort.

'Indeed they are pleasant for me, Mr Heely! I feel so comfortable with you. I like to sit on your lap this way. Sometimes . . . sometimes, though, I get feelings when I'm sitting on your lap that I don't understand myself. . . .'

I felt him start slightly.

'What kind of feelings, my dear?'

'Oh, I don't know . . . they're hard to describe . . . kind of trembly, warm feelings that go all through me. Like just now, when you were rubbing my leg. . . .'

'Are they pleasant feelings, dear?' he asked huskily.

'Oh, yes! Sometimes I think they are naughty feelings, and then again I think they can't be bad when they're so nice. Do you think they are bad feelings, Mr Heely?' I continued, watching him covertly for his reactions.

'My dear child,' he replied finally, taking one of my hands between his and squeezing it, 'I hardly know how to answer you. Madame Lafronde told me, if I remember correctly, that you are fifteen years old. At that age the promptings of Nature are to be accepted as an entirely normal manifestation of a healthy body, I would imagine. I have, I must confess, often doubted the prudency of Madame Lafronde's course in bringing you into surroundings and influences which I fear will tend to corrupt your thoughts. I wish . . .' he continued sadly, 'that it were possible for me to remove you from this questionable atmosphere, but if I were to suggest such a thing my motives would undoubtedly be questioned. So all I can do, my dear, is to offer you such counsel and advice as my more mature years may qualify me to give. I have never had any daughters of my own, and though I was once married, my wife was taken from me while we were both quite young. So now, in my old age, I have no one to hold on my knee but little Jessie.'

'Why, you're not old at all, Mr Heely!'

He raised my hand, which he was still holding, to his lips and kissed it. I was not so hardened as to be unmoved by his pathetic words, and I understood now for the first time with some degree of clarity, the exact situation.

Mr Heely's interest in me was unselfish in that it was not actuated by the desire to play any fantastic sexual game, but rather by the promptings of the vague and unsatisfied longings of a man who has lived a repressed and virtuous life, and who, in the eventide of his days, realizing that something vital has been missed, gropes belatedly and blindly for that intangible sense of fulfilment which can only come through bodily and spiritual union with the opposite sex. Too late he had found a compliment which could have satisfied the longings he himself would probably have refused to recognize as merely physical; he must now warm the fibres of his being with the dying embers of a fire disguised as paternal. This he could do without suffering the loss of self-respect or the sacrifice of dignity.

If I chose to continue accepting his bounty indefinitely without thought of compensating him in any way other than by dressing to suit his fancy and playing maidenly innocence, I could do so. He would never make any sexual advances toward me except those of the mildest and most indirect nature.

But I was not without conscience, nor did I lack an elemental spirit of gratitude. The man had been both kind and generous to me, and without hesitating long I made up my mind to find ways to provide this gentle soul with an occasional moment of happiness flavoured with just that degree of lubricity which would find an echo in his being, and leave him with a few soft memories with which to dispel the loneliness of his heart.

During the week which elapsed before his next visit I gave considerable thought to the subject, casting about in my mind for some formula which would fit the peculiar circumstances. Various ideas were entertained and discarded as unsuitable. But one afternoon there chanced to cross my thoughts the recollection of Mr Peters, the watchmaker who had boarded with us when I was a child. In a vague way, Mr Heely reminded me of Mr Peters. He was far more cultured and refined, but there was a certain similarity of characters which might have been much more pronounced had their social and educational status been parallel.

Submerged in memories of the past which the thought evoked I saw myself again a child of eleven, slipping surreptitiously into Mr Peters' room to be masturbated while I stood between his knees holding my little dress up. Again I saw his congested face and the tiny beads of perspiration which testified to the vibrant emotion he must have experienced vicariously through manual stimulation of my body. Had he not actually paid me to let him masturbate me and given other evidences of pleasue in realizing the act? And it had certainly caused me more pleasure than annoyance.

And mentally I began setting the stage for Mr Heely's next visit.

So it came to pass that after the customary exchange of banalities had been effected, I set about immediately to warm the atmosphere preparatory to the course I had elected to follow with Mr Heely.

'Mr Heely,' I began diffidently, 'you never have seen all the pretty things you had Madame Lafronde buy for me. They're so pretty they make my heart beat faster every time I look at them, and then I think of you.'

His face glowed with pleasure.

'I thought I'd seen all of them, my dear,' he answered, fingering the hem of my dress. 'I was just thinking today that perhaps you needed some new frocks. Madame Lafronde exercised very good taste in her selections and these black silk dresses become you wonderfully.'

'I don't mean the dresses alone,' I murmured, essaying a bit of bashful confusion. 'There were other things, beautiful things; you've never seen them at all, Mr Heely.'

'Ah, you mean underthings, my dear. Quite true, I didn't see them, but if they pleased you that is all that is necessary.'

'I never had such beautiful things in all my life, Mr Heely. Some of them have got the prettiest lace trimming, it looks just like handwork. Hester, my friend, says it's machine-made lace, but I want to show you, Mr Heely, and see if you don't think it's handmade.'

Without waiting for his answer I slipped from his knees and went to my clothes chest, extracted from among the garments stored herein a pair of dainty cambric panties, around the legs of which were attached narrow bands of expensive lace. Thrusting the intimate garment into his hands, I continued to expiate on the quality and beauty of the material.

'Don't you think that's handmade lace, Mr Heely?'

'Really, I'm hardly qualified to say, my dear,' he replied, as he gingerly fingered the garment. 'All I can say is that it seems to be well made, but whether by hand or machine I cannot say.'

'The ones I've got on are even prettier, Mr Heely.

87

I don't mind if you see them on me. I want you to see how pretty they are and how well they fit me.'

So saying, I raised my dress until a goodly portion of lace filigree and cambric panty leg, to say nothing of quite a bit of flesh, was revealed. Slowly I pivoted around on my toes so that Mr Heely might judge both the dainty workmanship of the garment, and in addition such physical allurements as might catch the eye.

His face flushed slightly, and he half-averted his gaze, but his next words assured me that I had not missed the mark at which I had aimed.

'My child, it is your pretty limbs which lend beauty to the garment. I have never seen a more charming picture.'

Visibly affected, he extended his arms and drew me again upon his lap. His arm prevented my dress from falling into place, and as I made no effort to adjust it I found myself seated across his knees with my legs exposed to the tops of my stockings and higher. I laid an arm over his shoulder and cuddled against him.

Soon I felt a hand lightly caressing my knee. It moved tenderly back and forth over the silken surface of my hose. I lay quietly with my head against his shoulder, my eyes half-closed. The hand moved higher and I sensed the tremor of its touch in a timid caress which dwelt a moment upon the bare flesh above the stocking. It receded downward to the knee, and after a brief hesitation again advanced until finally the palm lay cupped over the rounded curve of bare flesh. His other hand meanwhile passed under my arm, lay quietly and unobtrusively over one of my breasts.

Seated thus with nothing but the thin material of my panties and his own garments between the sensitive areas of our respective bodies I would have easily perceived anything in the nature of a muscular reaction to the erotic incitation to which Mr Heely was now being subjected.

That there was none confirmed my suspicions that either through physical weakness or possibly a purely mental inhibition he was incapacitated sexually in the more material sense of the word. For him naught remained but such secondary exultations as might have their birth in psychic stimulation, the last dispensation of benevolent old Mother Nature who, tempering the wind to the shorn lamb, concedes that minor consolation, a measure of bliss in the mere presence of contemplation of pleasure through the awakening of an echo, or the touching of a responsive chord in our sensibilities.

Certain now of my ground, I advanced boldly.

Snuggling closer to him, and tightening my clasp about his shoulder, I murmured in a low voice:

'Mr Heely, you have been so good to me, there is something I must tell you. I'm awfully ashamed to, but I think you should know, so you can tell me what to do. There is no one else I can ask, I just couldn't speak of it to anyone else but you. . . .'

His hand clenched about the flesh of my leg.

'What is it, Jessie, dear? I can't imagine anything you could tell me which should cause you to feel ashamed. As you know, I want you to feel perfectly free to tell me anything that troubles you.'

'Oh, Mr Heeley, when you know what it is, you may be terribly shocked, and not care for me anymore. I'm so ashamed to tell you I don't know whether I can get up the courage or not. . . .'

I dabbed at my eyes with a tearful gesture.

'But, my little Jessie!' exclaimed the now quite perturbed Mr Heely, 'I assure you from the depths of my heart that there is nothing, absolutely nothing which would lessen my regard for you. It hurts me that you can even entertain such a thought!'

'Oh, Mr Heely!' And here my sobs must have been quite convincing in their rendition. 'You think I'm a nice girl, and I'm not! I have the most terrible longings when I'm with you, sometimes I can't sleep at all after you've gone, and other times I have dreams, oh, such dreams, they wake me up and I lie in the dark thinking, and it gets worse until, finally, well, I just have to . . . have to. . . ?'

I paused, and after waiting a long moment for me to continue, Mr Heely whispered tensely:

'Have to . . . have to what, dear·'

'Oh, don't make me say it! You must guess . . . without my putting it in words . . . I don't want to do it . . . they say it ruins a girl's health . . . but I just can't sleep until I make that feeling go away! Now, don't you hate me, Mr Heely?'

The tension of his hand on my leg relaxed, and the hand moved gently back and forth over the flesh. I peeped at him through my eyelashes, his face was flushed.

'My dear little baby,' he murmured in a strained voice, 'and you thought telling me this would lessen my regard for you? Don't you remember that I told you the other night that certain emotions and impulses in healthy young bodies were quite natural? Of course, I never dreamed that I was unintentionally contributing to them, but I still don't think it serious enough to upset yourself about, except insofar as your rest and sleep is concerned. That . . .' he added in a troubled voice, 'is something we'll have to think about.'

'Then you don't think I'm bad for having those feelings, Mr Heely?'

'Nonsense, child! Every normal person has gone through the same experience in the period of adolescence. But you must exercise self-control and not fall into habits which will undermine your health.'

'But . . . but . . . Mr Heely, if I don't do that, it happens anyway while I'm asleep! When I wake up, it's too late to stop it from happening!

'Oh, Mr Heely there is something . . . I think . . . I know . . . would be good for me. It would smooth my nerves and take that feeling away . . . if only . . . but how can I ask you such a thing!'

'How can you continue to question my willingness to do anything in my power for you, my little Jessie?' the poor man insisted reproachfully. 'If I am in any way to blame for a condition which can only be relieved by discontinuing my visits I'll have to make the sacrifice. Do you think it would be better for you if I didn't come?' he asked anxiously.

'Oh, no, no, Mr Heely. That wouldn't keep me from thinking of you; it would only make things a hundred times worse!'

'What did you have in mind then, my dear?' he asked, vastly relieved. 'Speak frankly; I'll not be offended!'

'Oh, Mr Heely, it's something . . . it really happened in a dream once. I felt so much better that way than when I . . . you know what I mean . . . and the bad feeling didn't come back for a long time, but . . .' and I hid my face against his shoulder, 'it's dreadful to ask you such a thing!'

'Let's consider that after we know what it is!' he urged tensely.

'If you . . . if you . . . oh, Mr Heely . . . it sounds so terrible . . . but if you would . . . if you would just put your hand there where the feeling starts . . . if you would just put your hand there for a moment each night before you leave . . . I know the feelings would finish and go away and I wouldn't have to do that in the night!'

A tremor passed through his body, his arms gripped me convulsively, and though he spoke with forced calmness, I knew he was in exquisite torment.

'You think that would calm your nerves?' he asked in an unsteady voice.

'I feel sure it would . . . I know it would . . . if you wouldn't mind doing it!'

'Shall we try it tonight?'

'Yes, yes!' I whispered.

'Now?'

'Yes!'

So realistically had I enacted my self-imposed role of ingenuous impudicity that, unconsciously, it had quite taken hold my own imagination, and for the moment I was actually living the part I had assumed.

As I slipped from his lap I distinctly felt a tremor in my own knees, and the warm glow of sexual excitation was permeating my body. I had 'acted' myself into a real heat.

With trembling fingers I undid my panties and without troubling to remove my dress lay down on my back upon the bed. Shielding my eyes with a forearm and in a fever of anticipation I awaited his approach.

He rose from his chair and sat down on the edge of the bed by my side. He hesitated uncertainly for a moment and then slowly inserted his hand up under my dress. Seeing that he had not the assurance of temerity to throw the dress back and expose my body, and having succeeded in working myself up to a degree in which my own organism was now imperatively demanding satisfaction, I reached down and pulled up the dress myself, revealing my cunny which just that morning had received fresh depilatory attentions.

Just as an electric current is transmitted from one metal object to another by contact so does that mysterious force called sexual exultation communicate itself from one body to another under favourable circumstances. I had deliberately induced an erotic tension in this man such as he probably had not experienced in years. I had been actuated by kindly rather than lewd motives for, as a matter of fact, I had never felt the slightest sexual inclination toward him. Now, having succeeded by my sacrifices in exciting his sterile passions to an exquisite pitch, I found myself caught in my own trap.

A moment or two after I pulled up my dress I felt his hand on my cunny. I separated my legs a bit wider, lay back, closed my eyes, and prepared to yield myself up to the pleasurable sacrifice. I sensed my clitoris, now excited and swollen, pulsing impatiently in anticipation. It wanted to be rubbed and rubbed vigorously. But as I waited expectantly there came no motion in the hand which lay firmly, but inactively pressed against it. I waited a long minute and then moved my hips suggestively once or twice. The hand still lay motionless over the pubic mound with the fingers, likewise motionless, resting lightly along the extension of the crevice below.

It was tantalizing. Didn't this man know anything at all? I wriggled my hips again, once, twice, several times. I squeezed my thighs together, compressing his fingers between them, and still that hand remained impassively quiet.

The tension in my nerves was now such as to render further delay unendurable. I seized his hand in mine and forcibly imparted a rubbing motion as I pressed it harder against my clitoris. Under this friction and pressure the current of erotic sensation began to generate swiftly.

Having set his hand on the proper frictional course I released it and lay back again to savour the ravishing caress until the mounting sensations attained their maximum and, like a bursting rocket, exploded and hurled their melting fires through my body.

Mr Heeley was all tenderness and solicitude as he hovered over me, nor was it difficult to assure him that I now felt immensely relieved and was certain of a peaceful sleep and rest.

Needless to say, the 'treatments' were incorporated regularly as a preventative of further nocturnal disquiet, and thus, by the simple expedient of inducing the kind-hearted man to think he was safe-guarding my health and morals by masturbating me once a week. I found a way to warm the blood in his aged veins and recompense him in a small way for his generosity.

CHAPTER EIGHT

I had been with Madame Lafronde about three months when the patronage of Mr Thomas, another well-to-do but also middle-aged gentleman was steered my way by the astute old lady.

Things had run along in a pleasant manner; I had gotten along very well with Madame Lafronde. She seemed to take a genuine interest in my welfare, and some of the girls who had at first treated me with a certain coolness, doubtless inspired by the fear that patrons might be tempted from them by my juvenile coquetteries, had been won over and were now cordial and friendly.

Mr Thomas was too much a man of the world to be at all deceived on the matter of my alleged innocence, but beyond passing a few half-comical, half-cynical observations, he did not dwell on the subject.

Although the gentleman was fairly well along in years, he was hale and robust and had no physical deficiencies. My relations with Mr Thomas were so entirely normal, or so purely ethical, if I may use the term, that there is little to tell which would be of interest.

Like Mr Heely, he was a single man, but there the similarity ended. He had engaged my companionship for one quite specific purpose, and between times regaled me with piquant accounts of amorous adventures during his younger days in Ceylon. With apparently no qualms of conscience to disturb him, he told me of having fucked little native girls of eight, nine and ten years of age, of having two or three of them in bed with him at the same time, and of other salacious combinations.

I say he regaled me with these stories 'between times' because it was his regular and unvarying procedure to do it to me twice on each of his visits. He was entitled, by virtue of an exorbitant fee paid for my companionship, to pass the entire night, but he never stayed after the termination of the second act. He arrived generally around ten o'clock, spent an hour amusing himself in the parlour, and then came upstairs, when I was waiting for him. He was always prepared for an immediate encounter with a hard-on which belied his years, the potency of which was probably contributed to by aphrodisiacal sights, conversations, and liquor in the parlour.

When the first episode was concluded an hour would be passed in conversation, stories and banter while I sat on his lap naked. As he talked, his hands roved over my body, caressing my legs, thighs, and breasts, and lingering on my hairless cunny where the tantalizing touches kindled fevers in my organism while his own recovered its original potency. When he was ready for the second round we repaired again to the bed and I lay on my back with legs clamped around his middle and wriggled my bottom until I coaxed his second spend from him, whereupon he was ready to cry quits, and I was free for the rest of the night.

This man frequently disconcerted me with some outlandish story, told so seriously that I never failed to be taken in. While in charge of a plantation he had taken a baby, left to the vicissitudes of life through orphanage, and with no facilities other than those available in isolated bachelor quarters, had endeavoured to care for it and attend to its requirements.

What a kindhearted man, I thought, much impressed with the patience and benevolence the act implied, and passed some observation to this effect.

'She was a pretty little thing,' he concluded, puffing meditatively at his cigar.

'Ah . . . it was a girl,' I murmured.

'Yes. She had the most beautiful skin, a soft, olive tint. It was like silk to the touch. And her bubbies, not any bigger than orange halves, but as firm and. . . .'

'How old was that baby?' I interrupted.

'Oh, she was eleven or twelve, I guess.'

'It was indeed noble of you to have cared for her so tenderly, Mr Thomas,' I answered with heavy sarcasm. 'I presume dressing and undressing her, bathing her and so on must have signified quite a sacrifice of time and labour for you. Possibly you even had to share your bed with her?'

'Unfortunately, there was only one bed in the place. And I couldn't let the poor little thing sleep on the floor, of course.'

'Of course not!'

Next on the list came Mr Castle. This gentleman had a complex for strange and unusual postures in sexual intercourse, and also an itch to experiment along lines somewhat contrary to the plans of Nature. Only the fact that he was both liberal and possessed of unfailing good humour made assocation with him supportable. Had it been possible to offend him, my angry reactions to some of his droll impudences would quickly have terminated our relationship.

No sooner was the door closed behind us on the occasion of his first bedroom visit than I was startled to find myself suddenly seized from behind and tumbled forward so that while the weight of my body fell upon my hands and wrists, my legs were caught and held under his arms.

In this undignified position, with my short skirts fluttering about my face and head, and with my bare bottom and all there was between my legs exposed, I struggled and protested angrily, but to no avail, for with imperturbable aplomb, while still imprisoning my kicking legs under his strong arms, he unfastened the front of his trousers and in an instant I felt his cock poking against my inverted cunny.

I tried to evade its thrusts as I sputtered angry protests, but he had me in such a position that I was quite helpless and in another moment I felt it going in, in this upside down fashion. The whole thing was finished and over almost before I was conscious of the pain which his cock, pressing against the side of my womb in this unnatural position, caused me.

He was what is termed in professional circles a 'fast shooter,' one of those men whose orgastic reaction is to rapid as to require but a few thrusts. In the midst of my kicking and squealing I felt the hot gushes followed by the wet, sticky trickle of semen down over my stomach. A second later he released me and sank down on the bed, shaking with laughter while I, after regaining my feet, stood before him, my face flushed with indignation, protesting such cavalier treatment.

'Excuse me, Sister,' he gasped finally between gusts of laughter. 'I'm sorry I was so rude. It's a weakness I have . . . I just can't resist temptation!'

'Well, why are you laughing about it, then?' I demanded, only half-appeased by the doubtful apology.

'Ha, ha, ha! If you only knew how funny you looked, standing on your head, with your cute little cunny upside down!'

'Oh!' I gasped, my indignation mounting anew, but before I could formulate a sufficiently withering retort, he continued:

'There was something . . . something . . . ah, yes; how is it your cunny hasn't any fur? I've seen them shaved off before, but they're like a man's chin, you can feel the bristles even after a close shave. Your pussy felt as smooth as silk. Let's take a peek at it Sister!'

I was still palpitating with anger, but under such ludicrous circumstances it could not last long and finally I smiled in spite of myself.

'You're a very abrupt person,' I said. 'Since you believe in caveman tactics, it's a wonder you bother about asking me to let you see it.'

No sooner were the words out of my mouth than he acted on the suggestion. His hand closed over my wrist and I was jerked none too gently to the bed and tumbled over on my back. Again I raged helplessly while, shaking with irrepressible laughter, he adroitly subjected my wrists by holding them in one hand, and with the other pulled up my dress.

Apparently unfamiliar with the properties of depilatory agents, his visual and tactile examination seemed to convince him that the denuded condition was a natural one, which greatly intrigued his interest. While I continued to rage futilely, he felt and squeezed the naked lips and surrounding parts, and still not content, decided to have some more fun with me.

No one except a woman who had suffered the indignity can comprehend the conflict of emotions undergone in being jacked-off forcibly against her wishes. It is quite one thing to submit to the manipulation when it is desired, and another to be forced.

As the ball of the clown's finger rotated against my clitoris the treacherous little organ stiffened up in response, contrary to my wishes and despite all the mental influence I could bring to bear on it. When I breathed curses and demands for instant release it pulsed with increasing vigour under the friction, with the inevitable result that my resistance was suddenly stifled and my angry exclamations quite involuntarily changed into surprising moans.

The orgasm diminished my anger somewhat but I still felt resentful and complained bitterly of having been treated in such an outrageous manner.

'It was just the same as a rape!' I protested.

'Rape? Rape?' And again he burst into laughter. 'That's a new one on me, Sister! I never knew before that a girl could be raped by a finger!'

'Well,' I answered, my natural good humour beginning to assert itself, 'it amounts to the same thing. When you make a girl do something against her wishes, it's rape, even if you do it with your finger!'

It was impossible to stay angry with this comical buffoon, and being further mollified by a gift of respectable denomination, I found myself looking forward to his next call, if not with longing, at least with curiosity.

The next eccentricity he manifested was a desire to try an inexhaustable number of unusual and strange positions. Because of the rapidity with which orgasm overtook him, the only way he could avoid ejaculation and prolong these experiments was to take his cock out of me after making a few quick movements. Naturally, this was very tantalizing, for it made me hot without satisfying me, but I had to stand it as best I could.

Obligingly following his instructions I stood on the floor, bent over, my hands resting on my knees, and let him do it to me from behind. I lay doubled up in a ball on the bed with my knees crooked forward against my chest while he knelt in front of me. I sat spiked on his lap in a rocking chair, I lay on my back on a table with my legs over his shoulders and went through other equally strained and arduous exercises wondering all the while why a man should want to take such roundabout and complicated roads to reach a place which was accessible by shorter and easier routes. All these strenuous gymnastics just to make a few drops of semen come out of his testicles, a result I could have attained for him in ten seconds if left to my own devices.

But it wasn't until a subsequent visit that I found I had more objectionable things still to contend with.

This time he had me on my hands and knees on the bed and was kneeling behind me. This is the position known as 'dog fashion' in the social circles of prostitution, and insomuch as it projects a woman's cunt out quite prominently, she has to be careful that the man does not injure her by too deep a penetration, especially if he has a large cock.

I felt his cock pushing against me, but it was aimed too high, and was prodding my bottom instead of my cunny. At first I thought that this was just an accident and putting my hand behind me I shoved it downward and got it headed in the right direction. But after two or three vague pushes, it slipped out and again I felt it punching against my bottom, this time in such a determined manner that it almost got its head inside.

Again I reached behind me to push it away, but he resisted the effort, and leaning over my back, whispered:

'Don't push it away. Let it go in for just a moment!'

'I will not!' I exclaimed, and jerked free from his embrace.

'There, there!' he answered, soothingly, 'I was just

teasing you, Sis! Come on and let's finish. I have to get away early tonight.'

Rather reluctantly, and on the alert for a new attack on the unguarded spot, I again braced myself on my hands and knees, but this time he let Nature take her course in normal channels.

From this time on the man was unable to resist the temptation to try to do it to me in the bottom on every occasion which presented itself. Determinedly I resisted blandishments, coaxings, and even treacherous efforts to catch me unawares, but it got on my nerves and brought choleric protestations to my lips. In justice to Mr Castle, I must say that he took my angry rebuffs and blunt refusals to gratify his unnatural whim in good spirit and unfailing pleasant humour.

It was then I intimated to Madame Lafronde that it would not hurt my feelings were his affections tactfully transferred to some other girl, but I was ashamed to tell her the exact reason.

'Why don't you want him?' she insisted.

'Well,' I finally said, 'he has crazy ideas. The first night I had an appointment with him he stood me on my head and did it to me upside down!'

'What!' she expostulated. 'Is that the only reason you dislike him?'

Abashed, I made a clean breast.

'No, it isn't! If you must know, I'll tell you! He never gives me a moment's peace from wanting to do it to me in the bottom!'

I expected that this revelation would bring a decided expression of indignation from Madame Lafronde and that she would now be willing to concede that Mr Castle was indeed a most objectionable client.

But, after gazing at me a moment, she began to laugh heartily.

'And is that all that is wrong with him?'

'Isn't that enough?' I responded stiffly.

'My word, girl,' answered the old lady, 'there is no pleasant road to success in anything, not even in whoring. You're going to meet men far more difficult to deal with than this Mr Castle, so you must now learn how to get what you want from them and how to evade what you don't want by using diplomacy. They say the way to a man's heart is through his stomach. I don't know about that, I never did much cooking, but you can take my word for it that the way to his purse is through his cock. And his purse will stay open just as long as you keep his cock in a good humour and no longer!'

I was not too dense nor too stubborn to comprehend the wisdom of her philosophy and I did indeed learn eventually that more could be accomplished by cunning and diplomacy than by angry words.

'Sometime,' I murmured to Mr Castle one night as I deftly evaded a sly attempt on my bottom, 'sometime, I'm going to let you do that just to see what it feels like . . . but not tonight!'

CHAPTER NINE

When Mr Wainwright was added to my list of regulars I found need of all the philosophy I could muster. He was a suave, dapper little man, rather handsome in an effeminate way, but very nervous and emotional. He was not, I think, over twenty-eight or thirty.

There was nothing special in his appearance to suggest the possibility of any weird abnormality, yet here is what happened: As soon as we were alone in the seclusion of my room he went through a pantomine of courting me in the most exaggerated manner. Words of gallantry, adoration, and vows of eternal loyalty poured from his lips as he knelt before me, kissing first my hands, then my feet and legs.

In accordance with my usual custom when receiving new admirers for the first time, I was fully clothed, excepting one single garment which for convenience sake I left off, inasmuch as its absence would not be noted until the moment when its presence would be of no moment. Taken aback by this man's strange performance, and indeed not being sure that he wasn't simply trying to be funny, I remained silent.

Murmuring words of endearment and adoration his lips gradually ascended to my knees, whereupon he turned his face upward and begged in supplicating words:

'Oh, my Fairy Princess! Give me your permission to raise the hem of this robe so that your slave may cool his burning lips on the sweet freshness of your divine limbs.'

This was too much for me.

'Go ahead and cool them, Sweetie!' I giggled with a democratic sociability quite out of keeping with the regal estate he had delegated to me.

Ignoring the flippancy of my answer, he turned the edge of my dress up, not high enough to reveal the absence of the interior garment already referred to, but just high enough to expose two or three inches of bare flesh above the tops of my hose. Upon this isolated flesh he pressed more moist kisses, clasping my knee meanwhile to his breast.

'Beautiful Princess!' he sighed ecstatically, and then in humble, imploring tones, 'will Your Highness deign to repose upon the couch and let this faithful slave quench his thirst at the sweet spring of life?'

It was too ridiculous and I laughed hysterically, but supposing that he was now ready to 'quench his thirst' in the customary manner, I let him lead me to the bed and lay down, still laughing.

Disregarding my risibility he slowly and with exaggerated deference, raised my dress and folded it back. He gazed for a long moment at my denuded cunny which was now in plain sight, and then, before I guessed his intention, leaned down and placed his mouth on it.

Whether this was just a little frisking preparatory to an orthodox fuck I had no means of knowing at the moment, but in any event it was a pleasant variation, and I was agreeably surprised. I have been 'Frenched' on a few occasions even before entering Madame Lafronde's bordello, and sometimes Mr Hayden would tickle my clitoris with the tip of his tongue for a few moments when Hester and I were with him. I was peculiarly sensitive to the caress and sometimes felt an inordinate longing for it, but with the exception of Mr Hayden, none of my clients had ever taken the notion, and I, naturally, would never suggest it.

Consequently, when I felt this man's mouth on my cunny, and perceived the play of his tongue over the sensitive parts, I shivered delightedly, my clitoris stiffened up, and I relaxed my body to better enjoy the enervating caress.

It continued, actively, expertly. I felt my clitoris, now swollen and erected, clenched between his lips. A ravishing suction, was being applied to it, and my sexual organism responded by throbbing excitedly with a mounting fever of lascivious ebullition. Heavens, it did feel good. If it were kept up a moment or two longer, something would surely happen.

I tensed my body, lifted myself up slightly on my elbows, and glanced downward to my companion. Unobserved by me he had opened the front of his trousers, and was frigging himself violently. I sank back with a groan, my ovaries yielded to the intoxicating incitation, and in a second I was suspiring in the ecstasy of orgasm.

No sooner had my sexual forces expended themselves than a feeling of revulsion came over me. I do not know to just what event other women are similarly affected in this particular, but for several moments following ejaculation, the slightest touch upon my cunny causes me a disagreeable sensation. It passes quickly, but during those few moments I cannot stand even the softest touch or caress. As the last tremors of orgasm died away I put my hand on his head and gently but firmly pushed him away.

Yielding to the gesture, he released my clitoris from between his clenched lips. His face slid down a little and his lips attached themselves to the flesh on the inside of one of my thighs just below my cunny. This did not bother me, though I expected a discoloration would result from the strong suction he applied to the flesh as he continued meanwhile to masturbate himself vigorously.

The orgasm I had just experienced left me too languid to pay much attention to just what he was doing, though I was watching him through half-closed eyes. Suddenly, through his own lively handling, the jets of semen began streaking from his cock and flew all over my legs. And in the same moment, his teeth penetrated the flesh of my thigh where he had been sucking it.

Between pain and surprise I let out a shriek and sprang from the bed in a single bound. With mixed emotions of fright and anger I looked at him, uncertain as to whether I should fly from the room or demand an explanation of his brutality. He was lying on the bed, gasping and weltering in his own pollution, seemingly indifferent to my outraged feelings.

I raised my dress to examine the wound. It was less serious than I had first imagined, being quite superficial in character. He had bitten into a tiny fold of flesh, just deep enough to draw blood, which fact was attested to by several ruby drops which were slowly trickling down the inside of my thigh. When I saw that I was not wounded as badly as I had first supposed, anger dissipated fright, and I turned on him wrathfully.

'What kind of a crazy fool are you, biting me like that?'

He looked at me stupidly for a moment and then his gaze travelled downward to where the little red drops were visible between my legs. A look of contrition passed over his face. He flung himself at my feet, and clasping my knees to his breast, begged me piteously to forgive him. To my amazement his eyes were filled with tears.

'But why did you do that to me?' I insisted reproachfully.

'Sweet Princess,' he moaned, 'I did it unconsciously. Strike me, beat me, kick me, do what you will with me in punishment, but do not be angry with your slave!'

What could one do with such a lunatic?

'Well,' I said, finally, 'I'll forgive you, but don't ever do that again!'

When he had departed I gazed wide-eyed at the material evidence of Madame Lafronde's sage philosophy, for without bothering to count them, he had flung upon my dresser a little sheaf of bank notes which totalled an amount in excess of anything I had previously received.

After I had counted the money, I examined again the tiny laceration in the white flesh of my thigh. It had stopped bleeding and no longer pained. Money can indeed cure many ails and ills. It was an obsession the man was prey to, but lured on by the irresistible magic of gold, I risked further mistreatment and got it, and today, on the inner surfaces of my thighs just below my cunny, are several tiny white scars, each punctuating a moment of insanity during which the teeth of a sadist bit into my flesh while with his own hand he lashed his sexual fury into its final torment of expression.

During the later period of my incarceration in the reformatory, and for over five months of the time I was on Madame Lafronde's staff, I had no word of my foster brother Rene. Letters sent to the last address he had given me in Canada came back unclaimed. His silence worried me greatly. I did not know but what some grave misfortune had overtaken him, but I suspected that, unable to send me any money, he was ashamed to write.

While thinking about him one day I recalled that in our old neighbourhood dwelt a boyfriend to whom Rene was greatly attached, and it occurred to me to write this boy, or young man as he now was, if still alive, on the chance that he might have had some news of Rene.

I acted on this impulse, but the response, which came by return post was negative. He had not received any letters from Rene since the period which embraced that in which I had been in communication with him, and he likewise commented on the fact that a letter he had sent to the address last supplied him by Rene had come back to him unclaimed. Thus, my contentment and material success were marred by the preoccupation that something had happened to Rene, whose image was deeply impressed in my heart.

Accustomed to sleep until around midday or later, I was surprised one morning to be aroused from my slumbers by Madame Lafronde at the unusual hour of nine. When I was sufficiently awake to sit up in bed and ask what was wanted, she rather grumpily informed me that there was a visitor waiting for me in the parlour.

This was an unprecedented variation of the house regime, and I stared at her in surprise.

'Who is it?' I asked wonderingly.

'Don't sit there asking questions. Get up; comb your hair, put on a dressing gown and go downstairs.'

Plainly, Madame was not in the best of humour at having been obliged to get out of bed at this hour. There was something ominously mysterious about this matter. In my mind I endeavoured to find an explanation. With chilling apprehension there came across my thoughts the suspicion that it was in some way connected with the reformatory. Maybe they had discovered how I was living and had come to get me! My face paled and I glanced toward Madame Lafronde. Her expression told me nothing.

'Is there anything wrong?' I whispered.

'You'll think there's something wrong if you ever have anyone call here again at this hour!'

'But . . .' I protested, 'I have never made any morning appointments with anyone!'

'Oh, it's nothing serious. Here, slip this on,' she answered, holding my dressing gown for me. 'Tidy yourself a bit and hurry up so I can get back to sleep.'

Nervously, I tied my short curls with a ribbon, dabbed a little powder on my face and followed her downstairs where, after motioning toward the parlour, she left me and retired in the direction of her own sleeping quarters.

Still wondering who in the world could have had the temerity to upset the house traditions by calling at this hour, I pushed aside the curtains and entered the room.

Standing with his back toward me, looking out of the window, was the figure of a man I did not at first recognize. I approached hesitatingly, and as he heard my footsteps, he turned and faced me.

For a moment I stood paralysed, unable to move or utter a word.

It was Rene.

The letter I had written to his friend with seemingly fruitless results had in the end been the instrument of our reunion, for through the address I had given in the letter Rene had been able to locate me without loss of time or difficulty.

He had come directly to the house, and Madame,

on being informed that I was his sister, had consented to call me without delay.

In a flash we were in each other's arms, both talking at once. For an hour I sat on his lap, listening to the story of his adventures and misadventures. Shame-facedly, he confessed that, as I had divined, a long period of hardship, during which he had suffered many vicissitudes and disappointments, had been the cause of his silence.

'But, darling!' I interposed reproachfully, 'I could have helped you so easily. I have lots of money saved, if I had only known how to reach you I could have sent you some!'

Our conversation was interrupted by the maid, who had come in to clean the parlour.

'Come on up to my room, darling, we can talk there, and I'll have the girl send us up some coffee and cakes!'

With his arm about my waist we ascended the carpeted and padded stairs. Within my room I hastily gathered up such pieces of clothing as were lying carelessly about and straightened out my disordered bed while Rene gazed about in evident wonderment.

'Gee, this is a regular palace you're in, Sis,' he mused. 'Just what kind of a place is it? That old dame wasn't going to let me see you until I told her you were my sister.'

'Oh, Rene, don't you know what kind of a place it is?' I asked, in surprise.

'Well . . . I've got an idea. It's a kind of sporting house, isn't it?'

'Yes, it is, Rene.'

'Gee, Sis, I'm sorry. I'll find some kind of work and get you out of it.'

'But I don't want to get out! I'm getting along fine; its easy, and I don't mind it at all! Really, I don't!

Madame Lafronde is awfully good to me, Rene, and you'll be surprised when you see how much money I've got!'

'It's supposed to be a tough life for a girl, but gee, Sis, you look absolutely topping. Word of honour,' he added, standing in front of me and holding my arms, 'you don't look a day older than you did when I went away. In fact . . .' he continued, eyeing me in a puzzled way, 'you actually look younger!'

I laughed contentedly as he continued to look at me, perplexed.

'It's your hair, for one thing. Why did you cut it short? It's cute that way, but it makes you look like a kid!'

'That's what it's supposed to do,' I replied, giggling. 'Some of our most valued patrons are freaks that can't get a hard-on unless they think they're fucking an infant. Look . . .' I added, raising the short crepe-de-chine slip I had on under my dressing gown so that he could see my hairless cunny, 'more of my disguise!'

'Gosh!' exclaimed Rene, breathing harder, 'it gives me a funny feeling to see it like that, Sis! Reminds me of when it really was that way. But how did you get the hair off so smooth?' he continued, touching me gingerly with his fingers.

'It's some paste I put on it. It makes the hair come out clear down to the roots. Do you like it that way?' I asked, eyeing him mischievously. 'You used to think one wasn't much good until it had hair on it.'

'Gee, Sis, it looks good enough to eat! And your legs, why, Sis, you always did have pretty legs, but honest, they're perfect now; you're the best-looking girl I ever saw!'

What feminine heart wouldn't have thrilled at such sincere tribute as this?

112

'Oh, Rene, you old darling!' I murmured, half crying, half laughing as I put my arms around him and squeezed up to him. 'I missed you so much! I never have had a fellow half as good as you! I've just lain awake nights remembering all the things we used to do! Sometimes when fellows were doing it to me I closed my eyes and made believe it was you, but nobody could ever make me feel the same as you did!'

Against my stomach as I clung to him I could feel the warm pressure of something hard and rigid which was pulsing with enough vigour to make its movements perceptible through our respective clothing. I slipped my hand down inside the waistband of his trousers and sought out the disturbing element. A shiver passed through me as my fingers closed around the turgid object and a vertigo of longing which demanded immediate satisfaction overwhelmed me.

'Oh, Rene, darling, it feels so good to have this in my hand again! I'll bet it's been up inside lots of girls since I had it last, though. Are those Canadian girls very pretty, Rene?' I asked, the eternal feminine rising to the surface as in my imagination I pictured Rene with other girls.

'Some of them aren't so bad, but I never saw one that could hold a candle to you, Sis!' Rene replied uncomfortably.

'Come on, Rene!' I panted, 'let's do it quick! Nobody is up yet, but as soon as the girls are awake, I'll have to introduce you to them!'

I flung myself on the bed and in a jiffy the object for which I was palpitating with burning ardour was buried in my trembling flesh. With my arms entwined about Rene's neck I fluttered and moaned and received his thrusts in a regular frenzy of emotion. In it went, until I could feel his crisp hair pressed against my naked parts, and as if this penetration were not enough I hurled myself up against it and pressed with all my might so that it might reach the innermost depths of my being. Moaning, gasping, suspiring, and murmuring hysterical endearments, I clung to him, my arms clasped about his neck and my legs clenched over his strong back while my flanks quivered and strained to draw from him as quickly as possible the satisfying balm my body craved.

Hardly had I recovered from my first orgasm when there was a discreet knock at the door. While Rene hastily buttoned up his clothing I took from the maid a tray with coffee and toast. My hands were still trembling from the recent exhilaration, and my face was flushed and hot.

We lingered over our coffee for another hour, talking, laughing, reminding each other of little incidents which stood out prominently in our memories of the past.

'Do you remember when that little Marshall girl's mother caught you trying to do it with her in the coal shed?'

'I'll say I remember it! She gave me such a lacing with an old belt that I couldn't walk straight for a week. Do you remember how Mr Peters used to send me out on fake errands so he could have you alone in the house and diddle you with his fingers?'

And so, immersed in reminiscences of the past, some laughable, some pathetic, some tragic, the time flew by, and the sound of movement and conversation elsewhere in the house reminded me that it was high noon.

'I'm going to call Hester to introduce you to her. She's the girl that was with me in that darned old reformatory. She's my best friend; if it hadn't been for her, I don't know what would have happened to me.'

114

I jumped up and went directly to Hester's room. Finding her awake and languidly engaged in combing her luxuriant hair I danced up to her.

'Oh, Hester, I've got the grandest surprise for you! Powder your nose and come quick to my room. There's somebody there waiting to see you! It's my brother Rene, come back from Canada! He came at nine o'clock this morning and Lafronde woke me up! I bet you'll fall in love with him when you see him; he's the handsomest fellow you ever saw!'

My excitement was contagious, and Hester rushed to make herself presentable. As soon as she was ready I led her to my room where Rene was waiting.

'This is Hester, my very dearest friend, Rene. Next to you, I love her more than anyone in the world!'

'Gee, I don't blame you for loving her, Sis!' exclaimed Rene, as he jumped to his feet and admiringly appraised Hester's dark beauty. 'I could love her myself without half trying!'

'Well,' I said, judiciously, 'she's the only girl in the world that would be good enough for you, and you're the only fellow in the world that would be good enough for her, so that leads to only one logical conclusion.'

Hester stayed with us until, despite my protestations to the contrary, she felt that we might wish to be alone, and with a promise to see Rene again before he left, she slipped out, closing the door behind her.

Rene wished to leave around one-thirty, and anxious to be as close to him as possible during the remainder of his visit, I again sat on his lap. Before long, new temptation began to assail me. Tentatively, I felt around inside his clothing with my hand until I found what I was searching for. It stiffened out magically under my fingers. For a few minutes I squeezed

115

it, thrilling to the quick transformation and the significant throbbing which my touch had evoked.

'Once more . . . before we go?' I whispered, squeezing it tightly.

'Just what I was thinking myself!' he answered huskily.

'You lie underneath and let me get on top, like we used to do in the attic!' I suggested.

'Suits me, absolutely.'

And this is how it happened that Hester, returning to bid Rene good-bye as she had promised, on opening the door was confronted by a most poetic sight.

I, for greater freedom of movement, had thrown off the dressing gown and, crouched over Rene with my bottom in the air, was working frantically up and down on the pivotal point which projected from his middle.

'T-a-a-h!' she gasped, ' . . . I didn't think . . . excuse me. . . !' and she closed the door and fled precipitately.

'I forgot to lock the door!' I murmured, guiltily.

'Not the first time, Sis!' he retorted.

'Well, it doesn't make any difference here,' I answered resuming my efforts to attain the objective which had been uppermost in my mind up to the moment of interruption.

After Nature had taken her pleasant and satisfying course and the inward fires which consumed me had again been temporarily lulled with a copious shower of masculine sperm, Rene departed.

Hester had not returned, and so as soon as I had bidden him good-bye at the door, I returned to her room upstairs.

'Jessie!' she exclaimed, 'you could have knocked me down with a feather!'

'Oh, that was nothing,' I answered lightly, thinking

she had reference to opening the door without knocking. 'It didn't startle your modesty, did it?'

'But . . . but . . . your own brother!' she whispered, in low, shocked tones.

For a moment I failed to grasp the import of her words. When comprehension dawned on me, I burst into laughter.

'Didn't you know, ha! ha! ha! Didn't I tell you, Rene isn't my real brother, he isn't any blood relation to me at all, he's only a stepbrother!'

A look of relief passed over Hester's face.

'Jesse, no! You never told me that before! You used to talk about him in the reformatory, but you never said he wasn't your real brother. Gosh! I never was so surprised in all my life as when I opened the door and saw you on top of him, naked! I could hardly believe my eyes!'

'We were just renewing an old love affair.' I answered, laughing. 'What did you think of him?'

'Well,' she replied, smiling, 'let's go downstairs right now and tell Lafronde that we've just discovered we're lost sisters, so the next time he comes, he can be a brother to both of us!'

CHAPTER TEN

The days slipped into weeks, the weeks imperceptibly, into months, and almost before I realized it, a year had gone by. Barring the few disagreeable incidents of a minor nature such as those I have described, the time had been passed on the whole both pleasantly and profitably.

Miraculously, I had escaped all three of the afflictions whose menacing shadows are ever close at the heels of those who traffic with their sexual favours; syphilis, gonorrhea and pregnancy, the Three Horsemen of the Prostitute's Apocalypse.

My health was good, and I had gained in weight, having added several pounds of flesh which improved my figure even though at the cost of some of the juvenile slimness which in the beginning had been such a valuable asset. Nevertheless, I had for some time been observing a gradual change in my physical orgasm which was becoming more and more pronounced, and the condition was one which is not common in the walk of life I frequented.

I will speak plainly. Sexual sensibility, which is that capacity to respond easily and actively to erotic excitation, diminishes rapidly in the majority of professional prostitutes who are obliged to exercise their sexual functions with a frequency far in excess of the provisions of Nature. The sexual act becomes a mere routine in which pleasure or orgasm is only simulated to satisfy the customer's ego.

They moan and sigh and murmur passionate endearments, but if their minds could be read, the hollow mockery would be apparent, for one thought only occupies them: a wish to be finished and rid of the man as quickly as possible.

This is the rule which should have applied to me, but didn't.

Desires which should have been appeased by all too frequent gratification were quieted but for a moment, and almost at once flamed anew with increased insistence. And the tendency was growing. Strange as it may seem, sometimes after having had orgasm effected as many as half a dozen times in a single afternoon and evening, I was obliged to masturbate before being able to sleep. Pathologically and physically, I was oversexed, designed, seemingly, by Mother Nature herself, to be a whore.

Now in this propitious moment there entered into the horizon of my life, for the first time, a really sinister influence. And though in that influence I myself sensed a spirit of perversity, I was drawn toward it like a moth to the candle. Knowing that the destiny it signified was evil, I had no wish to resist it.

Montague Austin—what memories that name evokes. Memories of passion, cruelty, horror, blended with the cloying and intoxicating poison of a transcendental lust which knew no law other than that of gratifying its own frenzy.

I was supposed to have been infatuated with the man, but I never loved him, nor thought I did. No, I did not love him, but I did love the mad transports, the exquisite torment of lust which he, as no other man before or since, had the power to awaken in me. As an addict to the scented dreams of opium, so did I become an addict to Montague Austin. He was to me a fatal drug which held me a willing victim in its embrace.

For the first time, in broaching the subject of a new patron to me, Madame Lafronde manifested a doubt as to the expediency of putting my youth and inexperience to the test which she clearly thought an alliance with Montague Austin would signify.

I had seen the man but once; he was not a regular habituate of Madame Lafronde's house, but her facilities for gathering information were such that within less than twenty-four hours his social position, resources, and such portions of his history as were available on such inquiry were known to her. All the information, excepting that which related to his economic situation, was unfavourable. She summed up her opinion in the one expressive word—rotter. But he had money, and money covers as otherwise inexcusable number of objectionable qualities. Possibly by the exercise of tact and vigilance I could handle him.

As for myself, I was the last person in the world to doubt my own capabilities, so Madame Lafronde finally and with patent misgivings, yielded to my complacent and optimistic self-assurance.

Now let us glance briefly at the man himself.

He was, at the time our paths crossed, thirty-four years of age. The younger son of a titled British aristocrat, he had inherited both money and social position. The social position had been forfeited by dissolute escapades, the money dissipated in part, but enough remained to qualify him still as a rich man. He was married, but according to rumour his profligate ways had brought about an irreconcilable estrangement with his consort.

At first glance one would have marked Montague Austin as an extremely good-looking man. But a less

120

cursory observation would not have failed to disclose signs of a cynical and somewhat cruel character in his darkly handsome face and narrow mouth. A little above average height and signally favoured with regard to other physical characteristics, he was in truth a figure to intrigue feminine imagination.

In my brocade jacket, high-heeled slippers, and with my grenadier's cap tilted at a jaunty angle I was going through my customary antics one night when I suddenly felt myelf clasped from behind, and turning, looked into the cynically smiling face of a man I had not previously seen among our parlour guests. I paused, waiting for him to release me, but instead, he swung me around, dropped an arm under my hips, and hoisted me, cigarette tray and all, into the air.

'There is a tide in the affairs of men,' he quoted, 'which, taken at the flood, leads on to fortune. Baby, you're my tidal wave, the one I've been waiting for all my life!'

He got off this declaration with such well-simulated solemnity and impressiveness that all within hearing laughed, nor could I myself restrain a smile.

'I think you're the tidal wave,' I retorted, 'since I find myself quite swept off my feet. If you'll be so kind as to set me down, maybe I'll let you buy a packet of fags from me!'

'Lord love me!' he exclaimed tragically, 'she peddles fags while Rome is burning! I perish for a kiss, and she offers nicotine!'

'Oh, all right!' I giggled, and kissed him lightly on the cheek. 'Now be a nice man and let me down!'

He set me down on the floor, but will held me a prisoner with an arm under mine.

Yielding to his solicitation I unhooked the cigarette tray, placed it on a table, accompanied him to a secluded corner of the room, and let him take me upon his knee.

Dropping his bantering attitude he immediately became serious and asked for a room appointment. A shiver passed over me as his fingers boldly played with the nipples of my breasts. I glanced into his eyes but hastily lowered my gaze as something of the lustful obsession which was later to dominate me came into being. Sensing the absurdity of telling this man any fairy stories, I explained frankly that I was not permitted to make any appointments except through the intervention of Madame Lafronde.

'Ah, I see,' he answered, taking in the situation instantly, 'you're a special attraction. So much the better, I'll see her immediately, and I suppose there's no use of taking up any of your time until I do.'

'Any of the other girls can make room appointments.' I proferred.

'Thanks for the information,' he answered dryly, 'but you've wrecked their chances. I couldn't even get a hard-on with any of them now.'

'I've got a friend here,' I murmured, looking around for Hester. 'That's her over there by the door, the girl with the dark hair. She can give any man a hard-on. Shall I introduce you to her?'

'No thanks,' he answered with but a brief glance in the direction I had indicated. 'It's you or nobody now. When can I talk to your madame?'

'I'll tell her you want to speak to her, but I'm afraid it won't do any good.'

'Possibly she can be persuaded. What's your name, baby?'

'Jessie,' I replied.

'That's a nice name. Mine is Austin, Montague Austin, Monty to you. Skip along and tell the old lady I want to speak to her privately.'

The result of his interview with Madame Lafronde I have already made known. Insomuch as I had now become quite a parlour attraction, having in addition to my earlier accomplishments learned a number of naughty songs and suggestive dances, she was loathe to concede any of the earlier hours of the night, but an understanding was reached where Montague Austin, or Monty as I shall henceforth refer to him, was to enjoy exclusive prerogatives over my person one night each week after the hour of twelve.

A feeling of lascivious exhilaration was welling within me as I groomed myself for our first rendezvous. I had lately noticed that the craving for more frequently repeated orgasm was growing on me. It seemed that no matter how often I had it, the longing was never completely satisfied. Even the two or three patrons I had who were sexually potent now left me with the irritated feelings of a woman whose passions have been inflamed and then abandoned in a smouldering state.

The effeminate Wainwright, who still came regularly, caused me almost frantic torture with his licking, and sucking, and despite the preoccupations and the watchfulness I was obliged to observe to keep him from biting my legs, he left me in such a state that I nearly always masturbated as soon as he had gone.

It was a little after eleven-thirty. I had slipped out of the parlour, abandoning for the night my role of cigarette girl, and was making my toilette, preparatory to Mr Austin's promised call.

'How nice it would be,' I thought, as I fluffed violet talc over my body, 'if this Austin would suck me French style and then fuck me about three times afterwards.' My nerves tingled at the luscious vision thus evoked and a warm feeling crept through my body.

The little scarlet tips of my bubbies swelled up and in the upper part of my cunny I could feel something else getting hard, too.

A few moments, after twelve there was a discreet knock at my door and the maid appeared, inquiring whether I was ready to receive Mr Austin. At this moment I was standing before the mirror considering the dress I had tentatively chosen for the occasion, having yielded to an impulse to use one of the short black silk frocks which Daddy Heely had bought me. Just why it had occurred to me to put on this juvenile costume on the present occasion I could not say; some vague intuition probably, but as it turned out, a fortunate one as far as the effect of my new patron was concerned, though until the arrival of the maid I was still debating, undecided whether to wear it or change to something else more in keeping with the circumstances.

'All right, Maggie,' I answered, 'you may bring him up.'

I tied my short curls back in a cluster with a band of ribbon, sprayed them lightly with my favourite perfume, and was just adding a final touch of powder to my face when footsteps at the door announced the presence of my caller.

The door opened to admit him, closed again, and the steps of the maid receded down the hallway.

Mr Austin paused in evident surprise as he took in the scene which confronted him, then his face lit up approvingly.

'Are you the same girl I was talking to downstairs last night?'

'You mean that bold little hussy who runs around with a cigarette tray, showing her legs to everyone?' I answered jocularly. 'No, I'm her twin sister. She's off tonight, and asked me to entertain you in her place.'

'Well! I'm quite pleased with the substitution. You're much more attractive than your twin sister!'

'I'm glad you're not disappointed, Mr Austin!'

'Not Mr Austin; just Monty from now on, if you please!'

'Very well, Mr Austin . . . I mean . . . Monty!' I agreed demurely.

After a brief exchange of pleasantries Mr Austin proved again, as he had done previously, that he was a man who went promptly and without any unnecessary circumlocutions after whatever he wanted. With just the same directions as that employed to overcome Madame Lafronde's reluctance, he proceeded to take immediate advantage of the opportunity which was now his.

Abruptly he gathered me up in his arms and carried me to the bed. Seating himself on the edge he bent over me and his hand began to rummage under my clothing. With just the proper simulation of embarrassment I offered to undress.

'Not yet,' he answered, 'you're too pretty a picture just as you are.' But a moment later his questing hand encountered panties which, if not exactly finger-proof, were at least something of an obstacle to easy exploration. He fumbled with them for a moment, then flipped my dress up and on his own initiative set about to unfasten and remove the panties.

I laughed nervously as he pulled them down over my legs. Already I was on fire. My sensibilities were reacting to the brutally frank sexual influence which the man exerted, and covertly I glanced toward his lap. The cloth down the inside of one of his trouser legs were distended over an elongated swelling. It looked enormous. As though drawn by some inner

125

force I placed my hand upon it. It throbbed to my touch and I squeezed it through the clothing which concealed it.

Whether the thoughts that occupied my mind while I had been preparing for his visit were due to a premonition or mere coincidence I cannot say, but the wish I had expressed in thought was converted into a reality.

My dress was up, my cambric panties had been pulled down over my legs and cast aside.

Monty, on the side of the bed, leaning over my knees and supporting his weight on a hand which rested on the bed between my open legs had caught his first glimpse of my naked cunny. His eyes glistened and a faint flush crept over his cheeks. With one sudden movement his face was between my thighs and his mouth nuzzling my cunny. A warm, soft tongue penetrated it, tapping, touching, caressing, and then moved upward. The hot glow of the caress thrilled my senses and I relaxed in languorous abandon to the delicious ravishment.

His lips clenched my clitoris, it pulsed in response to the tugging incitation so vigorously that I was obliged to draw away to avoid orgasm then and there. I was torn between two impulses; I wanted to let it 'come' and at the same time I wanted the delightful ecstasy to last as long as possible.

The problem was not resolved by me, however, but by Monty, who raised up, ripped his trousers open and sprang upon the bed between my trembling legs.

Hard, rigid and hot I could feel it in there, distending my flesh to the limit of endurance, inspiring me with a wild desire to work on it rapidly, violently, until it poured out the balm which the fever within me craved. For an interval he remained poised above me, motionless, looking down into my face. His body did not move but within me I could feel the muscular contractions of the turgid thing which penetrated me. They followed each other with regular precision and each time I perceived that tantalising twitch my ovaries threatened to release their own flood of pleasure tears.

'Oh!' I moaned finally, and unable to resist the urge, moved my hips in pleading incitation. 'You've got me in such a state! Please do something!'

'All right! Come on!'

And in a second that rigid shaft was plunging in and out in a mad dance of lust.

'Oh! Oh! Oh!' I gasped, and as though incited by my fervour, the turgid arm drove home in shorter, harder strokes.

Higher and higher mounted the swirling tides, lifting me upon their crest, no longer resisting, but an eager, willing sacrifice, panting to yield up the store of passion with which I was surcharged.

I perceived the approach of the crisis, that delicious prelude in which one trembles on the brink of ecstasy, in which the senses seem to hesitate for one sweet moment before the breathless plunge.

And in that critical moment the throbbing weapon which was working such havoc within my body suddenly ceased its movement and was held in rigid inactivity.

Above me I saw a face which smiled sardonically down into mine and vaguely I comprehended that he had stopped his movements with the deliberate intention of forestalling my orgasm in the last moment. But he had stopped too late, the tide had risen too high to recede and with but a momentary hesitation, it swept onward and carried me, gasping, writhing and swooning in its embrace.

When the languid spell which always overcomes me

after a hard orgasm had passed. I found him still crouched above me and his cock, as stiff and rigid as it had been at first, still inside me.

'Why did you stop just as I was coming?' I complained weakly. 'You nearly made it go back on me!'

'That's what I was trying to do,' he replied cynically, 'but you put it over anyway. You know the old saying, baby, you can't eat your cake and have it, too. I like to enjoy the cake awhile before eating it.'

'That's all very well,' I rejoined, 'but when there's plenty more cake in the pantry, there's no use being stingy with it.'

'So!' he said, smiling, 'there's plenty more in the pantry, is there? I'm glad to hear it. But tell me this, does the second piece ever taste as good as the first?'

'And how!' I exclaimed fervently. 'The second piece tastes better than the first, and the third better than the second. The more I eat, the better I like it!'

He burst into laughter.

'You sound like you really mean it. I'd imagine that after a few months in a place like this you'd be so fed up on cake it would almost choke you. You're a cute youngster. You're wasting your talents here. What's the story? Innocence and inexperience taken advantage of by some bounder, I suppose?' he added quizzically.

'I'm here for two reasons,' I answered calmly. 'The first one is to earn money and the second one is because I like to do what I have to do to earn it.'

'Well, bless my soul!' he gasped. 'What refreshing frankness! And you really weren't seduced by a villain?'

'Seduced, nothing! I was the one that did the seducing.'

'Good for you! You're a girl after my own heart! You and I are going to get along famously, Tessie!'

'Not Tessie . . . Jessie!'

'Ah, yes; Jessie. Pardon me. Well, since you really like cake, how about another piece?'

'I'm ready whenever you are!'

'What do you say we get undressed, and really make a night of it? I didn't expect to stay all night, but I've changed my mind.'

'That suits me, Mr Austin. I'm yours . . . till tomorrow do us part!'

'Not Mr Austin . . . Monty, if you please.'

'All right . . . Monty!' I repeated, giggling.

Whereupon we untangled our respective anatomies, scrambled off the bed, and proceeded to disrobe.

That is, Monty stripped, but when I had gotten down to my hose and slippers he suggested that I retain these last articles of apparel for the moment. Odd, I thought, how so many men who get pleasure from the sight of a girl's otherwise naked body were so alike in preferring that she keep on the hose and slippers, and I murmured something to this effect to my new playmate.

'Very easily explained, my dear little girl,' he replied. 'Complete nudity may be as suggestive of cold chastity as obscenity, whereas, nudity supplemented by a pretty pair of silkclad legs and neat slippers is the perfectly balanced picture of esthetic lewdness.'

'But suppose one's legs and feet are pretty enough to look good without stockings? Everybody says I have pretty legs!'

'It's not a question of beauty, but of eroticism. I'll make a clearer illustration. Suppose we take two girls, each equally pretty. One of them stands before us entirely naked. The other is dressed, but she raises her dress and holds it up so we can see her pussy. Which of the two is the most exciting sexually?'

'The one holding up her dress,' I answered without hesitation.

'Right. And that's the answer to your question. You look naughtier with your hose and slippers than you would completely nude.'

My attention was now distracted from the matter of my own nudity to that of my companion. His body was well formed and in admirable athletic trim. Smooth, round muscles rippled under the clear white skin, a pleasing contrast indeed to some of my other paunchy, flabby patrons. But most impressive of all was the rigid weapon which, during the conversation and undressing, continued to maintain its virile integrity, standing out straight and proud from his middle. I glanced at it admiringly.

'How did you ever get that big thing into me without hurting me?' I commented, as I considered its formidable proportions.

'It carries its own anaesthetic, baby.'

'It looks strong enough to hold me up without bending.'

'Baby, it's invincible. I could put you on it and whirl you around like a pinwheel.'

'I'll take the starch out of it and make it melt down fast enough.'

'That's a big order. You may lose a lot of starch yourself trying.'

'Ha!' I scoffed, 'I wager it will be curled up fast asleep in an hour's time.'

A prediction which, as things transpired, turned out to be about one hundred percent wrong.

I returned to the bed and Monty, following me, placed himself on his knees between my outstretched legs. Gripping the cheeks of my bottom in his strong hands as he sank down upon me, he pushed home the lethal shaft.

Our previous encounter had hardly more than whetted my appetite, so, as soon as I felt his cock well inside, I raised my legs, hooked them over his back, and without loss of time began to work against him. Apparently satisfied with my initiative, he remained still and let me proceed unhindered.

Grinding my loins against him I could feel his pubic hair compressed against my cunny. Moving my bottom from side to side, then shifting into undulating, circular movements, I sought to capture a second instalment of the cloying sweetness with which Mother Nature rewards the efforts of those who labour diligently in her garden.

The first warning of the approaching crisis was manifested by the muscular quivering of my thighs, and Monty, still squeezing the cheeks of my bottom, commenced to raise and lower himself upon me with slow, deliberate thrusts. Now the length of the hot thing was entirely buried within me, distending my flesh to the utmost; I could feel it pressing my womb. Now, it was coming out, slowly, slowly, out until naught but the very tip lay cuddled against the quivering lips of my cunny.

A pause, a teasing agony of expectation, and it was going in again, in, in, until the crisp hair at the base was again pressed against my clitoris. Orgasm was creeping upon me, I could feel it coming, and in a frenzy of impatience, I launched my hips upward to meet the thrusts, but, instead of continuing its trajectory, it remained poised midway in its course. My orgasm was trembling in the balance. In desperation I brought it to its fulfilment with a supreme effort and fell back, half fainting.

'What is that, Mister, a system?' I panted when I

could speak. 'You played that same trick on me the other time!'

An hour later the suspicion was beginning to dawn on me that, in the realms of erotic prowess, I had met my master. Two hours later, I knew it for a certainty. I had experienced nearly a dozen orgasms while my partner's cock was still stiff and rigid as it had been at the start. On each occasion he had succeeded in making me have an ejaculation without himself rendering any accounting to Nature. It lacked but a few minutes to three.

'You look a bit fagged, baby,' he said smiling quizzically. 'Think you can stand one more piece of cake?'

'Yes!' I replied valiantly, although in truth I was beginning to feel like a squeezed-out sponge. For once in my life I had about had my fill.

This time he rolled me over on my side and with his stomach against my back and his legs pressed against mine, he put it into me from behind, spoon fashion.

I thought to turn the tables on him and, by lying perfectly still, oblige him to work himself into a spending heat. But it was unnecessary. He was done playing with me and went right to work on his own accord. Before long the pressure of his arms tightened about me and I tensed my body against the harder plunges as a hot flood was loosed inside me with such force that I could distinguish each separate gush as it flung itself against my womb.

I held rigid for a moment in my determination not to let myself go, but the feel of that hot stuff spurting inside me worked havoc with my intentions and about the time the fourth or fifth jet hit me, the brake slipped and I was off again!

The aftermath of this last orgasm was a feeling of extreme lassitude and I was entirely agreeable when my companion, having apparently no further immediate designs upon my person, suggested that we turn out the light and sleep. I dragged myself from the bed, attended to the customary hygienic requirements, divested myself on my slippers, and hose, put on a silk shift, slipped back into bed beside him, and in probably less than ten minutes was deep in sleep.

CHAPTER ELEVEN

I slept profoundly, dreamlessly, but not for long.

Something was pressing against my face, brushing my lips, with an irritating persistence which defied my mechanical, sleep-drugged efforts to shake away. I endeavoured to turn my face on the pillow away from it, and the knowledge that it was imprisoned so I could not turn it gradually crystalized in my mind.

As one coming out of a bad dream tries to dispel the lingering shadows, so did I try to free myself of something which seemed to be oppressing me, weighting me down, hindering my movements. I could not do it, and awoke to complete consciousness with a frightened start.

In the dim light which filtered through the curtains from the street illumination was revealed the fact that my erst-while sleeping companion was now straddled over me, a knees on either side of my body. His hands were under my head, which he had raised slightly, and against my lips, punching, prodding, trying to effect an entrance, was that invincible cock.

I struggled to raise my arms to push him away, and at the same time tried to twist my head sidewise. I could do neither. My arms were pinioned down by his knees, and his hands prevented me from moving my head. At my movements their pressure tightened, a sinister reminder of my helplessness.

Of course I realized what he was doing. He was

trying to fuck me in the mouth, something I had never permitted any man to do.

In prostitution, just as in other circles of life, there are social distinctions. The cocksucker is at the low end of the scale and is looked down upon with considerable scorn by those of her sisters who have not yet descended to this level. If among the entertainers in a high-class bordello one is discovered to be guilty of accommodating patrons with her mouth she not only loses caste but stands convicted of 'unfair' practice which makes it difficult for other girls to complete with her without also resorting to the same procedure.

This does not, of course, apply to those places known as French houses where cocksucking is the accepted practice, or to other places of a low and degenerate character wherein nothing is too debasing to be frowned upon.

These, together with the fact that I was both sleepy and exhausted sexually, were the considerations which inspired my efforts to escape the inverted caress which now threatened me rather than those of a strictly moral nature. The man appealed to me greatly in a physical way; I had reacted to his sexual advances with more passion and enjoyment than I had done before with any other person. Had he endeavoured earlier in the night to seduce me, with a little gallantry and coaxing, into sucking his cock. I might, under the influence of my exalted passions, have yielded. But I have always been quick to resent anything smacking of impudence or effrontery and, as I have mentioned, I wanted at that moment but to be permitted to sleep undisturbed.

'I won't do that!' I hissed angrily, as I struggled to free myself from his embraces.

'Oh yes you will, baby!' was the confident and surprising rejoinder.

His legs pressed tighter against my sides, constricting my arms so that I could not move them. He lifted my head higher. The end of his cock, with the foreskin drawn back, was right against my mouth.

'You . . . you . . .' I gasped, inarticulate with rage, as I was forced to clench my teeth to keep out the invader.

'Open your mouth, baby!' he ordered coolly, and gave my head a shake to emphasize his words.

When I comprehended that my wishes were to be ignored and that my efforts to dislodge him were useless, full rage took possession of me. For a moment I was on the point of screaming, but sudden recollection of the penalty exacted of girls who permitted scandals or disturbances to arise in their rooms at night stifled the cry in its inception.

We were expected, and presumed to be qualified, to meet unusual situations and resolve them with tact and discretion. Nocturnal disorders were unpardonable calamities and justified by nothing short of attempted murder.

'Open your mouth, baby?' he repeated, and shook my head again, this time with more force.

'All right!' I hissed, 'you asked for it!'

I opened my mouth. His cock pushed in immediately, and as it did so I sank my teeth into it. The intent was vicious enough, but the tough, resilient flesh resisted any actual laceration. Nevertheless, the pain inflicted by my small, sharp teeth must have been considerable.

He jerked it out of my mouth and simultaneously, withdrawing one of his hands from under my head, he dealt me a stinging blow on the side of the face with his open palm.

'Open your mouth, baby!' he repeated, undaunted, 'and if you bite me again I'll knock you unconscious?'

The tears started to fill my eyes.

'Damn you. . . !' I choked. 'I'll . . . I'll. . . .'

The hands subjecting my head were again holding it in a vicelike grip. His thumbs were pressing into my cheeks, against the corners of my mouth, forcing it open.

There was nothing to do but yield or scream such an alarm as would arouse the entire household.

I chose the more discreet course and, though almost suffocated with rage, opened my mouth in surrender to the assault which was being launched upon it. The big, plum-shaped head slipped in, filling the cavity with its throbbing bulk.

For a moment I tried to keep my tongue away from it, but there was no space in which to hide. His cock was so big I had to open my jaws to their widest, and my lips were stretched in a round, tight ring.

Further resistance was futile and anymore biting would bring a swift retaliation. So, still boiling inwardly, I relaxed, and let him go ahead.

A faintly pungent taste filled my mouth; the head of his cock, from which I could not keep my tongue, was wet and slippery. Every few seconds it jerked convulsively, forcing my jaws further apart. Pretty soon he began to move it, a short in and out movement. The foreskin closed over it as it receded, leaving only the tip inside my mouth, allowing me to relax my distended jaws momentarily. As it went in, the foreskin slipped back and the naked head filled my mouth again, forcing my jaws apart.

This went on for several minutes, and all the time he held my head with his hands. His cock seemed to be getting wetter but whether from its own dew or the saliva of my mouth I did not know. I wanted to spit, but he would not release me and I was obliged to swallow the excess moisture.

Finally, with the head just inside my lips, he paused, and after holding it still for a few moments, shook my face and whispered.

'Come on, baby! What's the matter with you? Are you going to suck it, or do I have to get rough again?'

I knew nothing of the exact technique of this business, though of course the very title by which the art was known indicated that sucking was in order. Choking, gulping, I tried to suck as it advanced into my mouth. Taking cognizance of my awkward efforts he paused again, and as though for the first time taking into account the possibility that I was in truth a rank novice, queried:

'What's the matter with you? Haven't you really done this before?'

Mutely, I managed to convey a negative by shaking my head.

'Lord love me!' he ejaculated, and then in slightly apologetic tones, 'I shouldn't have been so rough. I thought you were just stalling, my dear! However, it's something every young girl should know, and I'm glad to have the opportunity to be your teacher. Now listen: don't try to strangle yourself! You can't suck while the whole thing is inside! Wait. . . .'

He withdrew it until just the head was encircled by my lips.

'Now suck while it's like that, and run your tongue over it!'

'Well,' I thought in disgusted resignation 'the sooner finished the better,' and submissively I followed his indications. Vigorously, if not enthusiastically, I sucked the big round knob and rolled my tongue over its slippery surface.

'That's the way, baby!' he whispered tensely after a few moments. 'That's great! Now . . . hold everything!'

138

And while I remained passive, he worked in and out in short, quick thrusts. Thus, alternating from one to the other, sucking one moment, submitting to having it rammed down my throat the next, my first lesson in cocksucking continued.

I was still filled with resentment, but the first fury of anger had spent itself, and my thoughts were now concentrated on bringing the ordeal to a conclusion as quickly as possible. To this end I now tried to make the caress as exciting and fulminating as I could. I sucked the throbbing glans, curled my tongue around it, licking, sucking, coaxing . . . and the effect upon my companion was soon apparent. He groaned with ecstasy and from time to time jerked away from me so that the sensitive glans receded within the shelter of its elastic covering of flesh.

Perceiving that this manoeuvre was designed to delay an orgasm, I redoubled my efforts and when he again tried to withdraw I followed him by raising my head and with my lips firmly compressed around the neck of the palpitating knob, I sucked and licked without pausing.

The muscles of his thighs and legs, pressing against my sides, were quivering. Suddenly he withdrew his right hand from under my head and twisting sidewise reached behind him, groping with his fingers for my cunny. This was insult added to injury in my estimation and I tried to clench my legs against the invading hand. The effort was useless; he forced it between my legs and with the tips of his fore and index fingers he found my clitoris and began to titillate it.

Now began a new conflict. With every atom of mental influence I could bring to bear I tried to force that little nerve to ignore the incitation, to remain impassive to the friction which was being applied to it, to stay inert and lifeless.

I may as well have tried to stay the tides of the sea in their course. The traitorous, disloyal little thing cared not a whit for my humiliation and refused to heed the mental commands I was hurling at it. Despite the fact that it should have been as sleepy as I had been, it came almost instantly awake, hardened, and stood up stiffly.

He rubbed it in a peculiarly maddening way, a soft, twirling movement with the erected button lightly compressed between the tips of his two fingers. The little thrills began to generate, and communicated themselves to the surrounding area, up into my ovaries, down, seemingly into the very marrow of the bones in my thighs and legs.

Why say more? There was only one possible ending. When the ultimate capacity of resistance was reached and passed, and in the very moment in which my organism was yielding to the diabolical incitation, my tormentor, waiting apparently for this precise moment, loosed within my mouth a flood of hot sperm. I choked, gurgling and gasping, as part of it gushed down my throat and the rest, escaping my lips, ran in hot, sticky rivulets down the sides of my cheeks, over my chin. . . .

No sooner had the torrent subsided than he flung himself from me and lay panting on the bed by my side.

With the viscid stuff still dripping from my lips and its peculiar starchy flavour filling my mouth, I sprang from the bed and fled precipitately to the bathroom. First with water, then with tooth powder and brush and finally with repeated rinsings I endeavoured to purify my mouth.

When this was accomplished I went back into the

room, turned on the light, and flung myself into a chair where, for a few moments I sat silently glaring at my tormentor who, with drowsy indifference, contemplated me through half-closed eyes.

'Well,' I said frigidly, breaking the silence. 'Aren't you going to congratulate me on my graduation into the cocksucking class?'

He smiled dryly.

'Regular little powder magazine, aren't you, baby? Come on, kid, don't be a spoilsport. I'll admit I was a little rough, but that was a keen nip you gave me. I'll make things right with you. I like you, baby, you've shown me the best time I've had in a long while, and I'm not pulling your leg, either.'

'A nice time you showed me,' I observed bitterly, 'trying to fuck me in the mouth while I was asleep and nearly choking me to death. You know girls aren't supposed to do that! Why don't you go to a French house?'

This plaint seemed to afford him considerable amusement. He sat up in bed, laughing.

'Don't rate me so low socially, baby! I'm a sort of high-class chap with ecstatic inclinations!'

'I see; a special honour conferred on me. Quite a distinction. I must say.'

'Ha, ha, ha! Forgive me, baby. Word of honour. I'll behave quite properly in the future. Anyway, it wasn't so terrible, was it? Listen, I'll tell you a funny story. There was a young French girl just married and her mother was giving her some confidential advice. 'Daughter,' she said, 'the ultimate object of marriage is to have babies. Without the little dears no home is complete. However, the bearing and rearing of children is a confining task which imposes arduous and continuous obligations. It is my advice to you, daughter, that you do not have any babies during the

141

first two or three years. You will then, in after life, not be deprived of the memories of a few years of happiness and freedom from care to which youth is justly entitled.' 'Ah, mother dear,' answered the blushing maiden, 'you need preoccupy yourself no further on that score, I shall never have any babies!' 'Never?' gasped the mother, 'why do you say that you will never have any babies, darling?' 'Oh, mother,' answered the girl, hiding her blushing face in the maternal bosom, 'I shall never have any babies because I simply can't force myself to swallow the horrid stuff! I always have to spit it out!'

'And, so what?' I asked caustically, refusing to unbend at the ridiculous story.

'Don't you see, ha, ha, ha, don't you get the point? She didn't even know there was any other way of doing it. She thought she had to swallow the stuff to get a baby!'

Despite my efforts to remain haughty, my better humour was returning. I have always been like that, quick to anger, quick to forget. There was something about this man which was irresistible. Even his impudence had a saving grace, an ingenuous, disarming quality. Only the memory of the slap he had given me remained to irritate me. He sat there in bed, smiling, a sheet draped carelessly about him, half-concealing, half-revealing the smooth white muscles of his torso. His hair in its ruffled disorder gave him a boyish aspect, throwing a well-formed white forehead into relief against the background of bluish-black curls.

After all, what harm had really been done? And, I suddenly recalled, had he not earlier in the night given me a most delightful ten minutes by putting his tongue in my cunny? The service he had required of me was no less intimate. I shivered involuntarily at the recollection of the short but delicious episode. The last remnants of my resentment faded away. I began to feel slightly ashamed of myself for having made such a commotion.

'Still peeved at me, baby?' he inquired quizzically.

'No,' I answered, my lips twitching into a smile, 'only it was kind of . . . well, startling to be waked up that way from a sound sleep. I suppose you don't believe me, but I never did that before.'

'Of course I believe you, baby,' he interrupted, 'it was easy to see you hadn't any experience. Honestly, I don't know what came over me. You gave me such a stand tonight it came right back on me after I'd been asleep a short time, I woke up, and lay there looking at your pretty little mouth in the dim light, and the first thing I knew I got into a fierce argument with myself about it.'

'What on earth do you mean, an argument with yourself about my mouth?'

'Well, it was like this. At first I said to myself, it's too small, and then I said, no, it might be a tight fit, but it could be done. And the argument went on, until finally it got so hot it had to be decided definitely one way or the other, and so . . . and so. . . .'

'And so I got fucked in the mouth to settle it. Very well, Your Highness, shall we retire now, or is there any other way I can serve you?'

'Well, if it's not putting too much of a strain on your hospitality, I'd greatly appreciate a shot of brandy!'

I rang for the maid. After a long wait, she shuffled to the door half-asleep, took the order, and was back again in few minutes with the liquor. When this was consumed, we turned out the light and again composed ourselves for sleep.

The tumultuous events of the night, abetted perhaps by the brandy of which I also partook, were reflected throughout the remaining hours in a regular phantasmagoria of distorted dreams. In all these dreams, I was sucking somebody's cock. Strangely enough, in them I felt no inhibitions, no reluctance. On the contrary, I seemed to be doing something quite natural, and which caused me the most delightful erotic reactions.

At first it was Rene as I had last seen him, but with an incongruous discrepancy in time which took us back to our old attic playroom days. 'I'm going to do something nice to you,' I whispered, and placing myself on my knees before him I unbuttoned his trousers and releasing his erected cock, took it in my mouth. 'No, no, Sis!' he protested, but he made no effort to escape the seductive caress. The thrill of vicarious delight was trembling through me when I suddenly observed that Hester was standing nearby, looking at me reproachfully. I paused for a moment to tell her that it was all right, that Rene was only a foster brother, but even as I spoke, I saw that it was not Rene but Mr Hayden to whom I was ministering. From this confusing tangle of composite personalities, I drifted into another ambience. The effeminate Wainwright was licking my cunny deliciously, and as he paused for a moment to masturbate, I twisted around and cried: 'Wait! I'll show you a better way!' With my thighs across his face I took his small but rigid member in my mouth and sucked it until he had an emission.

When I finally awoke it was late noon and the echoes of some of these lurid dreams were still reverberating through my brain. I felt wet and sticky between the legs and my clitoris was in erection. When I had gotten my confused thoughts in order and separated the real from the unreal, I sat up in bed and glanced at my companion.

He was sleeping soundly and quietly on his back, his curly head high on the pillow, lips slightly parted over white even teeth. He had thrown the blankets aside and was covered only by a sheet. I glanced downward over the recumbent form. Halfway down its length the sheet rose sharply, projected upward in the form of a little tent. As I fixed my eyes on this significant pinnaclelike projection, I saw that it was jerking sharply at short intervals.

I lifted the sheet without disturbing him. That indefatigable, tireless cock was standing upright, as firm and rigid as a bar of iron. White and graceful the stout columns rose from the profusion of dark and tangled curls at its base, its plum-coloured head half-hidden, half-revealed under its natural envelope of satiny skin.

Still holding the sheet up, I looked at his face. It was in the peaceful repose of sound sleep. I thought of my curious dreams and wondered if he too was experiencing rare delights with some nebulous shadowland houri; maybe, even he was dreaming of me!

The thought set me aquiver. Softly I drew the sheet aside. I extended my hand, my fingers closed cautiously around the pulsing column. For a moment I was content to hold it thus, then, watching his face carefully for signs of awakening, I moved my hand up and down, slowly, gently, so that the silken foreskin closed over the scarlet head and then, receding downward, revealed it in its stark-nakedness.

Twice, thrice, I moved it so, pausing after each movement to see whether it was going to awaken him. At the fourth and fifth movement he stirred uneasily, murmuring some incoherent word. I waited, motionless, until his even breathing assured me that he was still deep in slumber, and began again.

'When he wakes up,' I thought. 'I'll make him tell

me what he was dreaming about that made his thing hard this way.'

My wrist slid downward, the white elastic skin descended, and again the scarlet head protruded nakedly. As I paused, holding it in this position, I saw a round, glistening drop of limpid transparency emerge slowly from the orifice at the tip.

As I observed this natural reaction to my manipulations a wave of lewdness swept over me, and in an instant I was in a state of passion bordering on nymphomania, dominated by but one thought, one driving desire, and that was to feel the rigid, pulsating thing plunging in my mouth, to suck it and lick it until the spurting essence brought relief to the frenzy which now possessed me.

I literally flung myself upon it, indifferent now as to whether he was awake or asleep, and engulfed the ruby head within the circle of my lips. In a regular fury of lust I suck and licked and bobbed my head up and down to approximate the motions of ordinary fucking.

Of course, this violent disturbance aroused my companion instantly, but I was too engrossed in my own passion to be hardly more than aware that he was sitting up in bed, and that his hands were clasping my face as though to guide the movement of my bobbing head.

Indifferent to all else I sought only to force the living fountain between my lips to pour out its elixir as quickly as possible. Instinctively I knew that when it spurted fourth, my own organism would yield in harmony. It was trembling now in that delicious borderland of anticipation, and needed but the final inspiration to precipitate its own shower of lust.

Between my thrusting, encircled lips the muscular flesh seemed suddenly to grow more taut. It held so

146

for a second, and then with mighty convulsions poured out in tribute, wave on wave of hot, pungent ambrosia. Gasping, choking with the deluge which threatened to strangle me. I writhed in the ecstasies of orgasms which came upon me in the same moment.

The reaction to this furious excess was a spell of enervating lassitude. As I came out of it and my chaotic thoughts took on a semblance of order, I was filled with amazement at the demoniacal frenzy which had taken possession of me. Next came the thought of what had become of the spurting jets that indomitable geyser had poured out. The odd, pungent taste was still in my mouth, but I recalled that I had almost choked with the quantity that had flooded it. When he had assaulted me the night before I had spit most of it out, though I had been forced to swallow some. I glanced at the bed to see if, unconsciously, I had ejected it. The bed was dry and clean. Seemingly, it had all gone down my throat.

I remembered the absurd story he had told me about the French girl.

'Well,' I observed, 'if it's true a girl can get a baby by swallowing that stuff, I guess I'm going to have one.'

'Kid, that was great!' he exclaimed. 'The first time in my life that I can recall that I really enjoyed being woken up.'

'I don't know whatever possessed me,' I murmured in some embarrassment. 'It came on me all of a sudden. I woke up and saw your thing sticking up. I knew you were dreaming something nice, or it wouldn't be that way. I thought. I'd tease you by frigging it while you were asleep, and then, all of a sudden I just got a regular fit to do that and I couldn't stop myself!'

'It was wonderful, kid, wonderful! I always get a

hard-on when I sleep late in the morning and there was something, oh, more than ordinarily thrilling in being woken up that way. I've had lots of women, but it never occurred to any of them to do that, I mean, while I was still asleep. It's something new to put in the book!'

'What book?' I asked.

'Oh, I was speaking figuratively. Something new to remember.'

'Did you really enjoy it so much?'

'Well, rather! If the old pego could talk it would say: 'thank you, a thousand times, Miss!''

'What were you dreaming about that was making it hard like that?'

'Well now, that's difficult to answer. Whatever it was it couldn't have been half as good as what really happened. I have funny dreams, but I can't seem to remember them clearly after I wake up. About all I ever recall is that there was a girl in them. I must have been dreaming about you this time. Do you have dreams . . . I mean, naughty ones?'

'I had some fierce ones last night,' I confessed. 'I guess they were mostly the cause of me doing that!'

'What were they about, baby? he asked curiously.

'Oh, mostly about you,' I lied, not wanting to say that I had dreamed of other men while sleeping at his side.

'Were they pleasant dreams?' he insinuated.

'Well, you saw what they made me do! I'll bet you think now for sure that I'm accustomed to doing that!'

'No, honestly, I don't, kid, I didn't give it a thought at first, but later I saw you weren't up to it. I felt kind of ashamed afterwards for having made you do it.'

'Oh, I was mad at first, but I don't care now. It gave me a thrill, too. It's the truth, though, I'd never done it before. But I'll wager you've done it that way to plenty of other girls.'

'You'd know I was lying if I denied it. And you wouldn't like me any better, even if I hadn't ever done it before, would you?'

'No,' I answered slowly. 'I don't blame a man for having all the fun he can. If I were a man, I'd do everything there is that's naughty. I'd do that to girls, and the other way, too.'

'What other way?'

'The way you did first last night . . . with your tongue.'

'Oh, you like it that way, do you?'

'It just sets me crazy.'

'Kid, I like your style. I made a deal with the old lady to have you once a week, but to tell you the truth I wasn't sure that I'd care about coming back even a second time. You couldn't shake me now if you tried. I like a girl who hasn't the silly idea of trying to fool a man with mock modesty.'

'You're married . . . aren't you?' I inquired tentatively, though I knew he was.

'Yes, I am, unfortunately.'

'Why unfortunately? Isn't she nice?'

'That's it, exactly. Too damned nice. She's the answer to why men like your kind of girl. She's an iceberg, a frigid monument to chastity in its most exaggerated conception. Everything related to sex is immoral. The only justification for a man getting into his wife's bed is when its for the purpose of creating offspring, and even then it's a nasty, degrading business.'

In my mind's eye there formed a picture of a pious, dour-faced female, embittered perhaps through the lack of physical attractions, whose life was dedicated to the suppression of all those natural instincts and longings of the flesh which contribute to make living worthwhile. I had heard of such.

'Good heavens!' I gasped. 'Why did you marry a woman like that?'

'Reasons of family,' he replied gloomily.

Of a naturally credulous and ingenuous disposition, my heart immediately swelled with sympathy for my companion's misfortune. I had yet to learn that there are always two sides to every story, and that one must know both to properly judge their respective merits.

'I'm sorry to know of that,' I said sincerely. 'When you come here I'll try to make you forget your unhappiness. I'm not cold-blooded, but I guess you know that already!'

'You're a fine kid and I won't forget you. Wish I could stay longer but I have an appointment at two o'clock and it's an important one. I'd better dress and toddle along before I weaken.'

With further desultory conversation we dressed and Monty prepared to leave. He held me for a moment in his arms at the door, lingering just long enough to lift my dress, slide his hand inside my panties and give my bottom a few lascivious squeezes.

'I'll see you next Wednesday night without fail.' And he was gone.

CHAPTER TWELVE

I stood for a moment thinking pensively of all that had transpired and then turned my eyes toward the dressing table upon which he had unobtrusively laid a bank note. It was for five pounds. I folded it up and tucked it in my stocking.

That afternoon I sat on Hester's bed, telling her about my new patron. She listened attentively, asked a few questions, and in a burst of confidence, I told her all that had happened.

'Oh, Jessie!' she exclaimed in genuine distress. 'You shouldn't have done that! I had a presentiment against that man the first time I saw him talking to you. I just had a feeling that he'd get the best of you some way! Lafronde shouldn't have given him any appointments with you!'

'What's the harm?' I answered lightly. 'He gave me five pounds!'

'What's the harm? There's plenty of harm! When a girl starts that, she's finished!'

'What do you mean . . . finished?' I rejoined sceptically.

'Why . . . why . . . it grows on you! You shouldn't have let him do that! You should have screamed!'

'Wouldn't that have made a hit with Lafronde, me screaming at four o'clock in the morning that a man was trying to do it to me in the month!'

'I don't care whether it would have made a hit with her or not! You shouldn't have let him get away with it! And then you did it again in the morning, of your own accord? Oh, Jessie!'

'Yes, I did! It wasn't bad . . . I like him. Anyway, what are you talking about? You've done the same thing with Mr Hayden. I've seen you!'

'Oh, Jessie, that's different. I never really did it with him. I just put it in my mouth for a moment to wet it. He never actually fucked me in the mouth and never wanted to. He's too much of a gentleman, and you know it!'

'Well, I don't see much difference.'

'Well, I see plenty, and I wish you had never met that man!'

'You're so funny, Hester. When I knew you in the reformatory I used to think there wasn't anything you were shy of. Now here you are preaching to me?'

'I'm not preaching, honey. It's just that I've had more experience than you, and I know what you have to watch out for!'

She smiled at me affectionately.

'Remember Heloise?' I asked teasingly.

'Yes; she was an example of exactly what I mean now. Fooling with some perverted idea until it takes a hold on you, and the first thing you know, you're a regular slave to it!'

'You did something with her and you didn't get to be a slave to it!'

'I just let her out of devilry and curiosity, and it disgusted me more than anything else. Just before you came here. I had some more of that same stuff, too. Lafronde sent me out on a call from a woman.'

'You never told me that! Who was she?'

'Oh, some man-hating female with crazy ideas. I've forgotten her name. She lived in a hotel. She telephoned here to have a girl sent to her rooms and

Lafronde picked me. I needed some extra money or I wouldn't have gone.'

'What did she want?'

'She didn't want much of anything except to lick another woman's cunt. It was perfectly disgusting, but I lay down and let her do it. She called back twice after that, and then she told Lafronde not to send me anymore because I wasn't 'responsive' enough. Lafronde asked her if she could send a different girl and she said yes, if she had one with a little life in her. Imagine that! There was a cute little witch here named Yolanda, very shy and quiet, but she was supposed to be one of those kind that like other girls. Lafronde asked her if she wanted to go out on the call and she said yes. A few days after that, early one morning, she sneaked her things out without saying a word to anyone and disappeared. So everybody supposed she had gone with this woman. Poor kid, if she did, she's probably on the streets now. Those kind of women are more exacting and harder to get along with than a man. They get tired of a girl quick and want new ones all the time. You see, Jessie, I know all about these things, and that's why I'm not in danger from them as you would be. You're an innocent little fool, and you'll fall for anything anyone wants to put over on you.'

'Well thanks, you sweet old thing, for your compliments, and for being so concerned about me. If I was a man, I'd do something nice to you right now for being so good to me.'

Hester laughed.

'I read in the papers that some doctor in Vienna has discovered how to change people's sex. If you'll let him change yours. I'll save my money to pay for it, and when you've got a nice cock we'll get married and live happily forever and afterwards!'

'O-o-o-h Hester!' I breathed in mock seriousness. 'If that doctor can make me have a six-inch cock and we get married, will you suck it for me every night?'

'You nastly little pervert!' she exploded, bursting into laughter. 'You take a suck of this!' She pressed her hand between her kimona-covered legs and rubbed two or three times. 'Since you've developed into a cocksucker you might as well suck cunts, too?'

'No, I won't suck your cunny, but I will suck your titties!' I exclaimed, and before she could defend herself I had tumbled her backward on the bed, pulled her kimona open, and gotten my mouth on the nipple of one of her bubbies.

'Stop! Stop! You're tickling me!' she cried, hysterical with laughter. 'Jessie, stop! You're making me have goose flesh all over my body! Stop it, will you!'

Resisting her efforts to dislodge me for a few moments, I clung to her titty and then releasing it, raised up to look triumphantly into her flushed face. She was still shaking hysterically, both her plump, round breasts protruding from the disordered kimona.

'Let's see if we can fuck each other!' I whispered teasingly.

'You crazy little fool! Get off me!' she gasped. 'Let me up! I can't breathe! You're pressing down on my stomach!'

'Come on . . . just for fun . . . to see if we can do it!' I persisted, now overcome with laughter myself at her comic, half-serious expostulations, and despite her efforts to stop me, I succeeded in pulling her kimona open entirely.

She had no panties on, but I, unfortunately did. To get them off, and prevent her from escaping while I was doing so would probably have been an impossibility. However, she suddenly relaxed.

154

'All right, you nasty little cocksucker! Let's see just how far you will go!'

This was a challenge which brooked no compromise, and though it was all in fun, I wasn't going to be the one to back down.

Raising up on one arm, I slipped my panties down and wriggled my legs free of them. When I nestled down again, our bare breasts and stomachs were together, and against my cunny I could feel the soft pressure of Hester's silky pubic hair.

'Now do you still want to see how far I'll go?'

'Yes, I do!'

'Very well; when you've had enough, you can say so!'

Whereupon I slid down a bit and got my legs between hers. This maneouvre brought our respective cunnies into still more intimate contact, and I rubbed mine against hers, pressing in as deeply as I could.

But I abruptly discovered that this was apt to be more devastating to me than to her because my clitoris and the sensitive parts of my cunny were exposed to the friction while hers were covered with hair. Furthermore, despite the fact that this had all started in fun, I was beginning to get hot.

Shifting away from her sufficiently to get my hand down to the source of the obstruction. I parted the soft hair with my fingers, separated the lips of her cunny, and then quickly pressed mine against the exposed membranes. She submitted to these manipulations without resistance, but flinched perceptibly as the moist flesh of our cunnies came together.

As for myself, I was almost instantly aware that this hot, moist contact of sensitive parts was capable of producing some erotic reactions I had not in the least suspected. I realized that they were not the normal ones which come through contact of opposite sex in

155

response to the laws of Nature, but rather the forced surrender of the senses to a purely mechanical stimulation, as in masturbation.

Nevertheless, a delicious sensation was the immediate result and it felt nicer than when I masturbated. I rubbed my cunny against hers as best I could it was an awkward proceeding and her hair kept getting in the way, obliging me to stop repeatedly to draw it aside. Had hers been free of hair as mine was, the contact would have been much more satisfactory. Even so, I was soon trembling, and Hester was moaning audibly.

In an effort to maintain a comical aspect to what had now ceased to be a joke, I managed to gasp:

'Do you . . . still want to . . . see how far . . . I'll . . . go?'

Her arms tightened about my shoulders.

'Don't talk! Oh! You're making me . . . ah . . . ah . . . a-a-a-ah!'

'Oh! You're making me, too! Press . . . right there . . . o-oo-o-oh!'

A few minutes later, flushed and dishevelled, we were looking at each other in comical and guilty confusion.

Hester jerked her kimona over the glistening curls between her legs, and very red in the face, exclaimed:

'I never dreamed you'd have the nerve to really do that or I wouldn't have let you start it!'

'Oh, shut up, you darned preacher. You wanted it as much as I did!'

'If anyone had seen us, we'd never have heard the last of it,' she murmured, glancing toward the door. 'Yes! That door was unlatched! Anyone could have walked in!' she added in consternation.

I giggled, recalling other doors which had been left unlatched.

'Like you did when Rene and I were saying good-bye.'

'Why don't you think of such things?' she asked reprovingly.

'Well, for heaven's sake! Am I the only one who's supposed to do any thinking! Anyway, nobody came in, so why worry about it now? And even if they did, this place isn't supposed to be a Sunday school exactly, you know!'

'Listen, you! Don't you ever dare tell anyone! It's something I never did before and I'm never going to do it again, either!'

'Don't be silly! You know I won't tell anyone!'

CHAPTER THIRTEEN

The week passed by and I was waiting for Monty's second visit. He had sent me a note, couched in affectionate terms, assuring me that he would be in without fail.

Of my earlier patrons but two continued to call on me with faithful regularity; Mr Thomas, and the effeminate Wainwright. Poor Daddy Heely was in a hospital, a nervous breakdown, according to reports. I wondered guiltily whether maybe the excitation my antics caused him had something to do with his condition. I had become quite fascinated with the Miss Innocence role I had built up for his edification, and had gone to extremes in thinking up erotic situations which could be presented to him in the guise of 'maidenly' confidences. He was physically unable to savour the more material delights of concupiscence, and I had supplanted the lack with artfully designed mental and visual extravaganzas. Probably I had overstepped the mark in my enthusiasm, and sent him into a psychopathic ward.

Mr Castle had simply disappeared. In addition to Monty I had another new patron of several weeks standing and indifferent qualities who had so far not distinguished himself by any eccentricities worth mentioning except one; he required that I be fully dressed on the occasion of his visits, and that I permit him to undress me. With ceremonial dignity by me, he divested me of my garments one by one until I stood before him, a modern Eve sans fig leaf. Thereafter, what took place was of orthodox regularity, a proceeding sanctioned by custom dating back into the most remote of prehistoric times as far as I know. In other words, he did just what men have been doing to girls since the dawn of time.

Monty had asked me to have a substantial supply of liquor available on his future visits and I had complied with the request. On a little taboret near the bed was a quart bottle of Scotch whisky of a mark he had indicated, together with a siphon of seltzer and glasses.

I hummed a song as I stood before the mirror for a last minute inspection to be sure that my hair was just right and that my face was properly powdered and my lips the correct shade of red. But my thoughts were not on the song, nor more than casually on the face that was reflected from the depths of the big mirror. I was thinking, with delicious little quivers of anticipation, of the several hours of unchastity which were in the immediate perspective. I was sure he would 'French' me again, for had I not confessed to him my predilection for the delicate caress? And if he did, and if he were nice to me in other ways, well, maybe I would repay him by doing again what I had done when I woke him up.

Hester said that after a girl started she was finished, because it grew on her. Nonsense. That might be true in some instances, and not in others. Hester meant well, but she didn't know me as well as she thought she did. She had a room engagement herself tonight, but had slipped away for a few minutes to speak to me.

'You be careful with that man Austin, Jessie! He's not your type!'

Not my type, indeed! What kind of a man did she

think my type was? A senile old innocent like Daddy Heely, or a perverted fool like Mr Castle whose one ambition in life was to do it to a girl in her bottom, or a semilunatic like Wainwright, who paid a girl to let him masturbate all over her legs?

From all of which it will be seen that I was pretty well convinced I knew better what I wanted than Hester did.

Reflected in the mirror, I saw the door opening gently and the face of the man I was thinking about appeared. I pretended not to have observed his entrance, and a second later he had clasped me from behind. With my knees hanging over his arms he lifted me into the air and buried his face in my bosom. I felt his hot breath on my breasts as he forced it through the texture of the scant garments which covered them.

'That's a nice way to come into a young lady's room, without even knocking,' I scolded playfully. 'Suppose I had been doing something I didn't want you to see?'

'In that case, I'd have shut my eyes!' he responded. 'But what would you be doing that you wouldn't want me to see?'

'Sometimes girls play with themselves when they feel naughty, and they wouldn't want a man to see that!'

'Ha!' he laughed, as he set me back on my feet and drew off his gloves. 'You're not confessing that you practice self-abuse, are you?'

'If I do, do you think I'd tell you?'

'Of course not! That's something no woman ever confesses to a man.'

'Well, prepare for a shock then. I do it often.'

'Amazing! I've known scores of girls and women and you're the only one that ever abused herself!'

'How do you know the others didn't?'

160

'Because I asked them and they said they didn't. Congratulations to you! Your score goes up another ten points!'

'Because I play with myself?'

'No! Because you admit it! Baby, you've given me an idea! I've . . . but wait . . . I'll speak of it later.'

'Tell me now!'

'No; let's get comfortable and have a drink first. I've got lots of things I want to tell you.'

'All right, but it's cruel to arouse a woman's curiosity and then make her wait.'

'Let your curiosity suffer for a few minutes. I'll dispel it pretty soon.'

'Well, then, let me hang up your things. Now sit down in this chair and make yourself comfortable. And here's that Scotch and seltzer you told me to get for you.'

'It's for you, too. You like it, don't you?'

'Yes, but the trouble is, after I've had about three glasses I lose all my maidenly modesty.'

'So much the better! Have three glasses right now!' I laughed.

'Here goes number one. My modesty is now one third dissipated. What is it you've got to tell me first? I hope it's something nice.'

'First, I want to tell you how absolutely topping you look. You're a good-looking girl no matter what you've got on, or haven't got on, of course, but those dresses, there's a sort of sophisticated childishness, about them that's irresistible. They're devilishly ingenious. Are they your own idea, or did somebody else think them up?'

The dress referred to, as you may have guessed, was another of the little-girl frocks Daddy Heely had paid for. I had worn one the previous week and as it seemed to have taken Monty's fancy, I had selected

161

another on the present occasion. It was a single-piece frock of black silk with a white belt, and long, tight sleeves. The cuffs, neck and breasts were lined with pleated ruffles and underlaid with cream-coloured lace.

To go with these dresses I had some dainty high-heeled Spanish slippers and black silk hose which I rolled just above my knees and fastened with elastic band garters. Except for one detail the costume was eminently respectable. That detail was the extreme shortness of the dress. It barely reached to my knees when I was standing, and when I sat in a normal posture there was no surplus material to be pulled down in a ladylike fashion. The dress was juvenile, but my legs were not. When I observed Daddy Heely's liking to sit on the floor at my feet I easily guessed the reason, and you can too.

Tonight, for certain optimistic reasons related to what Monty had first done on his previous visit, I had not put on any panties, and under the black silk frock was nothing except a diaphanous silk chemise, undervest, and brassiere.

I hesitated at this last question, not wanting to tell him the exact origin of the dresses, and so he did not press the query. I let it pass answered.

'What else have you to tell me?'

'Well, I must also tell you I've passed this whole blessed week positively thinking of nothing but you. I had such a ripping good time when I was here before that you've been on my mind ever since. The old pego has been in a continuous state of perturbation. Embarrasing at times, don't you know. Night before last I thought something really ought to be done about it. I tried the wife's door and it was unlocked, so I went in. She was asleep, or what I thought more likely, pretending to be asleep. The time is now, I thought, as I pulled the covers off her, the girl is here, and so is the place right there in the centre of her bird's nest. If I hadn't been well soused, I'd have known better. This is what I got?'

And turning his face sidewise he indicated something I had not yet observed; three long, partially healed scratches down the length of his cheek.

'My heavens!' I exclaimed. 'If she's like that, and you don't care for her, why do you want to do it with her?'

'Any port in a time of storm,' he answered ruefully, shrugging his shoulders. 'A man can't always make his cock behave.'

'Well, I think that's strange! If I were a man and I didn't like a woman, I'm sure I wouldn't want to fuck her!'

'That's what you think, baby. When a man gets in a certain state, he has to do something. When I was in South Africa I even fucked kinky-headed Kaffir girls. A half a loaf, or even a black loaf, is better than none!'

'And so, you got your pretty face scratched. It served you right. Is that all you got?'

'To all intents and purposes, yes. There were quite a few commmentaries and observations of an interesting nature thrown in for good measure.'

I couldn't help laughing but at the same time, deep inside me, a little canker of jealousy that he should have wanted to do it with her began to form.

'Is your wife pretty?' I asked suddenly.

'About as pretty compared to you as a moth is in comparison to a beautiful, exotic butterfly.'

His words relieved the vague foreboding which had come over me, and for the moment I forgot the matter.

'What else have you to tell me?'

'I want to ask you something. Suppose I should

163

want to take you out some night to a show, a cabaret, a party, or maybe pass the night in a hotel, could you get away?'

'I guess so, I'd have to ask Madame Lafronde. She doesn't like to have the girls go out, but sometimes she lets them. I've never been away all night. I suppose if you gave her something extra you could get her to let me, maybe.'

'All right; that's that. She can't hold you in captivity. If she gets rambunctious I'll take care of things. And now that the incidentals are disposed of, the momentous question is: how shall we pass the night to get the most fun possible out of it!'

I leaned over close to him, and cupping my hands around my lips, slowly spelled out my recommendation, in his ear; 'F-u-c-k-i-n-g!'

'Moved, seconded, and unanimously adopted! Let's start!'

'Shall I get undressed now?'

'No, I want to enjoy that dress awhile first, if you don't mind rumpling it. Let's lie down on the bed and just tease for a little while.'

'All right! But wait . . . you forgot something . . . you were going to tell me something else, you started to tell me and then you said you'd tell me later!'

'Ah, yes!' he exclaimed, laughing, sinking back into his chair. 'Before I mention that, I think you'd better take those other two drinks!'

'Oh! It's something that's going to put a strain on my modesty, is it?'

'Better not ask any questions until after you've had the drinks.'

'You're torturing me with curiosity! All right, here goes one . . . and . . . here goes the other. That makes three altogether. My modesty is now in a dormant state!'

'Well,' he said, still laughing, 'you put the idea in my head with your nonsense about playing with yourself. You made me think of something odd, a blank void in my life. I've been all over the world, I've lived with a dozen women more or less and enjoyed the transitory favours of hundreds of others. I've seen all kinds of naughty shows and exhibitions, and if anyone had asked me. I'd have sworn there wasn't a single act in the whole encyclopedia of sexual arts I hadn't witnessed. I've even seen actual rapes of young girls in show bagnios in Cairo. But while you were joking about abusing yourself it came over me that I never actually saw a girl masturbating herself, I mean, really by herself, just as though she were alone and nobody watching her.'

'Oh, heavens! I know what's coming! Give me another drink, quick! My modesty never lived through three before, but it's squirming and twitching now!'

'Listen, baby!' he exclaimed between convulsions of laughter, 'I've had something squirming and twitching all week on account of you! I had it pretty well under control the last time, but it's ready to go off on the slightest provocation now, and I think I'd better not expose it to any direct heat, that is, if I want to keep it in a playful humour for a few hours!'

'What a lovely way of saying you want to keep a hard-on! All right, where do I fit into the picture?'

'Well, with the idea you put in my head, and having in mind your inexhaustible resources, I thought possibly you might be kind enough to stage a little entertainment, enjoy yourself voluptuously, and at the same time gratify my prurient curiosity. Kill two birds with one stone, as the saying goes!'

I could not, of course, restrain my laughter, but at the same time the erotic titillations which the lewd suggestion evoked were vibrating through me and my face felt like it was on fire.

'I guessed it. In plain words, you want to see me masturbate myself! Well, I've done it when there was no man around, but it will be the first time I ever did it with one right by me!'

'Then you'll be accommodating?'

'Excellency, I'm yours, body and soul, and your slightest wish is my command! How . . . how . . . ' I exclaimed, again gasping with laughter, ' . . . how am I supposed to do it?'

'Don't ask me! I don't know how girls do it! I'm not even supposed to be here! You're doing it just as though you were alone!'

'Very well! but I'd better take another drink to make sure my modesty stays unconscious. It was never put to such a test before! Well, first, oh, ha, ha, ha, do I have to tell you what I'm thinking about while I'm doing it, too?'

'That would add greatly to the realism!'

'Well, first, I'm all alone, like you said, and I'm thinking about something I did with a man I liked . . . I'm thinking about what you and I did when you were here before. . . .

'Just a moment! I'm not supposed to be here, but you oblige me to obtrude for a second. What you and I did when I was here before . . . we did a number of things. Be more specific in the interests of lucidity and realism!'

'Well, ha, ha, ha, I'm thinking of everything we did, and especially what you did to me first, while I was lying on the bed here, before I undressed!'

'Proceed. I'm withdrawn from the room again.'

'I'm thinking about how you licked me down there, and it makes me feel hot. My little thing in the top of my cunny gets hard and I'm wishing you were here to do that again. And the more I think of it, the worse it gets, and pretty soon I think I'd better do something to relieve the feeling.

'I can't decide at first whether I will or not, and I walk over to my bureau and get these pictures and take this one out and look at it. . . .'

'Excuse me for coming in again, let's see that picture . . . u-um!'

'As I was saying when I was interrupted by a phantom voice. I look at the picture. It's a very nice picture of a naked man and a naked woman, and the man has got his face down between the woman's legs and he's doing something to her with his mouth. I think to myself I wish that woman were me and the man Monty. But they aren't, so after I've looked at it awhile I put it back with the rest of the pictures and hide them under the clothes in my bureau.

'I think, what's the harm, I might as well do it, a little, anyway. So I come back to the bed and lie down on my back, like this, with my knees up and kind of apart, and pull my dress up out of the way.

'Then I put my hand down like this, with my two fingers, oh, ha, ha, ha, and shut my eyes, and, ha, ha, ha, rub this little hard thing, kind of slow and easy, with just the tips of my fingers, and it feels awful good, and the more I rub it. . . .'

At this point the realism I had injected into the pantomine threatened to overcome me, and I paused, hysterical with laughter.

'. . . and the more I rub . . . the more I rub . . .' I gasped . . . 'the nicer it feels . . . until . . . until . . . the nice feeling . . . just seems to . . . burst inside me . . . OH! . . . like it's . . . DOING NOW!'

I wiped away the tears which hysterical laughter had brought to my eyes. My face was burning as I turned toward my companion. His face, too, was a dull red; his reaction to the lewd portrayal had not been much less than my own. He sprang toward me, and I knew what he intended to do.

'No, no!' I panted. 'Not now! Wait for me a moment! I'm dead down there now! Let me go wash myself and then I'll be all right!'

On unsteady feet I went to the bathroom and laved myself with tepid, scented water. Before I had finished my vitality was returning and the warm glow of voluptuous desire was beginning to reestablish itself.

'Well, Excellency, is your naughty curiosity satisfied? Now you know a girl's last secret!'

'Baby!' he answered in a tense voice, 'that affected me more than it did you, I think. I was so near going off I couldn't have held it another second! Look at this. . . .'

Unbuttoning the front of his trousers he took his cock out and displayed it, turgid and throbbing, to my eyes; he slipped the foreskin down and the plum-coloured head appeared, dripping with limpid moisture.

'Just sympathetic tears,' he murmured, 'I didn't come, but I was very close to it.'

I went again to the bathroom and brought a small wet towel and wiped away the tears. 'Careful! Careful!' he cautioned, as I fingered the palpitating column. 'It won't take much to release the trigger! I'll have to let the fire die down a little before I put it in you, baby, and meanwhile . . .' he smiled understandingly, ' . . . and meanwhile, you can lie down on the bed and take it easy while I pay you back for entertaining me in such a realistic way!'

'Shall I get undressed?'

'No, just lie down like you were a minute ago. You were really entrancing with your little dress up and the white of your bottom and thighs against the black background of dress and hose. That's it . . . just like you were before . . . with your knees up and your legs apart!'

He sat down on the edge of the bed, passed his fingers over the crevice between my legs in a lingering caress, and then his mouth descended on it.

What havoc an ardent, enthusiastic tongue can work in a girl's cunny! I tried to steel my nerves against it to prolong the exquisite sensation, but it was no use, I couldn't hold it back long and all too soon I was melting in his mouth. As the echoes died away, I pushed him from me to lie for a while in fainting languor.

It would take too long to relate all that transpired during those mad, sensuous hours, even if I could remember every act in all its lewd details. Suffice is to draw the curtain with the final scene, wherein, hours later, intoxicated both with liquor and lust, I perceived that Monty's face was again between my thighs, his hot lips pressed against my cunny. My dress, now displaced and rumpled, partly hid his face as he sucked and licked the avid flesh. He himself had long since disrobed and was completely naked.

As he crouched over me I could see his cock, still enticingly rigid, as it projected its muscular length outward.

'Turn this direction, Monty!' I whispered, 'so we can do it the 69 way!'

He reversed his position and the next moment it was touching my lips in a moist kiss as he knelt over my face and again buried his own between my trembling thighs. My lips shaped themselves in a tight ring around its mouth and neck and took the visitor in.

The odd, indescribable savour again filled my mouth, breeding within me, not distaste or disgust, but a wild hunger to feel it spurting like a hot fountain in my mouth and throat. So imperious was the urge that I scarcely now heeded the penetrating tongue which but a moment before had evoked such exquisite torment. I thought of nothing but to drain the nectar from the living flesh about which my lips were pursed, to receive its hot gushes in my mouth.

It would give me an orgasm even quicker than having my clitoris sucked. I felt it, I knew it, the poison had entered my soul, this, this was the supreme act of voluptuous delight, and nothing hereafter would ever give me the same thrill. All else would be incidental, superficial, this was the ultimate caress by the side of which all others receded into nothingness.

CHAPTER FOURTEEN

When I awoke, it must have been around noon. My head was aching dully and in my mouth was a queer, pungent taste which puzzled me for a moment, and then I remembered. I sat up in bed. I was stark naked, and I was alone. On the little taboret near the bed was an empty whisky bottle which accounted, in part at least, for the headache.

Draped carelessly over a chair were my clothes—dress, camisole, brassiere, and stockings. I had no recollection of having undressed nor did I know when or under what circumstances I had fallen asleep. Monty must have taken off my clothes and subsequently departed without awakening me. At what hour he had gone I had not the faintest idea.

Painfully I dragged myself from bed and went to my mirror. My hair was a tangle and there were violet shadows under my eyes. I shivered and pressed my hands to my throbbing temples. What a night! Monty had gone without awakening me. This reminded me of something, and I turned toward my dressing table. There were some bank notes there, weighted down with one of my perfume flasks, and under them a slip of paper with some pencilled scribbling.

'The next time, don't have on any lipstick. You left red rings all around it.

See you next Wednesday night. Love and Kisses. Monty.'

I rubbed my fingers over my lips and smiled involuntarily as I viewed the result. Then I tore the note into shreds and threw the pieces into the wastebaket.

I did not feel like dressing so I merely bathed my face, brushed out my hair, and went back to bed after ringing for the maid. She brought me some coffee and toast, and I asked her to tell Madame Lafronde that I had a headache and would not be be down until later.

About three o'clock Madame Lafronde came up to see me.

'What's the matter, Jessie? Anything wrong?'

'No; my sleeper kept me awake all night, and I've a headache, that's all.'

'You can rest up tonight. You needn't come downstairs if you don't feel like it. How are you getting on with Austin?'

'All right. He's not so bad, I like him. He gave me another five pounds.'

'Well, be smart, and keep him in a giving humour. I was rather doubtful about him at first. He's got a bad reputation.'

I stayed in my room the rest of the afternoon and evening, but along about ten o'clock I got restless, and hearing a great deal of laughter floating up from the parlour I decided to dress and go down.

Under the genial guidance of a gentleman who had just come from America, a game of 'strip poker' was in hilarious progress. Five girls were seated around a small table, cards were dealt to them, and the penalty of a losing hand was the removal of one of the few pieces of apparel the loser wore. To keep up the morale of the players, a grand prize to the winner, and consolation prizes to the losers were being offered.

Already one of the girls was down to her panties, and another to panties, brassiere and one stocking.

Even as I stood there trying to grasp the intricacies of the game, a shout went up, and the unfortunate in panties threw down her cards in disgust.

'Come on, Bobby! No welching! Take them off!'

Now it is one thing to take your panties off in the presence of a man in the privacy of a room, and quite another to take them off in front of a crowd of laughing people, and I smiled faintly as I watched the victim's flushed face.

But welching is an unforgivable sin in sporting circles, and she was game. Off came the little silk panties and the spectators, or the masculine element of them at least, had the pleasure of grazing on the patch of dark, twisted little curls that rose from the apex of her legs and spread fan-wise over her pubic mount.

'Now can I put my clothes on again?'

'No, no, no! Not until the game is finished!'

And so it continued, to the immense delight of the onlookers, until all but one of the scarlet-faced players were sitting around naked, some pretending a brazen insouciance, others trying to cover their cunnies and breasts with hands and arms.

'As insipid idea of fun,' I thought to myself as I looked on indifferently. 'Why are men so crazy to look at a girl's cunt? One would think it was the prettiest thing in the world. Whatever they find pretty about one must be in their imaginations. But . . .' I thought, continuing my mood philosophy, 'if men didn't think they were pretty, it would be just too sad for us.'

And an involuntary smile crossed my lips as there came to my mind the story about the orator for women's suffrage who shouted from the platform: 'After all, ladies and gentlemen, women are only slightly different from men. . . .' Whereupon a voice from the gallery interrupted: 'Hurrah for the slight difference!'

I lingered long enough to pick up some small silver in the form of a gratuity from a pleasantly inebriated gentleman who attached himself to me and could not be dislodged until I permitted him to put his hand down the front of my dress and feel my bubbies. He wanted very badly to go to a room with me, but I managed to divert his attentions to Hester and made my escape.

The next night was Wainwright's. He came punctually as always and went through his customary nonsense. Generally I extracted some amusement from my exalted status of Fairy Princess, and although I had always to be on the alert to keep him from biting me in the moment of ecstasy, there was something about the fantastic proceeding that left me in an excited condition.

He sucked me deliciously, but rarely continued it long enough to quench the fires the caress started. Before I could have an orgasm he would jerk away from me and masturbate.

This night I was in a particularly restless mood. The exhaustion following my orgy with Monty had passed away with a day and night of rest, and I was again charged with voluptuous longings.

Wainwright had concluded his preliminary gallantries and was crouched over his Fairy Princess on his knees, his head and shoulders inclined downward and his face between her open legs. His tongue had started its tantalizing manoeuvres, and the first shivers of lewd excitation were beginning to generate.

With languorous, half-closed eyes, I observed his cock sticking out from his middle. It was small and slender, much smaller than the average, but it was turgidly erect. It was like a child's in comparison to Monty's.

This assocation of ideas put into my mind the thought of how much easier I could manipulate so small a cock in my mouth. The thought took root and sent a hot glow through me, and in a moment it was no longer a thought, but a desire.

Without a word of explanation to the puzzled Wainwright I wriggled away from him, turned around on the bed, and got on top of him, straddling his face with my thighs. After a momentary hesitation, and with a clumsiness which betrayed his unfamiliarity with this classic position, his tongue again sought out my clitoris.

As soon as I perceived that its activities were in progress anew, I put my head down and took his little cock in my mouth. The mere fact that it contrasted so in size with the only other one I had dallied with in like manner inspired me with a sort of fascination, and I set to work on it with all my recently acquired skill.

But, alas, I suffered a deception which chilled and disgusted me. Like nectar turning to vinegar in the mouth, that erstwhile stiff little cock which I was so voluptuously sucking almost immediately began to wilt. From its former state of virile rigidity it degenerated into a flaccid, spineless, lifeless little worm, and the harder I tried to inspire it with a bit of manliness, the more fulminating was the disaster.

I released it from my mouth, disappointed, and emulating his own tactics, worked it patiently with my fingers in an effort to resuscitate it, but there was nothing substantial to grasp; it was like trying to make a piece of string stand up, so limp and flaccid had it become.

I could do nothing with it, and disgusted. I got up

from the bed. Wainwright's abasement was pitiful to behold.

'Oh, Princess!' he moaned. 'Beat me if you wish!'

He sounded as though he actually did want me to beat him. It came over me that if he left under humiliating circumstances he might not return again. He was too valuable a patron to lose. It had always been profitable to humour him; it might be wise to do so in this instance. As he grovelled on the floor at my feet I came to a sudden decision.

'I will beat you, you vile creature!' I cried.

Glancing hastily around the room I spied his own belt partly visible under the clothing he had placed on a chair. Snatching loose the strip of pliant leather I flew at him and began to belabour him across the thighs and buttocks.

'Take that . . . and that . . . and that. . . . ! I cried, 'you evil, depraved beast! If you ever do that again I'll . . . I'll . . .' and I paused to think of a sufficiently ominous threat.

'Oh, Princess! Oh, Princess!' he moaned, and turned over on his back apparently indifferent as to whether the blows fell on his cock and testicles.

Careful not to strike him in these susceptible parts I continued to rain blows on him. He grovelled, squirmed, and moaned, and suddenly to my great astonishment I saw that his cock was getting hard again. And there before my eyes was realized one of those strange, weird manifestations of sexual aberration such as delights the hearts of psychoanalysts and psychiatrists.

His hand descended to the reviving member which was now lifted upward in a half-erected state. His fingers closed around it, and while I continued to shower blows upon his naked body he masturbated himself to exhaustion.

176

A sight fit for a cabinet in Dante's Inferno would have been revealed had anyone unexpectedly intruded in those moments. The man, grovelling naked upon the floor, furiously masturbating, while I, with nothing on but shoes and stockings, my hair dishevelled, my face flushed, panting and crying imprecations, danced around him belabouring him frenziedly from all sides.

When it was all over and he was dressed and gone, I sank down on my bed. My heart was thumping and I felt half-suffocated. On the bed beside me was a heap of money. I figured it indifferently, and came to with a start. The man had literally emptied his pockets! There were bank notes, shillings, pence and even pennies, a total in excess of anything he had given me before. Surely the man was a lunatic!

There came an insistent tapping at the door, and Hester entered. She looked at me in astonishment. I was still naked, my face flushed my hair in disorder.

'Jessie! What's the matter! Did you have trouble with Wainwright?'

'No; no trouble.'

'We heard you whipping him and I was uneasy. You never did that before!'

'Oh, the damned fool,' I ejaculated, 'I think he's crazy.' And I related what had happened, omitting only the real cause of his having lost his erection. 'He couldn't get a hard-on without my whipping him and I did . . . with his own belt!'

'Did he give you all that?' she gasped, observing the pile of money which still lay on the bed.

'Yes,' I answered shortly.

'Gee! You have all the luck! I wish I had a regular who was crazy the way that fellow is! I'd even let him whip *me* for that much!'

'Well, he makes me dizzy. I'm still trembling.'

177

'I see you are. You scared me when I first came in, you looked so . . . so strange!'

'What time is it, Hester?'

'It's about two o'clock.'

'Are you going downstairs again?'

'No; there's nothing doing. I'm going to turn in.'

'Listen, Hester, I'm nervous. Sleep in here with me tonight.'

'All right, I'll get my . . . no! I won't either! I know what you're thinking about, you nasty little pervert!'

'Please, Hester!'

'I will not! Get the electric massage machine or jack yourself off if you're so hot!'

'Please, Hester!'

'What in the world is the matter with you, Jessie? Don't you ever get enough? You ought to have yourself castrated!'

'Please, Hester!'

'Oh, all right, all right, you disgusting little degenerate!'

CHAPTER FIFTEEN

Six weeks went by with Monty visiting me regularly, and week by week I found myself sinking deeper into the fatal fascination of the sexual perversion into which he had initiated me. I do not think he was responsible for the unnatural desire which was now dominating me, I think he was merely the casual and accidental medium through which existing but dormant instincts were aroused.

Like the Succubus of ancient Rome my sexual desires were now almost entirely concentrated in this one act. My inclinations for other forms of gratification were diminishing. Normal intercourse was only an aphrodisiacal irritant if it were not followed by cocksucking. I still masturbated to calm my nerves, but it was always with fellatio pictured in my mind as I realized the act.

In my hours of passion I felt an actual physical hunger for the spermatic nectar. It was as though it contained some vital, sustaining element necessary to my health and well-being, and the first taste as I perceived its saline presence in my mouth precipitated the wildest sexual frenzy. When it came pouring into my throat my own organism responded instantly, without mechanical stimulation of any kind. I no longer tried to spit it out as the hot waves laved my tongue; I drank it avidly, hungrily.

It is said that the cocksucking instinct is the heritage of children whose mothers, while in an advanced stage of pregnancy, and because of the discomfort or danger of normal intercourse while in this condition, have themselves resorted to fellatio, thereby afflicting the unborn child with the unnatural desire. Whether there is any scientific foundation for this theory, or whether it is mere superstition I do not know, but I feel certain, with respect to myself, that the instinct was inherent and not artificially created.

Without any special guidance, refinements and perfections of the art constitute in part its irresistible allure and enravish the masculine senses. Gently, softly and slowly realized, an orgasm effected in this manner sent the recipient, with few exceptions, into the seventh heaven of rapture. A soft, even suction, alternated with the teasing caress of an active tongue playing over the head and around the neck of the pulsing glans, supplemented with a slight up and down movement of the mouth soon had the object of these felicities groaning with erotic ecstasy.

If the subject was slow to reach orgasm, a more intense excitation could be induced by the use of the hand in addition. No normal man in a healthy sexual condition could long resist the luscious combinations of gentle fingers and warm, wet, sucking lips.

As the untouched chords of a harp vibrate in harmony with those which are giving forth their tremulous melody, so did my own organism yield up in its store of passion, an echo to the very paroxysm I provoked in another.

To Monty's manifest satisfaction the unique method of awakening him in the morning which I have previously related became a definite part of our erotic programme. I looked forward to it with a pleasant glow of anticipation, and the thought, implanted in my mind, caused me to wake earlier than I would otherwise have done.

He was a man of unusual virile potency whose sexual vigour reestablished itself quickly, even after the most enervating exhaustion, and he always had an erection when I woke up. Slyly, cautiously, inspired with a prurient fancy to see how far I could get with it before he woke up. I bent my head over the succulent fruit. But in a few minutes my cautious, discreet restraint gave way to more energetic movements as my own passions took the ascendancy. And as soon as this happened, instead of a sleeping subject, I had one who was very much awake indeed.

Week by week I looked forward to Monty's visits with increasing impatience. My other patrons I simply tolerated. The lack of interest in them, which I could not entirely conceal, became apparent and before long I lost Mr Thomas. Madame Lafronde commented on my petulant humour, and I told her I was tired of being merely an ornament and wanted as many men as I could get, like the other girls. Some of these, the more attractive, often had three or four different men in a single night. She was reluctant to change the existing order and evaded my request by telling me she would think it over.

I knew she felt that I was more valuable as an 'inspirational' attraction, and that she feared the complications and ill-humour which would inevitably arise when my younger and fresher charms were used to lure the fish from less attractive bait. Maybe, too, she was aware of or suspected my recently developed cocksucking proclivities, for little escaped her shrewd old eyes and if so, no one better than she knew what this would do to the peace and tranquillity of the house once the girls whose clientele I usurped discovered my technique.

In fairness to my sisters in vice, I will say that to most of them fellatio is abhorrent and practised only

181

under duress or the pressure of necessity when fading physical attractions render them unfit to compete on an even basis with younger rivals. Sacrifices must be made to compensate for advancing years and shrunken breasts.

Girls who are alert, good-looking, and possessed of attractive bodies do not need to practise fellatio to hold a clientele. But men are quick to take advantage of any weakness and if the caress be obtained once, either by duress or persuasion or voluntary indulgence, it is extremely difficult to evade further demands.

Monty's confidence to me regarding his conjugal unhappiness and differences became more and more candid. Wrapped up in the lewd fascination which the man held for me I gave no thought to the fact that only a bounder and a cad would have made his wife the subject of such intimate confidence to a whore, regardless of what personal differences may have existed between them.

He had explained the origin and significance of some long scratches down the side of his face, administered by his wife's agile fingers when he had tried to force her. And subsequently, there was a big, blue lump on one of his shins, the result of a well-placed kick received while trying to impose unwanted attention on her.

'Wait till she's undressed next time,' I commented viciously, 'or did you have her like me, with just her shoes and stockings on?'

He laughed cynically.

'I'll have to chloroform her first to see her naked!'

Apparently, some disagreement of two or three years' standing had arisen between them and she had consistently and determinedly repulsed all amorous advances since then. Picturing her in my mind as I did, an embittered, shrewish woman, I could not for the life of me understand how he was able to feel any desire toward her. But men are contrary brutes, and to make them want something desperately you have only to prohibit it. She didn't want him to fuck her, and presto, the wish to do so was never out of his mind.

These confidences affected me in a peculiar way. I wasn't in love with Monty in the true sense of the word, but when he told me such things I felt twinges of jealousy. It annoyed me that he should perversely want to do it with her. So distorted can one's perspective become that his inordinate desire to fuck the unfortunate woman inspired me with a feeling of personal animosity against her.

At first he had seemed to accept the situation with good-natured indifference, but lately I had perceived an undercurrent of bitterness and vindictiveness.

'Have you ever read De Maupassant?' he asked one night, after having told me of some domestic disagreement.

'No,' I answered. 'I've heard of him, but I have never read his stories. Why?'

'Well, among them is one with an idea I'd like to apply to her, with certain variations.'

'Tell me about it.'

'The story is a long one to repeat, but the essence of it is this: A young French noblewoman discovers that her husband is unfaithful to her. She decides to revenge his disloyalty in a manner as startling as it is unique. She hires some ruffians to enter the house and bind and gag him securely. When this is done she has him placed behind some curtains in her boudoir where he will, perforce, he obliged to witness all that transpires within the room, but without being able to move or interfere.

'Then she calls an old servant who has served her all her life and gives her some instructions. Following these instructions the old woman, after wandering about the streets for a time, accosts a young man of genteel appearance, and getting his ear, asks him whether he would appreciate an amorous rendezvous with a young and beautiful woman of nobility sufficiently to bind himself to certain simple conditions, viz: that he permit himself as he blind-folded while being conducted to and from the assignation; that during the amorous engagement he lend himself unreservedly to all the delicate refinements of eroticism for which the French people are noted.

'The first condition being one of no great consideration, and the second one which could be easily complied with if the lady were as young and fair and lascivious as the servant claimed, the youth, who was of a naturally adventurous and romantic disposition, did not hesitate long in accepting the mysterious assignation.

'Whereupon the old woman signalled a hack, and when he was inside blindfolded him and conveyed him to the lady's boudoir. Here the blindfold was removed and the young gallant found himself in the presence of a vision of nude loveliness which far surpassed his expectations.

'For an hour the youthful pair disported themselves with voluptuous abandon, neglecting none of the more delicate and refined artifices in which mouth and tongue play an important part.

'When the cup of love was finally drained to the last drop, the lady sprang from the bed and jerking some curtains aside revealed to the horrified gaze of the youth the securely bound figure of a man who glared at him with baleful eyes.

'What transpired later when the outraged husband was liberated is left to the imagination.'

'A very interesting story,' I observed. 'Get me the book so I can read it some day. But what has it to do with your wife? Do you want her to have you tied up and make you watch from behind a curtain while she Frenchies with some fellow?'

'Heavens, no!' he exploded, 'I'd tear her limb from limb if she were to play such a game on me. But there's no danger. She's too prudish. I was tickling my face with quite the reverse of the plot in the story, thinking what fun it would be to tie her up and then have some girl come in, you for instance, and do just what that French couple, did, right before her eyes. Maybe strip her clothes off first, so she'd enjoy it more.'

'What a horrible idea!' I gasped. 'Why do you want to torment and aggravate her? Why don't you leave her alone?'

'She's tormented and aggravated me plenty,' he growled vindictively. 'I'll get even with her, though. Do you know what I'd like?'

'Yes, I do! It's not a bit hard to guess! You'd like to fuck her, and you won't rest until you do!'

'Wrong, you little spitfire. I'd like to find some way to make her so hot she'd go down on her knees and beg for it, and when she did, I'd tell her exactly where to go.'

'Feed her some Spanish fly then,' I suggested dryly.

'By Jove! That's a dashed good idea! Wonder where one can get the bally stuff?'

'You'd better be careful. I heard a funny story once about a fellow who sneaked some into his wife's tea to make her passionate. He thought he'd better keep out of sight until it took effect so he went out and walked around the block a couple of times. When he came back he didn't see her around, so he looked in her bedroom. And there she was, on the bed, with her clothes up, and the butler on top of her. And the pantryman, the coachman and the gardener were all standing around holding their cocks, waiting their turn.'

'The moral being, that a chappie had better stick around after feeding his wife Spanish fly,' he laughed. 'I'll keep that in mind.'

'Well, come on, let's get started. I don't need any Spanish fly to make me passionate, I'm that way all the time.'

CHAPTER SIXTEEN

Through the damp London night a luxurious car sped
swiftly and surely, the soft purr of its powerful motors
hardly distinguishable above the swish, swish, swish
of rubber-shod wheels upon the wet pavement as they
flew onward toward their destinations.

Outside of the curtained windows a macabre fog
eddied and drifted, at times dimming the street lights
with its wispy, ghostly vapours. Within was snug
comfort, warmth, life and colour.

Had curious eyes been permitted to peek inside the
glass and curtain-shielded tonneau, a scene of revelry,
profanely at variance with the dismal exterior of the
night, would have been revealed.

Outside, the interminable procession of half suffocated lights vainly trying to pierce the grey shroud
which drew ever closer and closer about them; inside,
the ribald levity of alcohol-inspired abandon, the
sheen of silken hose on diaphanous garments fluttered
in careless disarray above the silk-clad knees.

There were four occupants in the seclusion of the
cosy, glassed-in, and softly lighted tonneau. Two of
them were gentlemen, modishly attired in the habiliments dictated by the fashions of the times for evening
wear, and two of them were young girls, whose
apparel, if not exactly that which would have been
considered in the best of taste by social arbiters, was
at least beautiful and colourful. The gentlemen,
regardless of their half-inebriated condition, were

patently at home in the atmosphere of luxury which both the car and their apparel suggested. The girls, had the imaginary observer surveyed them with a critical eyes and taken note of the exteme shortness of their dresses, the rouge upon their cheeks, the exaggerated scarlet of their lips and their indifference to the indiscreet disarray of their clothing, would have been catalogued instantly as ladies of that vast assembly politely described as 'not nice!'

One of the gentlemen was Monty and one of the girls myself. The second gentleman was another scion of aristocracy known only to me by the nickname Zippy, and his companion was a young Spanish girl of saturnine but piquantly beautiful features named Carlota.

This was not the first nocturnal outing I had participated in. Yielding to the influence of the magic wand of gold which Monty had waved before her eyes. Madame Lafronde had consented to this departure from the accustomed routine.

'I don't want to stand in the way of your doing the best you can for yourself, but watch your step, girl, watch your step!' were her final words on the subject.

Tonight we were to be present at the clandestine showing of some naughty moving pictures which Zippy had arranged for with an exhibitor at some obscure point far over to the East Side of London. After the show we would dine in the seclusion of a private room in a popular resort.

Zippy was a genial chap of very likable personality. He was possessed of a humorous and witty disposition. His droll witticisms and antics kept one constantly laughing, and when he was half under the influence of liquor, he kept those around him fairly convulsed.

Carlota, whom I had met a few hours before, constituted something of an enigma. Her attitude toward me was perplexing; I had always been able to make friends easily, but my overtures to her left her unresponsive and I sensed some coldness, the reason for which I could not imagine. At times I found her looking at me covertly and imagined there was something baleful in the glint of her dark eyes.

Thinking that maybe she regarded my acquaintance with Zippy as a possible menace to the security of her domains in his affection, I was scrupulously careful not to presume upon the bon-homme spirit of the four-cornered friendship, and still this explanation did not seem to fit the circumstances exactly, for she seemed peculiarly tepid in her demonstrations of affection for the good-looking young aristocrat.

Tonight, however, she had apparently cast off her moody lack of animation and had entered into the festive spirit of the occasion. A silver-covered flask was being passed from hand to hand as the smoothly humming motor carried us onward toward our destination. Ensconced in one corner of the luxuriously upholstered seat, Monty leaned back with me on his lap. At the other end of the seat, Zippy held Carlota in a similar fashion. A supple, beautiful arm was curved lightly about his neck, and a small, piquant face was snuggled against his.

In the pleasant spell of a mild alcoholic langour, I watched them dreamily. I felt happy, contented, and was looking forward to a night of joyous abandon with no premonition or presentiment of evil to mar my lightheartedness.

Carlota's skirts were up over her knees, revealing a brief extension of flesh which glinted ivorylike in the soft light and was accentuated by the black sheen of her silk-clad legs. The metallic clasps which engaged the tops of her hose, holding them smooth and tight about her legs by means of elastic garters which ascended upward and disappeared under filmy garments, sparkled like jewels as the movement of the car caused the light to vibrate against them.

An inquisitive hand, lured on, no doubt, by the seductive disarray of garments, fell upon her knees and began an insidious exploration upward, its movements contributing further to the disorder of her clothing and the revealment of more ivory thighs. Of the hand itself soon nothing was visible but portions of a white cuff, the rest of it being lost to sight among the filmy undergarments.

Carlota giggled nervously and pressed her legs together, by virtue of which manoeuvre the invading hand was firmly imprisoned between walls of warm, living flesh.

With my head resting on Monty's shoulder, I watched this lascivious play with half-closed eyes. What a pity, I thought, that Carlota was not always jolly and happy. When she was like this, she was really beautiful. What pretty legs she had, too, so slim and graceful and softly curved. When girls had legs like hers no wonder men admired them. Mine had been like that when I was younger, but during the last year or two they had filled out, become more solid, more suggestive of maturity.

I straightened my own legs out and contemplated them pensively.

'What are you doing, baby? Admiring your legs?' murmured Monty.

'No; I was admiring Carlota's, and comparing mine with them.'

'Oh, envy! Thy name is Woman! Do you think Carlota's legs are prettier than yours?'

'Yes,' I said, candidly. 'I do. Mine are getting too matronly.'

'Bosh,' answered Monty, and he plunged his face

between my breasts and set me to giggling by blowing hot, whisky-scented breath through the cloth over my bubbies. 'You're just fishing for compliments, and out of pure obstinacy, I refuse to bite.'

'The only time to properly judge a lady's legs,' expounded Zippy solemnly from his corner, 'is when they're around your neck. I maintain that Carlota has the nicest legs in the world.'

Monty and I burst out laughing and Carlota jerked upright in pretended indignation.

'Oh! What an insolent inference! I never had my legs around his neck in my life.'

'In my dreams, my dear, in dreams! A man has a right to dream anything he wants to, hasn't he?'

'No! Not such defamatory dreams as that! If you want to dream about me, dream something decent! And . . . o-o-oh! . . . take your hand away from there! Stop! . . . stop! . . . you're going to make me wet my panties!'

The sudden slowing of the car, followed by two long and two short blasts of the siren warned us that we had reached our destination and Carlota, escaping from the fervid embrace, straightened out her clothing preparatory to leaving the car.

As it rolled to a stop, apparently in accordance with prearranged plans and in answer to the signals of the siren, the figure of a man materialized from the fog-enshrouded night to guide us to the rendezvous where the entertainment was to take place.

We were conducted to a room improvised to represent a theatre in a crude way; a few chairs, a small platform elevated two or three feet above the floor, and back of this a white curtain. The projection machine and operator were hidden from our view in an adjacent room whence the pictures would be flashed through a small round hole cut in the intervening wall. There were no other spectators present as Zippy had arranged for an entirely private showing.

The exhibition lasted for about an hour and a half and consisted of several different films, some of them allegedly taken from real life among the apaches of Paris and which ran the gamut of every imaginable sexual indulgence and perversion. Another, based superficially on the question of whether or not it is a physical possibility for a man to be raped against his wishes, had as its theme the sequestering of a young man on his wedding day by a group of jolly, fun-loving friends.

Snatched from the side of his bride of a few minutes, he is carried away, stripped of his clothing, and chained against a wall in an upright position with his arms elevated and his legs separated.

Under these undignified circumstances he is turned over to the mercies of a bevy of girls who, with lewd acts, dances and other artifices, endeavour to make him have an erection. For a while this modern St. Anthony is able to subjugate any erotic reactions and successfully resists the wiles of the sirens. But alas, the flesh is weak, and despite his determination to withstand the impure temptations, Satan, in the guise of a beautiful young girl with nimble fingers, forces his cock to awaken from its lethargic slumber and raise its head in obeisance to the powers of Evil.

With this disaster, the battle is practically lost, for once a man's cock is turgidly erect not even the chaste determination of a Galahad can control its subsequent actions nor stay the course of lascivious Nature.

Raising her dress, the temptress turns around and stooping over, with her hands on her knees, backs her round, white bottom up against the rigid spike. Closer and closer she presses, until the treacherous obelisk, following the narrow road downward between the plump cheeks, reaches and penetrates the natural haven between her thighs, and naught remains to complete the victory of sin but the slow, weaving circular movement of her bottom.

By hand frigging, by sucking, and by other lascivious arts the unfortunate victim is subjected to further depletions of his sexual vitality as the sirens, one after another, drain him to exhaustion, until at last his cock is reduced to a state of unconsciousness and inertia from which no seductive feminine enticements on earth could arouse it, and when this is apparent, the luckless (?) groom is released and permitted to go on his honeymoon.

The entertainment terminated with a horrific exposition of a girl and a diminutive Shetland pony. It was incredible, unbelievable, but the evidence was there, clear, distinct and indisputable in the moving photographic reproduction upon the screen.

When the show was over we returned to the car and half an hour later were at a restaurant where a small private dining room had been reserved for us. We enjoyed a nice dinner, followed with exquisite wines, over which we lingered, joking, teasing, and otherwise enjoying ourselves. After the dinner, we would part company. Monty and I going our way and Zippy and Carlota another.

But it was very pleasant and comfortable in the little dining room. We were all in the roseate state of semi-intoxication in which everything is just right and everything that is said excruciatingly funny. So we dallied, telling naughty stories, rumpling each other's clothing, and indulging in all kinds of lascivious nonsense, while Monty and Zippy continued to drink until they had passed the half-way stage of intoxication.

'On an occasion of thish nashure,' declaimed Zippy,

taking advantage of a lull in the conversation, 'ish an invariable, not to shay an inviolable cushtom for each guesh to relate in hish own crude way the chircumstances and detailsh of hish or her firsh sexual experiensh.'

'What he meansh,' interrupted Monty, condescendingly, 'ish: everybody tell about their firsh fuck!'

'I believe I . . . hic . . . made myself clear without . . . hic . . . the necesshity . . . of an . . . interpreter!' protested Zippy with great dignity.

'You're half intoxshicated!'

'I resent that inshinuation! I insist that I'm not half intoxshicated. On the contrary, I'm half sho . . . sho . . . sober!'

'Shut up, both of you! You're both intoxicated! If you start any arguments, Carlota and I are going to beat it!'

'What wosh thish argument about in the firsh playsh?' interrogated Monty, scratching his head in perplexity.

'Oh, Zippy had an idea for each of us to tell about our first sex experience, and you interrupted him.'

'That wosh a good idea. I mosh humbly beg hish pardon for my intrushion. It would be mosh interestin' to learn under what unforshunate chircumstances you two young ladish losh your maidenheadsh. I nominate you to tell the firsh story.'

'Oh, no!' I protested, laughing, 'it happened so long ago I can hardly recall the circumstances. Let Carlota tell hers first. While she's telling hers, I'll try to remember mine! That is, if you two men will stop drinking. There's no fun telling stories to people who are too drunk to listen.'

'I shecond the movement,' interposed Zippy solemnly. 'Everybody lishen now, while Carlota tells ush about her firsh romansh.'

"Ah,' murmured Carlota dreamily. 'Until now I have kept the secret of my misfortune and the circumstances under which my ruin was accomplished locked in the innermost recesses of my heart, nor did I think ever to reveal them.'

She paused and remained pensively silent for a long time.

We waited expectantly.

'I was the only child of wealthy parents who showered upon me every care and blessing which loving hearts could devise,' she began. 'We lived on a beautiful estate in the country where the art and handiwork of man was supplemented by every beautiful and exotic creation of Nature. Close to our home was a charming wooded fairyland in which wild flowers abounded in bounteous profusion, and through which a little brook of clear, limpid water rippled on its way to the distant sea.

'From my earliest days I recall with what delight I wandered through this miniature forest, listening enraptured to the lilting songs of the birds which lived in its green boughs, gathering a scented flower here and there, watching the big black and gold bees as they skimmed the blossoms in their eternal quest. . . .'

'Thersh too many birdsh and beesh and flowersh and not enough fucking in thish story . . .' growled Zippy discontentedly.

'Hush up, Zippy! Let her tell the story in her own way!'

'Up until the time I was fifteen years old,' continued Carlota, unabashed by the interruption, 'I was as pure and innocent as driven snow. My parents had carefully shielded me from every contaminating influence; I knew nothing; I was ignorant of all the true facts of life. . . .'

'Terrible mishtake parentsh make,' observed Zippy sadly.

'To that lack of knowledge, which I was old enough to rightfully possess, I ascribe the fact that my pure innocence was trampled in the mire of lust and my fresh young girlhood blighted forever,' continued Carlota, her voice husky with emotion.

Monty wiped away a tear and Zippy turned his head to cough suspiciously.

'I shall never forget the day; it is burned into my soul with letters of fire. I had just passed my fifteenth birthday; I was a woman in body, but an innocent, unsuspecting child in all else. I thought that babies were brought by fairies who left them upon the doorstep in baskets woven from flowers and vines.'

Monty was sniffling audibly. Zippy reached surreptitiously for a bottle and succeeded in pouring himself a stiff drink before I could wrest it from him.

'Got to have some kind of stimulation,' he protested aggrievedly, 'thish story ish breaking my heart.'

'I had discovered a limpid pool among the rocks into which the water eddies so gently that the sandy bottom could be seen through the crystal-like depths. Several fish inhabited this little pool and it was my delight to lie on my stomach and watch them swimming lazily about, with the sunlight, which penetrated the translucent water, causing their iridescent scales to shine with all the colours of the rainbow.

'It was to this pool I hurried that fateful day, eager to see my little pets, each of which I had endowed with an affectionate name. I had brought some bread with me, and as I lay there watching them dart at the slowly sinking crumbs, I was startled to hear a voice close by me, 'Ah, little Miss Narcissus,' it said, 'does your pretty face enchant you so that you linger over its reflection in the water?'

196

'I looked up into the smiling countenance of a handsome young man who was standing there regarding me curiously. I was startled, but not frightened. I knew nothing to be frightened of. 'No, Sir,' I replied, 'I was looking at some fish that live in this pool. They are really very beautiful. Their scales shine like rubies and emeralds and sapphires in the sunlight.' 'So?' he answered, peering into the pool. 'You have to lie down and put your face close to the water to see them,' I explained.

'Whereupon the young man, who was an entire stranger to me, accommodated himself upon the rocks in a position similar to my own, and together we gazed into the limpid pool while I identified the various members of my adopted family.

'His interest in the fish waned quickly and he began asking me questions which I, candidly and ingenuously, answered without hesitation, thereby revealing to him my childish simplicity as well as my identity.

'I thought I had never seen so handsome a young man. He was much older than I, five or six years, at least. 'Do you come here often?' he asked. 'Every day,' I replied, 'unless it rains.' And then, my curiosity overcoming my diffidence, I asked: 'Who are you? You don't live near here, do you? 'No,' he replied slowly, 'I come from a far-off city. It is a secret, but I will confide in you for I see you can be trusted. You must never tell anyone I listened with breathless interest. 'I am an emissary of the king. I am sent here to see that the animals and birds and flowers are not molested. When the little birds fall out of their nests I put them back, and when the chipmonks can't find enough acorns, I feed them.' 'Oh, how wonderful!' I breathed ecstatically. 'May I help you sometimes? Some wicked boys place traps to catch little bunnies, but whenever I find the traps I throw rocks on them and break them up!' 'Quite right, my dear little Carlota (he now knew my name), I will be very happy to have you assist me in my search for hungry chipmunks, and if we find any bunny traps we will assuredly destroy them. You may meet me here at this pool tomorrow, but remember, not a word to anyone, not even to your parents. The king would be very angry.'

'And thus, with a joyous secret clutched to my trusting heart, and in the happy anticipation of accompanying this wonderful young man in his search for little birds which had fallen from their nests, I ran home. . . .'

'Mosh touchin' story I ever heard,' mumbled Zippy, 'but. . . .

'Hush up!' I hissed. 'I want to hear the rest of this story without anymore interruptions!'

'Sure enough, he was there waiting for me the next day, and what a delightful time I had, wandering through the woods with him, exploring little glens and shady bosques where the vines and leaves were so thick. I had never attempted to penetrate them alone. But it was easy with someone to hold the vines back, to lift you over fallen logs, and carry you across wet places where little green snakes might be hiding.

'There was a place where the brook spreads out, standing several inches deep in the lush water grass. Across this swampy terrain was a leafy hummock which I had seen from a distance but had never approached, not knowing how deep the bog might be around it. I pointed it out to my companion and without a word he picked me up in his strong arms and started across the intervening swamp.

'There was a strange, sweet sensation in being carried this way, one which I had never experienced before. It filled me with a soft, melting languor, impossible to describe. As he strode along, he shifted his hold to ease my weight and his hand, under my swinging knees, came in contact with bare flesh where disarranged clothing left it exposed.

'A gentle, tingling warmth began to generate there where his hand was supporting my legs, and an overpowering emotion gradually stole over me. I closed my eyes and abandoned myself to the unknown but delicious sensations, languishing, half-fainting, oblivious to everything else in the world.

'My subsequent recollection of what transpired was dim and vague. In a half-unconscious state I was dreamily aware that we had reached the hummock, and that he had laid me down on the soft grass and was doing something with my clothing. Indescribable ecstasies were being provoked by some mysterious caresses between my legs, right there when they came together, caresses productive of sensations so overpoweringly sweet that I neither questioned their propriety nor even wondered how they were being effected.

'Suddenly the delicious spell was broken by a short, quick stab of pain. An involuntary shriek of anguish escaped my lips, but the pain passed almost before the sound had died away, and again a flood of warm delight permeated my being and seemed now to be projected clear up inside my body. So intense were the sensations which were now being provoked that I fainted dead away.

'When I recovered consciousness with all that had occurred impressed on my memory only as a vague and indefinite, but delicious dream, I found myself in a peculiar situation. I was lying upon the grass with my head resting on my companion's folded coat. My dress was up and my panties had been removed. My companion was engaged in sponging my thighs with a handkerchief he had apparently moistened in the brook. As he squeezed the water from it, I perceived that it was stained with a dull red.

'I sat up and felt a twinge of pain and an odd, swollen sensation between my legs. I tried to stand up, but I was dizzy and weak. What had happened? Ah, my friends, there is no need to tell you what had happened. In that unguarded moment the heritage of purity had been snatched from an innocent trusting maiden; she had been robbed of that priceless jewel which once taken can never be replaced; her virginal chastity was gone forever.'

Carlota choked, overcome with emotion.

'Dishpicable, unprinshapled scoundrel,' groaned Zippy, 'robbing a young girlsh pryshless jewel. . . .'

'Misherable king's emishary ought to be imprishoned for life!' exclaimed Monty, bursting anew into tears.

I was the only one whose heart remained untouched. As the narrative seemed to have come to an end, I murmured:

'That was a beautiful story, Carlota. Now tell us the real one.'

'The real one isn't nearly as beautiful as the one I told you,' answered Carlota, who had now regained her composure.

'Wosh the idea?' growled Zippy, sitting up suddenly, 'Imposhing on our shimpathies in such a . . . hic . . . inexcushable manner?'

'Thash what I shay!' echoed Monty, with an aggrieved expression on his face. 'Wosh the idea?'

'Shut up, you two! We'll make her start all over again, and if she doesn't tell the truth this time, we'll do something to her!'

'Oh, well, if you insist on the truth you can have it, but I warn you, the circumstance was quite devoid of romantic interest. Fiction is always more interesting than truth!'

'Thash what we want, the truth,' exclaimed Zippy with renewed enthusiasm.

'Never mind the romantic interesh!' recommended Monty.

'Well, let's see . . . I guess I was twelve, or very close to it. My Aunt Carmen and my little cousin Ferdinand were staying with us for the summer. One afternoon Mamma and Aunt Carmen went to the city, leaving Ferdinand in my care. It was just such an opportunity as I had been wishing for. A girl playmate had whispered some interesting facts to me confirming pretty well-defined suspicions I had already formed regarding certain phenomena of nature.'

'I hope there isn't going to be any birsh and beesh in thish story,' murmured Zippy uneasily.

'Before Mamma and Aunt Carmen were out of sight I had made up my mind that I was going to find out all about it. Ferdinand was nine, just young enough to accept my leadership in everything, and just old enough to keep a secret when warned that its discloure would bring parental vengeance.

'He could be trusted, and so as soon as Mamma and Aunt Carmen were at a safe distance, I locked the doors, invited him to come with me to my bedroom, and under the pretext of teaching him a new game, got him to undress and did likewise. The game wasn't exactly a new one, but it was the first time either he or I had ever tried to play it, and we were a little awkward.

'By working his little dangle with my fingers, a process I had to repeat several times, for it persisted in going soft on me, I managed finally to get it stiff enough to fulfil its proper functions, and after a few erratic efforts, it suddenly slipped into the hole

201

between my legs with an ease which rather surprised me.

'And this, dear friends, was the simple and unromantic circumstances under which I was fucked for the first time, though in truth it should be put the other way around, for it could more properly be said that I was the one who did the fucking. I hope you're satisfied. As a matter of fact, the first story I told you was also true, except in some minor details.'

'What were those minor details, if I may ask?' I inquired politely.

'Well, in the first place, I wasn't entirely unaware of what was going to happen when he laid me down on the grass and took my panties off. In fact, I was rather hopefully anticipating it, for I had felt something hard rubbing against my thigh all the time he was carrying me. In the second place, I wasn't by any means unconscious while he was doing it to me, though I pretended to be. And in the third place, as I have just related, it wasn't my first fuck, or my second either for that matter, even though he did make me bleed a little because of his size.'

Carlota tossed off a pony of brandy while Monty and Zippy remained pensively silent.

'Now,' she observed, clasping her hands behind her head and leaning back in her chair, 'let's hear yours!'

'Mine,' I answered, 'parallels yours . . . I mean your true one . . . so closely that I would only have to reverse the ages of the participants, for I was the younger, by several years. Which reminds me of something I intended to ask you in view of your experience . . . can you get my juice out of a nine-year-old cock?'

'Gosh, I don't know,' confessed Carlota. 'It always seemed to be wet when it came out, but whether it was boy-juice or girl-juice I don't know because I was twelve years old at the time, the hair was beginning

202

to grow on my cunny, and the juice might have been all mine. But don't fool yourself, a kid nine years old can have an orgasm, whether he squirts anything or not.'

At that moment a waiter, after knocking discreetly, opened the door to murmur apologetically that it was well past closing time. A hasty glance at the timepiece on the wall showed that it was indeed two o'clock in the morning.

We gathered up our effects and prepared to depart. Both Monty and Zippy were tipsy. Carlota walked in the peculiar fashion of one who is not quite sure of the footing, and I myself found when I stood up that I was far from steady on my feet.

Monty's chauffeur, who was huddled up in his seat half-asleep, came to life, jumped out, opened the door for us, and stood patiently awaiting instructions.

For several minutes we stood there debating further exploits. For my part I was in favour of going directly to my room with Monty. My blood was heated and in my fevered, half-inebriated state I pictured several hours of delicious sexual abandon. But I was overruled by the others, who were still in an adventuresome mood. They wanted to go somewhere else to pass another hour or two before separating, and each had different ideas.

'Listen, everybody!' finally announced Monty with drunken determination. 'We'll go to my housh! I've got a nish, comfortable room where everybody can relaxsh and enjoy themselves!'

'Oh, so, we can't do that! I protested hastily. 'Your wife will have us thrown out!'

I could not have voiced a more ill-advised objection. Monty instantly became stubbornly resolute.

'Listen!' he said with injured dignity, 'a mansh housh ish hish cashel!' When he wansh to entertain dish in hish cashel thash hish . . . hic . . . ina . . . inalienable right!'

Nobody could offer a valid contradiction to this time-honoured philosophy, and though the chauffeur looked startled when he received his instructions, we were soon on the way. Though even in my beclouded state I could not repress certain misgivings, I lulled them with the thought that his wife would undoubtedly be asleep at this hour, and I would think up some pretext to get them to leave as quickly as possible.

But, alas, under the effects of the silver flask and other stimulants which were drawn forth from hidden recesses in the car, the warning sense of caution diminished and before long I hardly remembered where we were going and by the time we got there I was nearly as drunk as the rest and but dimly aware of the surroundings.

The next thing I knew we were within the beautiful room which Monty had modestly described as 'nish and comfortable.' The feel of rich, thick carpets was underfoot, and about us every luxurious comfort and adornment which money could command. The soft nightlight which was burning gave way to a brighter illumination as crystal chandeliers burst into life. In an immense open chimney firewood was laid to light, and in an instant this stately, beautiful room became the scene of riotous revelry.

Carlota and I flung ourselves upon gorgeous divans while Monty and Zippy divested themselves of their hats and top-coats and placed upon an inland table the several bottles, some full, some partially depleted, which they had carried up from the car.

A sleepy butler appeared unsolicited, and stood with gaping mouth in the doorway.

'Go 'way! Go on back to bed!' ordered Monty. 'This ish a private party, we don't want any intrushions!'

The man retired hastily.

There was an interlude during which events remained only in my mind in a nebulous blur. Here and there were incidents which stood out in relief, surviving the chaos of the night. Of course, it was inevitable under the circumstances that Carlota and I should be wheedled into disrobing, for no drunken orgy is complete until the women have exhibited themselves naked, and when the cataclysmic hour struck, she was down to her slippers, hose and a short undervest, while I, more circumspect, had removed only my panties.

Across the room where the shaded glow of a rose-tinted light fell softly on her naked thighs and pointed, cone-shaped breasts, her head on Zippy's lap, Carlota lay, alternately shrieking hysterically and moaning as he realized some occult operation between her legs with his finger.

Upon the velvet cushions of another divan an equally exotic scene was revealed. Cuddled in Monty's arms I rested my head languidly on his shoulder while he fingered and played with one of my bubbies which he had succeeded in exposing by the simple expedient of tearing open the front of my dress.

My own fingers were clutched around something stiff and round and hot which projected upward from his unbuttoned trousers. I slid the satiny skin slowly up and down, and each time the rosy head emerged from its shelter of flesh the rigid column jerked like a live thing I squeezed it tighter, gripping it with all the strength of my fist, and still the spasmodic throb was strong enough to break my grasp as the plum-coloured head was forced through the tight ring formed by my thumb and index finger.

Each mighty convulsion awakened a corresponding throb in my own sexual organs, and an inordinate longing began to assail me. I wanted to feel that luscious, throbbing thing in my mouth, to run my tongue over its wet surface, to lick it and suck it until it burst.

What difference did it make that Carlota and Zippy were there? They were too immersed in their own pastimes to pay much attention to what I was doing. Very likely, too, they already knew I was a cock-sucker, for Monty was very indiscreet with his talk when under the influence of liquor.

In another moment, doubtless, the luscious fruit for which I was panting would have been between my lips had it not been for an interruption.

That interruption was the quiet opening of the door which gave access to the beautiful but now disordered and bottle-strewn lounge. I was the only one directly facing the door and I was the first to perceive a new arrival.

I froze in rigid attention.

In the doorway, surveying us gravely and silently, stood a woman, Inasmuch as this woman was the direct opposite of the mental picture I had formed of Monty's wife I did not for a moment or two even consider the possibility that it was she. I simply wondered who she was.

The woman who stood there regarding us with a calm, almost expressionless face was young, not much older than I, probably. An embroidered robe of rich, wine-coloured material was drawn about her and fastened with a loosely knotted, tasselled rope of silk. Under its lower hem, the lacy edge of a white garment, a nightgown, without doubt, peeked. She wore no hose, but on her feet were dainty, high-heeled bedroom sandals.

She was superbly, radiantly beautiful, a blonde of perfect type whose skin was suggestive of peaches and cream, and whose loosely coiled hair glinted in the light like spun gold.

So silent had been her entry and so quietly did she stand that for several moments no one but myself was aware of her presence. Monty, his attention finally attracted by my tense attitude, turned his eyes in the direction I was looking, Zippy in turn glanced casually toward the door, and started abruptly. Carlota, facing the opposite direction was still moaning and suspiring audibly. Zippy shook her significantly and murmured a warning 'S-h-h-h!' She looked at him in surprise, and then turned her head to see what was holding his attention. When she saw, she sat up hastily, drawing her one diaphanous garment down over her hips as far as she could.

It must have been three-thirty or later. Monty was the first to break the silence.

'Wosh the idea of thish intrushion?' he demanded thickly.

For a long moment there was no answer from the immobile figure. She continued to regard us, coolly, unemotionally. Then:

'Take your disreputable associates out of this house immediately.'

The words were spoken in a quiet, dignified voice, low and musical, but firmly resolute.

By this time realisation of the intruder's identity had dawned upon me and surprise gave way to a rapidly growing feeling of resentment and anger. In a confused, startled way, I comprehended that I had been cheated and imposed upon. So firmly rooted was the conception I had formed of this woman, a conception in which she appeared as a flat-chested, sour-faced misanthrope, devoid of seductive feminine charms, that to find her in every respect the exact antithesis of all I had been led to believe, or permitted to believe, was at first a shock, and as this was assimilated, cause for rage which grew quickly to consuming proportions.

In some way, not yet clearly defined in my mind, I had been misled and hoodwinked. I had been permitted to assume that I had a rival unworthy of serious consideration, much less to be jealous of. Once, impelled by some vague uneasiness, I had asked Monty whether she was pretty. His answer leaped into my memory. 'About as pretty, compared to you, as a moth is in comparison to a beautiful, exotic butterfly!' The recollection brought a new surge of anger, for it suggested that I had not only been deceived but likewise made the victim of my own ridiuclous vanity. This woman was regal with a loveliness which made mine look like cheap tinsel, and I had the sense to realise it.

In the baffled, frustrated, angry grouping of my thoughts, I included her as well as Monty in my resentment. I had pitied her before, but I hated her now with all the bitter venom which jealousy can brew in the heart of a woman confronted by the superior and invincible charms of a rival. I could have sunk my fingernails in the soft bloom of her cheeks with vicious delight, I could have clawed the full, voluptuous breasts which swelled the dressing gown outward in twin globes with infinite satisfaction. I fairly suspired to hurl myself on her and disfigure every inch of her golden beauty.

Dimly, I was aware that Monty had lurched to his feet and was advancing toward her angrily.

'Lishen! Thesh ladiesh are my guesh! Wosh the idea of inshulting my guesh? Wosh the idea calling my guesh dish . . . dish . . . reputable?'

She stood her ground, receding not an inch before

the menacing gesture of an upraised hand. No emotion was visible in her face except that of cool disdain.

'Remove these people from here instantly,' she repeated 'I will not tolerate their presence here.'

'Shay! Wosh housh ish thish? I refush to be embarrasshed in the presensh of my friends!'

He made an unsteady lurch, and the sharp sound of a hand in contact with flesh was heard. He had slapped her in the face with considerable force.

A wave of cruel pleasure crept over me with the sound of the impact and the hot blood tingled in my cheeks. Across one of hers a dappled, reddish outline appeared to mar the white purity of her skin. But she did not flinch. With outward calm and dignity she remained motionless. There was a moment of deadly silence, and the low voice spoke again.

'Take your degenerate friends with you and leave this house or I will go myself.'

What followed can only be told in a summary fashion. My own emotions were so violent that I saw everything through a sort of red haze and the details were blended in a confused blur of movement and action.

Monty had seized her in his arms. They were tussling and swaying in the doorway, she trying to escape his grasp and he apparently intent on dragging her into the room. No words were spoken; there was no sound except the heavy breathing, the swish of garments, and the scuffle of moving feet deadened in part by the thick carpets.

The pallor of her face had given way to a vivid flush which burned in either cheek. One of her bronze slippers had been dislodged in the scuffle and she was panting audibly. With a violent effort she succeeded in wrestling an arm free from his clasp, and placing the palm of her hand against his chin she forced his head back. For a moment it seemed that she was about to free herself from his drunken embrace.

As she strained to loosen his grasp, the sound of ripping cloth was heard and the neck and upper part of her robe and nightgown were torn open. The folds sagged down over her shoulders and arms, and one white breast was exposed.

I can see it yet, that proud breast of alabaster whiteness protruding from the ravished garments, its rosy nipple standing out prominently.

The sudden yielding of the garment caused her to lose her balance and the temporary advantage she had gained. She tottered backward and before she could recover herself she was again helpless in his arms. But she did not cease to struggle as she was dragged toward the centre of the room.

The blood was singing in my head. I felt choked, suffocated, and was breathing in short, dry gasps. Zippy and Carlota sat stiffly erect, watching with bulging eyes, but I gave them hardly a thought. Remembrance of his cynical admission of attempts to fuck her was simmering in my brain. Well, he would never lay hands on me again. Let him fuck her if he could, and let her claw him to shreds while he was doing it if she wanted to. That was what he had on his mind now. I knew he was going to try to fuck her right there in our presence.

The sound of more ripping cloth bore out the supposition and testified to his lust for the woman who had spurned him as he tried drunkenly to disrobe her. The kaleidoscopic, shifting blur of movement now revealed her half-nude as the entire front of her dressing gown was ripped open and the torn fragments of the nightgown underneath tangled about her legs.

I clenched my fists and bit my lips. My face was burning hot and my head felt light and dizzy.

As the torn fragments fluttered about her shapely limbs, he lifted her up. She managed to slip from his arms and regained her feet, but as she did so what remained of the garments was stripped upward and for a moment, not only her legs, but her bottom as well was left naked. As she twisted about the light shone full on the patch of little bronze ringlets of hair at the base of her stomach. Another violent movement and pieces of her torn garments again covered the exotic sight.

She was panting, choked, inarticulate, but as if aware of her half-naked condition she gathered herself for a supreme effort and placing both hands against his chest she shoved with desperate strength. Doubtless, divining what was in his mind, she put every ounce of her failing energies into a superhuman effort to escape the humiliation. She succeeded in pushing him from her. He clutched at her in an effort to regain his balance, tottered uncertainly for a moment, and fell backward. His head struck the edge of the iron grating in front of the fireplace. His body twisted once or twice, straightened out, and remained motionless.

There was a momentary silence, broken only by a faint, peculiar whistling sound from the lips of the fallen man, a sound which I and probably both my companions, assumed to be more an indication of drunken stupor than anything more serious.

But the woman standing there panting beside him, looking down into his face, suddenly began to scream. In an instant the servants, who had probably been hovering around close at hand but loathe to interfere, rushed precipitately into the room.

'Call a physician! Call a physician! Call the police! Get these people out of here!' she screamed, repeating the words over and over.

While two servants lifted Monty from the floor to

lay him upon a sofa, another scurried to telephone a doctor, and another addressed himself to us.

'I'd advise you to retire as quickly as possible. The Marster appears to be in a very bad condition. He's not responsible under the circumstances, and you'd better be off, seein' as the Mistress is quite 'isterical!'

It was a sober and quiet little procession that filed down the stairs and out into the night air. Monty's faithful chauffeur, aroused by the sudden movement and lights about the house, inquired anxiously:

'What's happened?'

'Oh, Monty staged a row with his wife. He fell down and hit his head on the fireplace grating,' Zippy answered gloomily.

'Is he hurt?'

'I don't think so. Get us away from here as quickly as you can.'

The uneasy chauffeur hesitated a moment but finally decided that the best course was to do as suggested. He put the motor into movement and the car slid off down the quiet street.

As my thoughts cleared I became aware that Carlota was putting on her clothes, and for the first time realized that she had left the house clad in nothing but a silken shift, though she had remained sufficient presence of mind to grab her clothes and bring them with her, which reminded me that my own panties were still decorating a chair back there in the house.

I was not tempted to return for them. The wild emotions of the past half-hour were passing and I felt weak and faint. A fit of trembling seized me and I began to cry.

Carlota turned suddenly on me and I was electrified to hear her hiss:

'Damn you! If it hadn't been for you this would never have happened!'

'What on earth do you mean?' I gasped, hardly able to believe my ears. 'What did you have to do with it?'

The only answer was a string of curses and maledictions that left me petrified with astonishment.

Zippy tried in vain to quiet her. She began to shriek.

'Let me out!' she cried hysterically, 'let me out!'

Thinking that the excitement and liquor had thrown her into some kind of a fit, I put my arms around her and tried to soothe her. She shoved me away with a violent gesture and screamed:

'Keep your hands off me, you damned little cocksucker, keep your hands off of me!'

The chauffeur, who of course could hear the clamour, slowed up the car, and opening the glass window at his back, peered in.

'Here! Here! What's going on?' he exclaimed anxiously.

'I want to get out! Let me out!' cried Carlota.

'Certainly, you can get out if you want to!' answered the man with alacrity, and he jumped from his seat to open the door for her.

Carlota literally hurled herself from the car, and sobbing brokenly, ran off and disappeared in the darkness.

'What . . . what in the world came over her?' I whispered dazedly, turning to Zippy. 'What will happen to her, running around in the dark in a drunken fit?'

'Don't worry about her, Jessie. She can take care of herself.'

'But . . . but why did she say such awful things to me? Why doesn't she like me? I've never offended her or done her any harm!'

'Don't you know, really?' he asked.

'No, I don't! Do you?'

'Why, she's jealous of you. That's what's the matter with her.'

'Jealous of me? Why should she be jealous of me?'

'Well, you see, Jessie, she was Monty's girl before he met you.'

'Why! I thought she was your girl!'

'No,' he answered with a resigned gesture. 'Monty shoved her off onto me to keep her pacified. I did the best I could, but I wasn't up to it.'

'Oh!' I gasped weakly, 'Oh!'

Zippy placed an arm over my shoulder and patted me sympathetically. 'Monty is a good scout but he takes some wild chances. We all must have been crazy to let him take us to his house tonight.'

'I didn't want to go; I tried to talk him out of it, but I'm glad now I went. I found out several things I didn't know before. I never want to see him again.'

Unable to control my feelings, I began to cry again.

'Cheer up, kid. Don't let yourself get upset. You have to take things as they come in this life, the bitter with the sweet!'

His arm tightened about me and unresisting I let him draw my head over against his shoulder where I continued to sob until I was able to restrain myself. This Zippy was a nice chap. I had always liked him but had never permitted myself to be more than discreetly friendly with him on Carlota's account. There was comfort and consolation in the sympathetic pressure of his arm, and soon I felt better.

'Will you come to see me sometime?' I murmured. 'I'm not going to have anything more to do with Monty.'

'Of course I will, if you want me. I couldn't ask you before because, well, it just isn't cricket to poach on another man's preserves.'

'That's how I felt about Carlota. What a dummy I

was! I knew from the way she acted there was something wrong, but I didn't have sense enough to suspect what it was. No wonder she didn't like me!'

The big automobile was rolling along smoothly and quietly and within another twenty-five minutes or so I would be back in my room.

Dawn was not far off, but it was still dark outside.

CHAPTER SEVENTEEN

So quickly does the heart respond to kindly words in moments of distress that already a tender feeling for Zippy was taking root. He was really nice and he was good-looking too. I put my feet up under me on the car seat, and cuddled down against him with my head resting on his lap. The soft vibration of the car was soothing to the nerves and soon I felt quite comfortable.

Under the pressure of my shoulders on his lap I became aware of a disturbing element which started a new train of thoughts. I moved my body so that I could lay my hand on the disturbance, even squeeze it softly. It immediately became more pronounced and grew into a small riot. For several minutes nothing was said.

The next thing I knew his trousers were unbuttoned, the cause of the agitation was out in the open and my head was being impelled down over it by hands which exerted a firm pressure.

I was surprised at such directness, but not displeased.

'The chauffeur?' I whispered questioningly.

For answer Zippy reached over me, manipulated a switch, and darkness equal to that outside descended upon the interior of the car.

Some fifteen or twenty minutes later two discreet notes of the siren advises us that my destination was near. When the car stopped and I stepped out, the sky was tinted in the east. The night was lifting. Dawn was at hand.

I ran up the steps, rang the bell, and after a long wait the door was opened by the night maid. Within less than ten minutes all told, I was in bed and sound asleep.

I slept for at least five hours, but I would have sworn that it was not over five minutes before I was dragged from my lethargic slumber by a violent shaking and insistent voices which continued relentlessly until I finally sat up to protest the commotion.

'Wake up, Jessie! Wake up!'

It was Hester who was repeating the disagreeable phrase and shaking me insistently, but as my vision cleared I saw Madame Lafronde standing nearby, and several girls besides.

There was something in their faces which dispelled the last vestige of sleep, and I now saw that Madame Lafronde was holding a newspaper.

'Wake up, Jessie! Wake up!' pleaded Hester. 'Are you awake?'

'Yes! I'm awake! What's the matter?'

'Oh, Jessie, were you with Montague Austin last night? Something dreadful has happened!'

The blood drained from my face.

'What is it?' I whispered.

'He's dead, Jessie, he's dead! There was some kind of trouble in his home last night or early this morning; there were some girls there, the police are trying to find them! We thought . . . we were afraid . . . maybe you were mixed up in it! You were out with him last night, weren't you? The paper says there were two girls!'

'Let me see the paper!' I gasped, without answering her questions.

Silently, Madame Lafronde placed it in my hands.

Big black headlines screamed at me from across the top of a column on the front page:

MONTAGUE AUSTIN DIES UNDER MYSTERIOUS CIRCUMSTANCES.

I clutched the paper with trembling fingers and tried to read the smaller print, but my mind refused to concentrate upon the long drawnout recital and only blazing fragments detached themselves here and there to impinge on my consciousness.

'Youngest son of late Sir Weatherford Austin died at an early hour this morning as the result of injuries sustained in his own home. Wife in hysterical collapse unable to give coherent account of tragedy . . . not known whether fall was accidental or whether he was knocked down . . . died without regaining consciousness . . . conflicting stories told by domestics suggestive of bacchanalian revelries motivate investigation by Scotland Yard . . . empty bottles and whisky-flasks . . . intimate garments left behind . . . half-naked girls flee with male companion . . . identity of man unknown . . . chauffeur to be interrogated today . . . victim has figured in many sensational escapades . . . '

'Now, Jessie,' said Madame Lafronde not unkindly, seating herself on the edge of the bed, 'for the good of all concerned, let's get the truth so we'll know what to do. Just answer my questions. Were you there?'

'Yes, I was! But I didn't . . . none of us . . . even dreamed he was badly hurt!'

'What happened exactly?'

'He was fighting with his wife. He was drunk and he slipped and fell and his head struck against the fireplace grating.'

218

'What were you doing in his house while his wife was there?'

'Well, I . . . we were all of us half-drunk and he insisted on taking us there! I didn't want to go!'

'Who are these other people?'

'A girl, named Carlota, and a fellow, a friend of Monty's, everybody calls him Zippy . . . I don't know his right name.'

'Who is this Carlota?'

'I don't know her full name, either. I'd met her two or three times before when I was out with Monty and Zippy. I didn't know it until last night, but she used to be Monty's sweetheart.'

'Do either of these people know your name and where you live?'

'Zippy does. Carlota . . . I don't know. Monty might have told her.'

'How did you get here this morning?'

'Zippy brought me . . . in Monty's car.'

'In Monty's car? With his chauffeur?'

'Yes; you see the chauffeur . . . none of us . . . knew there was anything seriously wrong when we left.'

'Then the chauffeur knows this address too?'

'I guess he does now, all right.

'All right, kid. If you step fast maybe you can be out of here before the doorbell starts ringing, and maybe you can't. There's no hard feelings, but you know how it is, I can't afford to have any of my girls mixed up in anything like this.'

'I understand. I don't blame you,' I answered dully, and got out of bed to dress.

'I'll have your money ready for you as soon as you're dressed and we'll slip you out the back way . . . just in case. I'll give you some address where you can get on easy if you want to get a new place, but use a different name and don't mention having worked here. If you do, there's a good chance you'll be picked up. The police are going to find out all they can about this affair, and if they get you, there's no telling what you'll have to go through.'

Hester went with me to carry some of my things and to help find a room where I would be safe from annoyance. We found one which appeared to be suitable, and though the landlady looked askance when she heard I was to occupy it alone, her misgivings were calmed by the sight of sufficient money to pay a month's rent in advance, and my assurance that I would be receiving no 'visitors' other than Hester.

The room was cosy and comfortable, but after Hester had gone, such a feeling of loneliness and wretchedness welled up in my heart that I threw myself on the little bed and had a long cry.

The next afternoon Hester returned to tell me excitedly that within less than fifteen minutes after our departure the police, who had extracted the address from Monty's chauffeur just as Madame Lafronde had anticipated, were there looking for me, and in addition two barristers had called repeatedly in a vain effort to see me. I shuddered and from then on the little room seemed more like a haven of refuge than a lonely exile, for I entertained a profound horror of police and jails, the long months of deadly monotony in the reform school never having been forgotten.

'They found that girl Carlota, too. She used to be a dancer in a music hall. And who do you suppose your mysterious friend Zippy turned out to be?'

'I don't know,' I answered. 'Who?'

'No less a personage than that polo-playing Lord Beaverbrook! I've seen his picture in the papers lots of times. I think the whole thing will be hushed up soon. They know it was an accident and that nobody was much to blame but Austin himself.'

True to Hester's prediction, references to the scandal disappeared quickly from the press and no great efforts were made to locate the missing witness. For à time I entertained the hope that Madame Lafronde would relent and call me back. But the hope was dissipated when Hester sadly informed me that it was futile. She herself had tried to pave the way for my return only to be told by Madame Lafronde that though she liked me, I was a 'firebrand' and in the best interests of the business its doors must remain closed to me.

Hester came faithfully to visit me for an hour or two every afternoon.

'Did the papers ever hint what Austin and his wife were quarrelling about?' I asked her.

'Yes; she objected to his having you and those other people drinking and carousing in the house. Wasn't that it?'

'Partly, but there was something else . . . something lots worse than that.'

'What was it, Jessie?'

'He had her half-stripped. He was going to fuck her right there in front of all of us.'

'Oh, Jessie! What did I tell you about that man? Why wouldn't you listen to me?'

She was on the point of tears again and I hastily endeavoured to turn the conversation into a lighter vein.

'Don't worry so about me, you sweet old thing! I'll listen to your advice in the future. But it's fierce to be here all alone. Maybe I'll pay you to come and sleep with me some night. I've got lots of money. I'll telephone Lafronde and disguise my voice and ask for a girl, and you can volunteer.'

221

'No! I won't sleep with you, you perverted little woman-fucker!'

'Not even if I pay you?'

'No! Not even if you pay me!'

'That's nice! You'd go to a hotel with some woman you don't even know and do things with her, but you won't sleep with me!'

'Jessie, how can you even think of such things after what's happened?'

'Let's get undressed and lie down for a little while. You haven't anything to do this afternoon.'

'Are you in your right senses?'

'Listen; if you'll stay, I'll do it like Heloise did . . . only nicer!'

'Oh! You're one of those, too, are you? Well, thanks, I don't want any today. When I do, I'll let you know. How much do you charge?'

'I'll bet I could make it last you a whole hour!'

'No!'

'Please, darling, sweet Hester! Think of me, locked up here alone in this room by myself day after day!'

'No! And if I did, you'd be sure to leave the door unfastened so anyone could open it and walk right in!'

'Look!' I exclaimed, and jumping up I twisted the key in the lock and held it up before her. 'I'll even hang up a towel over the keyhold so nobody can peek at us!'

'Well, come on, then! I just want to see if you're really capable of doing that, too!'

I had paid a month's rent, but by the time two weeks had passed I found the loneliness and inactivity intolerable. Hester had brought a list with several addresses which Madame Lafronde had prepared, and feeling now that there was little likelihood of being

222

bothered by the police, I set out one afternoon to see if I could find a place.

With one swift glance of appraisal the madam of the first house on the list invited me to a room, had me undress for a survey of my physical assets, and immediately began to ply me with flattering and enticing inducements to join her ménage. I was rather taken aback by such unexpected eagerness and the assurance of profitable earnings, but anxious to settle the matter of immediate occupation I accepted her offer without delving into promises which seemed somewhat exaggerated.

The bargain was struck. I was shown the room which would be at my disposition and introduced to several of the young ladies who would be my future companions. They were a slightly faded lot, considerably below Madame Lafronde's standards, and the depressing thought came over me that my entry into this second-rate bagnio signalled another step downward towards the abyss. But I shrugged the thought aside; I could always leave it if I didn't like it, and told the woman I would bring my effects in the morning.

Before opening the door for me to leave, she detained me a moment in the hall.

'Listen dearie,' she murmured in low, wheedling tones, 'I forgot to mention . . . I don't suppose it will make any difference . . . but I've got a special class of trade here . . . this isn't a French house exactly, but you know how it is . . . most of my best paying regulars like a little out of the ordinary . . . you understand. All the other girls here do it. You won't mind that, will you dearie?'

Ah! As I digested this bizarre announcement, which fully explained the cajolements and flattery and alluring promises, the woman watched my face anxiously, as though to read therein some sign which would tell her whether the bird was going to fly off affrighted or remain in the trap.

For a long moment I stood pensively silent. I knew from the dejected aspect of the place, the sallow-faced girls, the tarnished furniture, that the type of men who frequented it would be far, far different from those I was accustomed to dealing with. Up to the present, my cocksucking inclinations had been exercised voluntarily, to satisfy my own sexual cravings. Here, I would be obliged to do it, whether I felt so inclined or not. I hesitated uncertainly, and then, with a gesture of indifference, replied:

'I'll give them what they want.'

And thus, with six short words, did I seal my pact with hell, and bind myself henceforward to madden the brains of men and corrode their souls with the bittersweet poison of my sucking lips.

THE AMATORY EXPERIENCES OF A SURGEON

Anonymous

CHAPTER ONE

Not all the glowing descriptions of amatory writers, nor the inspired breath of passion itself, can truly, and in sufficient degree, estimate the force of those desires and the intoxicating delirium of that enjoyment in which the softer sex plays so important a part, and in the gratification of which it relishes a more than equal degree of pleasure.

Were I to cover these pages with descriptions of the most seductive or lascivious scenes, I should fail to realize its full effect.

Language stops short of the reality. No words, however passionate, however glowing, could transport the bosom and enthrall the frame like the one, magic, soul-dissolving sensation experienced by lovers in the celebration of these mystic rites; but if my readers will follow me, while I tell them of some of my amatory experiences, their own feelings may perhaps enable them to sympathize with mine; and thus, by analogy, enjoy again some of the most sensual and moving incidents in their own careers.

To say that I was born of respectable parents would, in the full acceptation of the words, be false. My mother was of that disgraced and neglected race, a discarded mistress; my father, a nobleman of the first rank, while still a young man, full of the fiery vices of youth, had caught her eye; his handsome form and noble bearing won her simple love.

The old story followed. He seduced her, kept her

awhile to be his toy, and at length, grown tired of her society, threw her off as a plaything of which he was weary.

She died, but he lived on to break the heart of many other innocent creatures.

Whatever may have been his errors, among his redeeming points must be reckoned his care of his illegitimate child.

After my mother's death I was sent to a boarding school, and at the age of fourteen had grown a tall, well-made, and genteel-looking youth.

It is needless to say that it was here, in the society of other lads, many of whom were my seniors, that I was first made acquainted with all that is necessary for men to know from a theoretical point of view; of practice with the opposite sex, I knew nothing, but my ardent imagination pictured ecstasies that fell but little short of the reality, and was further assisted in its expanded ideas by the scenes we boys enacted among ourselves.

All that we could do we did, and we gave each other as much amusement as we knew how to administer.

It was no uncommon thing for us to wander into another boy's bed, and each taking in his hand the warm, half-stiffened, little member of the other, to produce by pleasing friction that overflow which, feeble substitute as it was, caused us so much enjoyment.

Often, too, would one of the bigger boys wantonly insert his glowing affair within the lips of some fair-haired youngster, and there lie and permit himself to be titillated in the most agreeable manner possible.

These pastimes were so common that we scarcely ever passed a night without the repetition of some of them.

I was not fully initiated into all the mysterious practices of the elder boys till my sixteenth birthday, when they admitted me as a member of the upper class, as all above that age styled themselves. Their custom was that each lad, on attaining the age of sixteen, had to give the upper class a banquet to inaugurate his admission amongst their privileged circle.

My particular chum, Bob Ferguson, had for some time whispered to me, when he played with my prick, that there was a great surprise in store for me on my birthday.

Well, at last the momentous night arrived, and being the best provided boy in the school (as to pocket-money), thanks to the liberality of my father, we had a really splendid banquet, which they all declared quite eclipsed any previous affair of the sort.

On those occasions our master, usually a strict disciplinarian, generally gave us permission to enjoy ourselves and make as much noise or have what fun we liked in the big boys' room. Little could he have ever dreamed of the excesses that were actually enacted at these birthday feasts.

After stuffing ourselves with cold game-pie, tarts, and champagne, the real business of my installation commenced by all stripping off their clothes.

Even now my soul thrills as I recall to mind that room full of handsome, naked youths, several of them as handsome as Adonis himself, some of the eldest having quite a beautiful growth of silky hair ornamenting their pricks, and my readers may be sure that inflamed as we were with feasting and wine, the sight of one another's charms made everyone rampant and ready for action.

A couple of them now began to handle my tool, gently frigging and pulling back the foreskin as they passed their hands up and down the stiffened shaft; next they proceeded to anoint it with some pomade, and one of the biggest boys presenting his bottom as he stooped forward on a chair, they made me shove into him, till I was fairly in. The delicious warmth of the tight sheath that held me was so exciting, that without further instructions I fucked him as naturally as possible, clinging tightly to him with my arms, and thoroughly enjoying it. Presently the captain of the class, a fine handsome youth of eighteen, attacked me in the rear; the pricking pain attending his first insertion was rather sharp, but being well lubricated, he was soon in full possession, and my double position of fucker and fuckee soon drove me almost mad with delight. I seemed to spend my juice again and again every time; he delighted me with his warm overflow in my bottom. At last I fairly fainted from excess of emotion, and when I came to myself found I was lying on one of the beds with Bob Ferguson's cock in my mouth, whilst the captain was deliciously sucking my reinvigorated tool.

What an orgy of lust we enacted that night! It seemed to me heavenly at the time, and even now as I write these lines, my old cock stands at the remembrance of it.

Soon after this I left school, preparatory to commencing the career of life, which had been marked out for me; but after a while, finding the occupation of dispensing medicine too irksome, I obtained the permission of my noble parent to study for the medical profession.

Accordingly I went to London, and after several years studious application at the hospitals, I received my diploma from the Examiners at Surgeons' Hall, or in modern parlance, from the Royal College of Surgeons.

A short time after that I settled in a small practice,

at the village near which my paternal patron had his principal estate.

It is needless to say that our relationship was kept as secret as the envious gossips of the place could reasonably desire; all they knew was that Lord L—— had extended his patronage to me, and that was enough to excite the jealousy of the tuft-hunters of the neighbourhood.

Notwithstanding these ill-natured people however, my lord's patronage was quite sufficient to bring me plenty of practice, and within a time I became the fashionable doctor of the district.

This was not entirely owing to the reasons, cogent as they were, I have above detailed; to a very natural desire to succeed, and to attention to my patients, combined, I flatter myself, with no mean professional ability, I added the graces of a manly, robust, and genteel person.

To this later circumstance, I think, I owe in a great measure my renown amongst the fairer portion of my patients. My success with these, in love as well as physic, was really marvellous, and I have had as many as three or four people coming to my house in one day for medicine, not altogether of a nauseous description.

My father at this time was living at Broad Heath, his residence in the locality; there he kept a mistress, and being himself a bachelor, he spent the most of his time in her society. In my capacity as medical adviser to the family, an office which carried a key to fit all doors, I had frequently seen and spoken to this lady; she was a woman of perhaps nearly thirty years of age, tall, slender, yet not thin, carrying in all her movements that particular grace which is only possessed by females of this stamp; far from dark, yet sufficiently inclined toward the brunette to prevent her being called fair, she had large and full brown eyes, in which floated constantly the light of youthful desire, unsullied by contact with the ruining hand of public prostitution, and fresh from her native atmosphere; her manners were easy and graceful, and her conversation charming.

With this lady my fancy soon found a resting place, and full of notions of revenging Lord L——'s desertion of my mother, I allowed myself to cherish ideas of putting in practice a signal retribution.

Adelaide—that was the name of this full-blown rose—exhibited in all her intercourse with me so much condescension and regard that I had but little difficulty in persuading myself that her conquest would prove an easy victory.

I endeavoured to insinuate myself into her confidence, and hitting upon a few of her weak points, I soon found myself in a position to open the breach.

Gradually allowing my feelings to become visible, and watching the effects upon the lady, she appeared to me to be flattered by partiality and she smiled on my suit. Opportunity only was now wanted to complete the adventure, and it was not long before it occurred.

One day I was making my usual afternoon's round among my patients, when on passing the gates I perceived the chariot of Lord L—— emerge with his lordship seated alone with it. Waiting until it had turned an angle of the road and was well out of sight, I went up to the house, and asked for his lordship—of course he was not at home—and as I was turning, as if to depart, I suddenly asked for the lady, making an excuse about some flowers I had promised her.

Being admitted, I found her seated alone, having just parted from my father; we entered into conversation, and I studied to improve the opportune chance by every means in my power.

Not to weary the reader by detailing every passing compliment or meaning look, suffice it to say a quarter of an hour found us side by side upon a sofa, with my arm tenderly pressed round the waist of the lovely woman. From this position it was easy to snatch an occasional kiss, and finding no great resistance to this liberty, I proceeded cautiously to others still more daring.

My hand wandered over the palpitating bosom of my fair friend, and I gradually turned myself toward her, until our faces met and my chest pressed her softer charms beneath it.

Our eyes met: there was no necessity for words; the soft, voluptuous languor in her humid optics was far more expressive than words of the amorous storm within that tumultuous bosom.

Fierce lust now took full possession of me, and no consideration, however sacred, would have prevented me from gratifying my burning passion upon the person of the lovely being before me.

I sought and found the hem of her dress and, without experiencing much opposition, succeeded in passing my hand up to her knees; it did not stop there, but with redoubled ardour it aspired to take possession of things above. A thigh of large and beautifully moulded proportions ravished me with its softness; yet further, a mossy growth of fine downy hair rewarded the boldness of my searching hand.

Wound up to a fearful pitch of excitement, I worked my finger into as charming a little recess as ever tempted man.

Delays are dangerous, more especially in love, so say the eager, and so thought I, as stealthily unbuttoning my nether garments, I slyly introduced my firm and excited weapon to the lovely spot. A voluptuous shudder passed through her frame at the first touch. I press forward, a murmur of resentment breaks gently from the lips of my companion; I feel the commencement of the soft insertion, and bursting with impatience, I bury myself in the body of the dear girl.

Once fairly in, how I did revel in charms of such a luxurious nature. Fiercely did I move in and out of the tight, lusciously clasping case, which clung so amorously with its soft, juicy folds to the shaft of my delighted weapon of love.

At each thrust she sighed more deeply, and as the maddening moments passed, and the intense enjoyment lashed our passions into fury, she hugged my form closely to her, whilst low murmurs of wanton pleasure escaped from the dewy lips which had just previously essayed to express her resentment at my outrageous conduct.

Nature could no longer restrain her tribute to the efforts of love, which now produced their usual effect, but in a more exaggerated form. I felt the approach of those moments during which we die a thousand deaths, as the fires of fierce lightning dance through every nerve. It came; I fell forward. Description is vain to paint my feelings. A quivering agony of pleasure seized us both—a delirious desire to press our souls and bodies closer in communion, a mutual rush of that hot balm, which finally relieves excited nature, closed our transports and left us breathless, hot, and moist in each other's arms.

We remained for some moments closely entwined in each other's embrace, and exchanging those gentle little tokens of gratified passion that usually mark the period of listlessness, succeeding the fierce energy of previous action.

At length we separated, but only to adjust our somewhat ruffled habiliments. She then made me sit down by her side, and it was not long before I found my champion growing restive beneath the touches of the soft, warm hand she had inserted into his nest. Not contented, however, that he should remain thus concealed, she with a slight jerk brought my stately toy into daylight, then proceeded to examine it in every direction.

This amusement I found highly gratifying to my own senses, and soon induced such a state of erection as to give fair promise of a refreshing spurt to the lovely operator.

A new idea seemed to strike her, and sliding onto her knees between my legs, she wantonly caressed my member, all hard and excited as it was; and after lengthened kisses, she slowly let it slide into her mouth, and then so tickled it with her tongue, and pressed it between her moist lips, that I was fain to cry 'hold!' and abruptly withdrew my instrument for fear of a discharge. But if I deprived myself of one opportunity, I quickly found another opening, not less delightful than the less usual entrance I had just quitted.

We gave ourselves entirely up to the rage of our voluptuous sensations; I wriggled and pushed, until I lay gasping on her breast in the soft agonies of a bountiful emission.

Again and again I cooled my raging lust in the arms of this charming woman who was ever ready to respond with all the ardour of her sensuous nature to the continued resurrections of Cupid's battering ram, which she laughingly assured me was a perfect phoenix of its kind.

At last, exhausted nature refused longer to sustain my desires, and after much loving dalliance and promises of a speedy reunion, the high-mettled pego had to confess himself vanquished, and slunk away crestfallen from the field of love.

CHAPTER TWO

When Sappho loved a fair being of her own sex even to madness, she doubtless found a means to gratify the passion with which she burned, although to us men, and more especially to medical men, it is surprising how a perfect enjoyment could be arrived at, without a penetrating power on either side.

Woman is formed to receive within her the all-important member of the other sex, and if she is deprived of that, there is but one substitute to compensate for the loss, and that is imagination. But the inspired poetess possessed imagination in an inordinate degree, and no doubt she brought it into play in those soft encounters of which the old Greek writers tell us, a sufficient amount of that essential to constitute a pleasure no less keen than novel.

And so in the present day, what is wanting in absolute reality is an imaginative mind supplied by the fancy. When a man gives himself up to the pleasures of self-enjoyment, does not the idea that he is procuring these agreeable sensations by unnatural means tend to heighten his feelings? And does he not try to picture—aye, to a marvellous exactness—how he would feel, were those finishing throbs of ecstasy experienced upon the panting bosom of the lovely being he is lusting for?

Even so, this pleasure, in whatever degree it is experienced, is ever to be increased by the action of the mind.

You are mounted on the body of a woman of pleasure, you imagine, perhaps in ignorance, that you are the first to pluck the maiden flower from a lovely and innocent girl. Have you not precisely the same sensations that would be experienced in the actual deflowering of a maid? Of course you have; and in no case can the adage be more properly applied than when in allusion to such a deception it is remarked: 'Where ignorance is bliss, 'tis folly to be wise.'

The mind has everything to do with the action of the body in matters of this nature, as in all others, and in none in a more direct degree.

It is the knowledge that you are engaged in an act of the greatest indecency; that you are in fact uniting the most outrageously sensual part of your body to that of a no less sensual part than the closest recesses of a woman's person; that you have pushed that lascivious instrument of yours to the utmost within her belly; and that you are about to flood her very vitals with a stream of that all wondrous fluid with which man is endowed. That is what constitutes the zest of enjoyment with a man of sensual mind, and any pictures that add additional piquancy to the act are provocative of increased ardour and enjoyment.

I have wandered out of the course of my narrative in rather a discursive manner, but I must beg forgiveness of my readers for the foregoing homily, as it may explain in some measure the acts which are to follow and which might otherwise appear purposeless.

With my fair friend of the preceding pages I passed the following morning. In her arms I wantoned away a couple of hours; again she gave me the same pleasure, and once more she received the strong champion of her desires between other lips than those naturally formed for it. This time I was resolved to let matters have their course. She sucked and pressed my prick with her lips and tongue—and it grew excited; still the delicious friction was continued, and new excitement added, until I was obliged to caution the fair girl of the inevitable result. She redoubled her caresses; nature could stand it no longer, and with a fierce cry of furious delight I discharged in her mouth, which was filled with the creamy proofs of my perfect enjoyment.

She far from resenting this premature result, she evidently relished the termination of the scene, and swallowed the sperm with the gusto of a determined votary of Priapus.

Since this adventure I have known many women who prefer by far to have the seminal shower bestowed upon their mouths, rather than receive it in their cunts, and I have enjoyed in more than one instance the pleasures of a similar penchant.

Although my conquest pleased me at the moment, I soon found the temperament of the lady was not such as to ensure a lasting ascendency over me, and about two months after our first embraces, we were parted in a rather unexpected manner.

I had gone one day to visit Adelaide as usual, at a time when I knew Lord L—— was absent, and I was about to enter the conservatory, on my way to the drawing room, when the sound of voices in that apartment made me pause. They appeared to be those of a man and woman, and I had no difficulty in recognizing the latter as belonging to my fair friend.

Curiosity and a stronger feeling caused me to approach cautiously; as I advanced, I heard evident sounds of ardent osculation, and placing myself behind the half-opened door, I plainly saw a scene I shall never forget.

Lying on a sofa, her plump buttocks elevated upon the round end, and resting herself on her chest and elbows, with her clothes thrown over her back, disclosing all her most secret treasures, was Adelaide; while standing behind her bottom, his trousers about his legs and his prick standing up in front of him like a constable's staff, was the six-foot butler, a tall strapping fellow of most important dimensions. As may be readily supposed, he was not long idle; making a passage between the cheeks of my little Adelaide's bottom, he plunged his tremendous prick up to the hilt in the cunt of my young lady, who, by the wriggling of her buttocks and the low murmurs of delight which I could distinctly hear as she endearingly besought him to push and give her all he could, was evidently greatly relishing the assault of her huge antagonist.

At it they went: he all fury and lust, and she not in the least less wantonly excited.

As the huge yard moved in and out of its moist sheath, it literally glistened in the sunlight, while the beams of old Phoebus were full upon them. (What luscious sights old Sol must often enjoy, and he deserves it too, as but for his enlivening warmth we—poor mortals—should be little fitted for the pleasures of coition.) I saw the stretched lips of her delicious cunt close on his prick with such a force of suction as I knew would soon prove their amply sufficient power to bring him to a crisis, but, alas! infidelity, at least in this instance, was to meet fitting reward.

As the sturdy butler drove against the yielding bottom of the fair girl, the concussion caused the sofa to move forward by slow degrees, carrying with it its lovely and wanton burden, until it reached a small table, whereon was placed a set of Chinese chessmen, arranged for battle on the ivory board. As the sofa reached this table, a tremendous lunge from the now dreadfully excited fuckster overturned the obstacle with a loud crash, and my lovely but faithless Adelaide, raising her head to discover the cause of the disturbance, overbalanced the sofa, making it rear up on one end, just as the crisis of the stalwart champion approached, and bringing the frightened girl bodily upon him; in fact, at the very moment of the coming ecstasy of emission, when quite unprepared for such a shock, she fell back and carried her companion to the floor as well, where he lay with her upon him in a half-fainting state as he still lightly clasped his love around her buttocks, his instrument of pleasure standing up between her open legs and inundating her belly, neck, and even her face with a copious shower of sperm.

It was in this position that I surprised the combatants on entering the room; imagine the horror of the big butler, and the confusion of Adelaide!

Gathering up his trousers, the guilty domestic made a rapid exit, and I was left alone with the softer culprit, who, between rage and terror, could hardly contain herself. She reproached me with intruding on her privacy.

'Yes, my pet,' I replied. 'I am so sorry for having disturbed such a truly delightful séance of love. I owe you a thousand apologies, my dear Adelaide; may I be allowed to atone for it by finishing what Perkins was prevented from thoroughly accomplishing?'

My satirical smile, as I said this, drove her almost beside herself with rage. She ordered me to leave the room, and continued relentless in spite of my assertion that I loved to go in directly after another man.

'Wretched spying beast,' she hissed between her clenched teeth.

Turning on my heel with a cynical observation that I thought in her case the Eastern girdle of chastity would be very useful to her lord, I left her to her own reflections, resolving in my own mind that, as my father's place was so well filled by his butler, it was no longer necessary for his son to try to compensate his fiery mistress for that which he could only administer in insufficient doses, not enough to satisfy the craving appetite of his fair protégée.

I now renewed my application to my professional studies, succeeding in effecting several cures in cases of importance, where the remedies applied by many eminent members of the art of healing had failed.

Among my patients, some of whose cases were successfully treated by means of a rather novel expedient, were two sisters, the daughters of a gentleman of property in the town, the particulars regarding whom are, I consider, of sufficient interest to be related in the next chapter.

CHAPTER THREE

It is one of the requirements of society that the feminine portion of it should wear, at least to outward gaze, the semblance of virtue; yet there is nothing in female human nature which is more difficult to adhere to.

Among the males, society tolerates vice of all kinds, which does not actually bring the perpetrator within the pale of the law; but with woman, one false step—nay, the very breath of slander—is sufficient to cast her, a degraded being, without the pale of its magic circle.

Can we picture a more pitiable position than that of a young woman, in the prime of her youth and beauty, condemned to await in silence the advance of the opposite sex, with the knowledge that the person whom she is prevailed upon at last to accept may, after all, turn out to be an impostor, totally disqualified for performing those functions that are necessary to the happiness of married life.

We medical men are not ignorant of the secret pangs and unruly desires that consume the bashful virgin, and that society with its ordinances prevents her from finding a safe vent for. We have often the means of tracing all the passionate thoughts, and sometimes the secret wanton doings, of those whom kind society has condemned to disease, rather than to allow nature to take its own proper course and allay those symptoms so detrimental to young girls.

Who shall say how many victims have been sacrificed on the altar of mock modesty for fear that the disgrace of the only natural cure for their complaint should blast their characters?

I have alluded to the circumstances which have come to my knowledge from time to time, with reference to the expedients made use of to allay those raging fires which in too many cases prematurely exhaust the constitutions of our young women; and one of these cases will suffice to prove how ingenious are the designs to cheat society of its whimsical requirements.

A young lady, not yet eighteen years of age, was under my care for a complaint of the bladder, in which the symptoms denoted the presence of calculus, or stone. An operation became necessary, which the patient underwent with unexampled fortitude.

I could not conceal a suspicion from the first that the young girl could, if she choose, enlighten us to the nature of the case; but strange to say, she absolutely preferred to submit to a painful and dangerous operation, with the knowledge that death might possibly ensue, rather than render us any information which might lead to a correct conclusion.

The operation was performed successfully. A mass of calculus was removed, and as these formations never take place without something to build up a 'nucleus,' we began to search.

We recommended the usual examination, only to discover that the formation had for its nucleus a hairpin, which must have been introduced by the fair hands of the young patient herself, doubtless not without a sufficient covering to render the insertion tolerably agreeable.

The result was that the inexperienced girl had allowed the hairpin to become disengaged, and instead of getting into the entrance she had intended, it had slipped into the urethra, and thence into the bladder, from whence the very nature of its shape had prevented its returning.

This instance is only one of a number I could give my readers, illustrative of the shifts young ladies are frequently driven to in order to satisfy, in secret and by illicit means those desires which they are prevented from openly exhibiting and which they dare not appease by nature's only fit and proper remedy, connection with the other sex.

I have promised in these pages a faithful recital of events that, having befallen me, have left a sufficiently warm interest in their remembrance to entitle them to a place here; and true to this promise I am about to relate my adventure in the case of the sisters before alluded to.

As I have already stated, they were daughters of an opulent resident in the town. They both inherited the pretty face and elegant form of their mother, who, when they were quite children, had committed them in her last hours to their father's paternal regard.

I was the medical attendant of the family, and as such it fell to me to be depository of such little complaints as these two young beauties had to make.

At the time I write, the elder was just sixteen and her sister not yet fifteen.

I had of late observed in the older those usual indications of approaching puberty that disturb the imagination of young girls, and I knew from her symptoms that nature was working powerfully within her to establish her claim to be treated as a woman.

One day on calling, I found that Mr H—— had gone out hunting, and would not return until late in the evening. It was then four o'clock in the afternoon of a hot and close summer day. The two young creatures were alone, and received me with the modest grace so captivating to a young man.

I stood and chatted until the time for paying my other visits had passed, and as none of them were pressing and could as well be paid the following day, I remained to tea.

After tea the younger of the two girls complained of headache, and after a little while she went upstairs to lie down, leaving her sister to sustain the conversation.

I played the agreeable with all my powers of attraction. I gazed on her with longing eyes. My looks followed every movement of her body, and my wandering fancy drew an exquisite picture of all her concealed beauties.

Gradually love grew into ardent desire—a desire so strong that I had some difficulty to keep my seat, while my rampant member stood beneath my trousers with the strength of a bar of iron.

Each moment only served to increase my fever, while I fancied I observed an embarrassment on her part, which seemed to hint that she was not ignorant of the storm that raged within me. Innocent as she was, and all inexperienced in the ways of the world, nature stirred within her powerfully and doubtless whispered that there was some hidden fascination in my gaze, something wanting to content her.

At length, tea things were sent away, and I could find no reasonable excuse to linger longer by the beautiful being who had so fiercely tempted me.

I rose to go. She rose also. As she did so, a certain uneasiness in her manner assured me that she had something to communicate. I asked her if she felt unwell, pretending that I observed an unusual paleness on her lovely face.

She said she had something to tell me, and

proceeded to detail the usual symptoms of a first perception of the menses, which had occurred a few days previously and which had at first much alarmed her.

I reassured her on this subject, explained the cause, and promised relief. And on taking my departure I requested her to come to my house on the following day, and said I would then investigate her case.

With what impatience I passed the interval may be easily imagined by any of my readers who have been similarly situated. But as the longest night must have at length an end, so did this, and morning broke to dispel the restless dreams of unruly passion that had held me enthralled.

I anxiously awaited the time of my young patient's arrival, and my heart danced with joy as I heard her timid knock at my street door.

She entered—heavens! how my prick stood—how beautiful she looked.

I stand even now when I think of that sweet vision.

Over a plain skirt of black silk she wore a mantle, such as becomes young ladies, with a neat little bonnet. Pale kid gloves set off her exquisite little hands, and I noticed that her feet were encased in boots any lady might have envied.

I hastened to make her take a seat in my study. I entered fully into the particulars of her case. I found, as expected, that she was experiencing the full force of those sensations which were never intended to be borne without relief, a relief I was panting to administer.

I told her of the cause of her own symptoms. I gradually explained their effects and, without shocking her modesty, I contrived to hint at the remedy.

I saw she trembled as I did so, and fearful of over-reaching my purpose, I broke off into a warm condemnation of that state of society that allowed such complaints to blast in secret the youth and beauty of young girls like herself.

I went on to hint at the evident necessity there was for the medical man to supply those deficiencies that society left in the education of young ladies.

I spoke of the honourable faith they maintained in such cases, and of the impossibility of anything entrusted to them ever becoming known.

I saw that she was so innocent as to be ignorant of my purpose, and burning with lust, I determined to take advantage of her inexperience, and to be the first to teach her that intoxicating lesson of pleasure which, like all roses, is not plucked without a thorn.

I gradually drew near her. I touched her—she trembled. I passed an arm around her slender waist; the contact literally maddened me. I proceeded to liberties that to a more experienced girl could have left no doubt of my intention.

Upon her my touches had only the effect of exciting more strongly within her breast those sensations of which she already complained.

I was now fairly borne away by my passions, and throwing my arms round the innocent beauty, I covered her face and neck with fierce and humid kisses.

She appeared to be overcome by her feelings, and seizing the moment, I lifted her like a child from her chair and placed her on a couch. I removed her bonnet and without meeting with any resistance from my victim, for contending emotion had rendered her all but senseless.

I carefully raised up her clothes. As I proceeded, I unveiled beauties enough to bring the dead to life, and losing all regard for delicacy, I threw them over the bosom of the sweet girl. Oh, heavens! what a sight met my gaze as, slightly struggling to escape from my grasp, she disclosed fresh secrets.

Everything now lay bare before me—her mossy recess, shaded by only the slightest silky down, presented to my view two full pouting lips of coral hue, while the rich swell of her lovely thighs served still further to inflame me.

I could gaze no longer. Hiding her face with the upturned clothes, I hastily unbuttoned my trousers. Out flew my glowing prick, standing like a Carmelite's. I sank upon her body; she heaved and panted with grave terror. I brought my member close to the lips. I pushed forward, and as I did so, I opened with my trembling fingers the soft folds of her cunt.

I repeated my thrusts. Oh, heavens! how shall I describe what followed? I gained a penetration. I was completely within the body of the dear girl.

I sank upon her, almost fainting with delight, my prick panting and throbbing in her belly. Oh, the ineffable bliss of that encounter. My pen trembles as I revert to the scene.

What followed, I scarcely know. I pushed again and again, until I felt myself getting dangerously near the crisis.

I observed her soft and still gloved hand beside the couch; I seized it, and covered it with kisses.

Heavens! what fire ran through me. I burned; I was on the point of spending.

Not unmindful of her reputation, even at that intoxicating moment when I felt the approach of the blissful moment of emission, with fear I thrust once more. My prick seemed to traverse the full extent of her belly.

Then, groaning in the agony of rapture, I drew out my bursting member, and falling prone upon her, I drenched her little stomach and thighs with an almost supernatural flood of sperm.

I lay for some time so utterly overcome with the intensity of my feelings that I could only close my eyes and press the dear girl to my breast.

At length I rose; carefully removing the reeking trace of victory, I adjusted the tumbled clothes of my companion, and taking her tenderly in my arms, I placed her in an easy chair.

I shall not attempt to describe all the degrees she went through before she came finally to herself and to a full knowledge of her complete womanhood. That she never blamed me for the part I had acted was the best guarantee that she had not regretted the accomplishment of my pleasing conquest.

On recovering from the confusion and dismay consequent upon the event I have just narrated, my fair patient lost none of her volubility, but talked away on the subject of our recent encounter, and asked so many questions that I had hardly time to reply to them ere she puzzled me with fresh ones.

Before she left me, I had initiated her into the exact proportions and nature of that potent invader whose attack she had so lately sustained.

The handling to which my prick was now subjected in no way reduced its desire for a second engagement, but a consideration for the delicate state of my new-made disciple, and the tender condition which I knew her very little privates must be in, induced me reluctantly to postpone any further attempt, and she departed from my house, if not a maid, yet a perfect woman.

CHAPTER FOUR

Nothing could exceed the caution with which we concealed our secret enjoyments from every jealous eye, and yet I trembled lest my indiscretion should become known.

There was only one thing for which we both panted, and that seemed too dangerous to be put into execution. Julia had often received the entire length of my large member in her little cunt, but that was the sum total of our bliss; to emit there was more than I dared.

Several weeks had elapsed since the commencement of our intercourse, and during that period I had been unremitting in my attentions to the youthful charms of my new acquisition.

She pined for the enjoyment, but I knew the risk of indulging her in her desires.

Fear of getting her with child was with me always paramount, for although as a medical man I might have enabled her to get rid of the burden before maturity, yet I was alive to the dangers attendant on so serious an undertaking.

One day, as with many sighs and much regret on both sides we proposed to omit the most usual way of finishing the performance of the Cyprian rites, Julia gave vent.

Julia, worked up almost to frenzy by the sweet friction, refused to permit my withdrawal, and throwing her arms round my loins, she finally detained me, while with wanton heaves and every exertion in her power, she endeavoured to bring me to the spending point.

I was alarmed for safety, and vainly struggling to free my rampant prick from the warm, sticking folds that environed it.

The more I struggled, the closer she held me, and the closer I drew to the dreaded moment, the more she exerted herself to produce the feared emission.

'Stop, stop,' I cried. 'Julia, my darling girl, I shall do it, I know I shall. Oh!'

I could say no more, but with a violent drive forward I sank, spending on her belly; my prick fairly buried in her up to the hair, the semen spouting from me in torrents.

As for my wanton companion, she threw back her head, and received the dangerous fluid with as much enjoyment as if it were herself who was trembling in the rapturous agony of its emission.

Trembling in every limb, as much from the fear of the result as from the excitement of the act, I rose and helped the tender Julia to her feet.

As she got up, a heavy pattering sound announced the return of the fluid, which ran in large drops upon the carpet and ran in rills down her beautiful thighs.

A few days after this affair we were diverting ourselves with sundry little freedoms one toward the other, when Julia, seizing my prick in her soft, white, little hand, threw herself upon the sofa and, drawing me to her, commenced to kiss and toy with my member. This, as may be supposed, afforded me considerable pleasure, and I let her do what she pleased, wondering all the time what her next gambol would be.

From kissing she took to sucking, and this delicious

touch of drawing lips soon inflamed me beyond all restraint.

Again she took it between her lips, and holding the loose skin tightly in her grasp, she made her hand pass rapidly up and down the huge white shaft until, heated to the utmost and almost spending, I jerked it out of her grasp.

'Ah, my lad, you were afraid it would come out, were you?'

I replied that I was only just in time to prevent it, upon which with a laugh and a smack on the ticklish part in question, she exclaimed: 'Well, then, my fine fellow, we shall see what we can make out of that large round head of yours.'

Then, suiting the action to the word, she again commenced the agreeable titillation, until with nerves strained to the utmost pitch of luxurious excitement, I felt the approach of that rapturous ejaculation. Jutting out my member before me, I heaved my buttocks up and down, and with a few motions of her hand Julia fairly brought me to the emitting point.

With a sigh of heavenly enjoyment I let fly the hot gushes of sperm on her bosom, while her fair hand, retaining hold of my throbbing prick, received a copious flood upon its dainty surface.

After this we would frequently lie down together on the soft hearthrug and, each with a caressing hand on prick and cunt, produce in one another those delightful effects which, say what people will, give a spur to the passions no man our woman can resist.

We would operate on each other in this way until prudence compelled us to stop for fear of the concluding overflow, and then, waiting for a few minutes, would once more bring our senses to the verge of the impending flood.

These hours were wiled away until a serious cause of anxiety arose to put an end to our security.

As I had feared, Julia proved with child; how could she be otherwise, with such an opportunity?

As soon as she made me acquainted with the fact, I prescribed for her, but without effect. The prolific juice had taken firm hold, and nature was progressing in the formation of the little squalling consequence of our amour.

My anxiety was now intense lest the discovery I saw impending should, in spite of our endeavours, overwhelm us.

Under these circumstances I determined to take a resolute course. I operated on my little Julia. I succeeded. I brought away the fetus, and removed with it all danger of discovery.

The result was not so favourable with regard to the health of my patient. Our overheated passions had put an end to youth's dream of uninterrupted enjoyment in a continual round of sensual pleasure, and Julia had now to reap the harvest of her indiscretion. She soon fell into a weak state of health, and I recommended immediate change of air.

Her father, alarmed at her indisposition, took her to Baden, and after a residence of some months there, the roses again revisited her cheeks.

At Baden she was greatly admired, and soon received an offer for her hand, which her prudent father did not feel justified in refusing; she became the wife of a Russian prince, who, if he did not get with her that unsatisfactory jewel, her maidenhead, at least became possessed of a cunt well practised in all the arts of love and lechery.

Thus terminated my amour with one of the most agreeable and most salacious girls I have ever known, and my prick still stands at the recollection of the various luscious scenes in which we were mutually carried away by the violence of lust in its most enticing form.

CHAPTER FIVE

I now gave myself up with reserve to the pleasure of love.

All my patients who showed the least susceptibility were overcome by my potent argument, and vigorously fucked.

I varied my pleasures in every possible way. Nothing that could enhance the enjoyment did I scruple to call into action. I fucked. I kissed. I sucked. I underwent all these operations myself, and I found a delicious retreat between the buttocks of one of my fairest patients. I hesitate not to own it. I penetrated those regions intended by nature for further purposes, and I declare that the pleasure I derived was proportionally as great as the act itself was indecent.

I became a lover of this mode of dalliance and never spent with so much relish and impetuosity as in the beautiful bottom of a fair woman.

And it must be owned that these parts themselves are wonderfully well adapted for the purpose. The natural construction of the entrance, the soft interior, and the length to which they are capable of receiving the longest male member, render the art unique; while the fiery heat experienced by the operator and the accumulation of delicious sensations produce in their turn a stiffness, a vigour, and an enjoyment without parallel.

One of our greatest poets, he whom no censor, no authority could debase to mere conventualism, extols in his own fervent, gloomy strains the much forbidden pleasure:

> Oh, lovely woman, by your maker's hand,
> For man's delight and solace wisely planned;
> Thankless is she who nature's bounty mocks,
> Nor gives love entrance wheresoe'er he knocks.

A considerable portion of my pleasure consisted in reading and showing to others curious amorous works. Of these I possessed a large collection. Several of them were in themselves a budget of exciting literature of a rare and costly description.

One of them was the celebrated work of the Marquis de Sade, over which it is said that extraordinary man went out of his mind.

I allude to *Justine*, and if the quintessence of sexual excitement and glowing scenes that beggar description can be productive of sufficient effect to produce such a result, even to the author himself, this rare and fearful work is certainly the one capable of doing so. The wonderful descriptions it contains, the fiercely exciting scenes it depicts, and the exhibition of so many varied means of producing the acme of enjoyment, render it no less valuable for its deep effectual influence over the passions than for its deep philosophy and wonderful power of reasoning which stamp it as the work of a genius of extraordinary talent.

Satiety, that enemy to the indulgence of the soft enjoyment, now attacked me; I wanted a change. My powers were naturally great, my health robust. My member became sick of sliding in and out of places so often visited and in which it had so frequently left his tears of gratitude.

I longed for a ripe young beauty to caress, to lie with, to suck. I found a lovely little girl of sixteen years of age who had been under my care for a spinal affliction, in the treatment of which complaint I had been for a long time acknowledged a successful practitioner.

She had been an inmate of my house in order to be more fully under my care. Her friends were resident in another county, and had such confidence in my discretion that I believe had I even proposed to have slept with their neice, they would have thought it was only a part of my system.

Mary had been with me about a week, when I found so much pleasure in her society that I began to feel a curious sensation about the region of my privates on beholding and listening to her sometimes of an evening.

I made her sometimes sit with me by the fire, when I would place her on my knee, so that her sweet little bottom would be immediately over my stiffened member, which by its throbbing and jerks caused her to sit rather uneasily, and thereby induced a gentle friction that was highly agreeable to me.

One evening, having been more than a week without food for my passions, which were becoming riotous, I could restrain myself no longer. I began to play and romp with my companion in such a manner that I frequently had my hand on her naked knee, and even once or twice on her thigh.

Her flesh felt soft and warm, and my desires began to master my reason. I tried further advances, taking care not to startle the innocent girl out of her confidence in me.

By degrees, under the pretense of tickling her to excite her laughter, I reached the goal of my desires. My hand—the tip of my fingers only—touched her pouting, beardless cunt. A thrill shot through me at the contact. It was as soft as her damask cheek, and the warmth of its velvet skin sent fire through my veins.

I now endeavoured to advance, but she held her legs firmly together, apparently not altogether relishing the tickling sensation my intrusion produced.

She was an excitable girl, however, and soon, by suddenly pretending to throw her backward, I got her to open her legs. And then, oh! how I stand when I even refer to it. I placed my smooth fingers in the open slit; it was as moist as the interior of her lovely mouth, and the opening was small and apparently intact.

My readers may wonder perhaps at the above remark, but my experience has shown me that in very many cases young girls, long before they reach the age of sixteen, cannot strictly be said to be possessed of a perfect maidenhead.

The cause is this. What with the early efforts prompted by nature to break through the restraints she has herself placed in that tender spot—by the self-introduction of their fingers and other, inanimate objects, and the effects of the society and even the bed-fellowship of boys—young girls on reaching puberty are seldom possessed of the imaginary jewel in its full perfection, at least so far as regards the lower and the middle classes of society.

But to return to myself and my playmate:

When she found my hand in possession of what she had no idea of the use of, she tried all in her power to disengage herself, but I took care her struggles should be unavailing, and at length she laughingly ceased them.

I now roamed over her charms at leisure, but my prick was up, my boiling point was reached, and I cautiously laid her lengthwise on the sofa and, getting on her, pulled out my stiff-standing member. Moistening it well with saliva, I put it to the tender orifice and pushed.

Up to this time my young companion had no idea of my intention, and wonderingly submitted to my caresses. She now felt the painful pressure I was causing with the large head of my prick, and would have diverted my attack but that I kept her steady with my left arm round her waist.

Again and again I attempted the entrance. I was foiled, until suddenly a squirt of sperm came to my assistance. Once more trying the now moistened barrier, the head of my prick went gradually in as far as its junction with the shaft. There it stuck, and my excitement being now at its height, I spent. The hot, thick fluid escaped from me in streams, and inundated the soft and stretched interior of her plump belly.

During the emission I gained about another inch, but no more, and only at the expense of much pain to my youthful mistress.

In the course of the following day I repeated my attempts upon Mary's little fortress, and at length demolished her natural defenses, and plunged the whole length of my machine into her vagina. The enjoyment was extreme, and the tightness of her little unshaded cunt soon brought on a most plentiful shower of semen, which I freely poured into her.

Mary, once her passion had been thoroughly aroused, proved to be most lasciviously inclined. For fear of injuring her back or putting a dangerous strain upon her tender spine, I made her lie as still as possible, which position was delightful to me to stir up her vitals by the gentle movements of my big prick, which would quickly come to the crisis of emission, so deliciously tight did her little cunt cling round its ruby head.

She was one of the most apt pupils I ever had in

the art of gamahuching. We used to do the double, both of us stripped perfectly naked on her bed (this was only done when I visited her in her room, after my household had all retired for the night); then she would reverse her position and lie over me, burying my face between her thighs whilst I returned the attentions she so delightfully bestowed on my prick, by sucking and tongue-fucking both her pink little cunt and her rosy, wrinkled, little bottomhole, until she spent over and over again in my mouth, each pearly drop as precious to me as the most veritable elixir of life, for streams of sperm literally spouted from my prick in response to these proofs of her ardent enjoyment. How she sucked my prick first, and then cuddled it between her throbbing titties, till it came again! What transports of ecstasy seemed to carry us both away it is impossible to describe in these pages.

She told me that she longed to feel me move within her with all the furious energy of which she knew I was so capable; that her having to keep still, and my gentle movements when I fucked her, only seemed to excite without giving her that full satisfaction that she instinctively felt could only be obtained by giving full licence to all our desires by a perfect abandon of voluptuousness in those ecstatic conjunctions of which I had hitherto so imperfectly given her an idea, of the heavenly joys she yet anticipated to receive in my arms; adding that she had most enjoyed it when I completed her ravishment on the second day of my attempt, and that although she had actually fainted under the excruciating pain caused by the entrance of my big affair into her tight little cunny, yet in her trance-like swoon she had experienced such supernatural pleasure as she had never felt since.

'Do, darling,' she added, 'fuck me with real energy, if only for once; do let me feel what the ecstasies of sexual conjunction are really like; let me die of love for once, if I am never able to bear it again. You know the complaint, my spinal affliction, will never let me recover sufficiently to be married.'

Thus appealed to by the loving Mary, I consented to fuck her properly, but only on one condition—that she allow me to tie her facedown over the couch in my surgery, so that I might give her every possible satisfaction by my own movements, and yet be sure that she would not injure herself by twisting about, as I knew that otherwise in the abandon of her ecstasy she would be almost certain to do.

The next afternoon, just as I was certain all the morning calls were over, and was looking over my notes to see what visits I had to pay, a gentle tap at the surgery door reminded me of my promise to Mary.

She entered, saying with a most bewitching smile on her usually pensive face: 'Now sir, I mean to keep you to your word; do you think I will let you go round and fuck half a dozen of your lady patients first? Why there would be nothing left for poor Mary. I want every drop of that life-giving fluid; if I die, you shall be as dry as a stone before you go out today.'

My time was really precious, but there was no gainsaying the darling, so after many preliminary kisses and endearing touches, I first locked the door. Then we both divested ourselves of everything we had on. My impediments were only dressing gown and trousers, whilst Mary was also in equally light marching order.

The couch I proposed to lay her down upon was a veritable battleground of Venus, having been made for my special use, according to ideas that I furnished to my upholsterer; and could my readers but have the experience of that sofa, instead of this partial scrawl, they would indeed have a repletion of luscious adventures, *ad nauseam*.

To return to my tale, this couch was very wide, with no back, and a scroll-head at one end, whilst what would be considered the foot was half-moon-shaped, so that when a bottom or a pretty cunt was exposed to my attack, I could stand well between the open legs of my fair patient and administer my natural clyster with the greatest possible ease to myself, either standing or kneeling on a hassock.

This couch had a most beautiful springy motion when under a pair of lively lovers, being constructed with a special eye to luxurious effect, and it had also screws at each end and in the centre, so that I could elevate the head, bottom, or body of my patient to suit the ideas to be carried out.

Mary was all docility, and quietly placed herself on her belly upon this throne of love; using silken cords to secure her by the wrists and ankles, I then finished the tying by firmly fastening her body down by means of a long sash passed under the sofa and over her back.

'Now, my darling, you are completely at my mercy!' I exclaimed with a laugh. 'I think I ought to birch* that naughty little bottom for you, but instead of that I will kiss it.'

Kneeling down, I adjusted the height of her delicious little cunt till it was exactly opposite my eager lips, so also was that ravishing little wrinkled orifice which nature placed so close to it that it is

---

* I used this couch sometimes to tie down and flagellate several of my old male patients, whose early excesses had made them too used up for the sport of love, and could only enjoy the pleasures of emission under the stimulating effects of the rod. It was one of the most lucrative branches of my profession.

impossible not to believe it ought to have its due share of attention from both prick and mouth.

She was already spending in anticipation. My tongue revelled in that creamy emission till she was almost beside herself, and actually screamed for me to let her have my prick.

'Oh! Oh! darling, I must have the real thing at once. Oh, don't tantalize me so, dearest!'

But that was not my intention at the moment. I wanted an even more luscious enjoyment—to take her second maidenhead, in fact. Leaving her delicious cunt, my tongue titillated that other rosy aperture till she was almost mad, her appeals for satisfaction were getting quite piteous.

'May I go in here then, darling?' I asked. 'You will find that it surpasses anything you can imagine, love.'

'Yes, oh, yes, anywhere; kill me, if you like, but make me feel that ineffable pleasure that I know only a prick can give; you drive me wild!'

Cold cream was handy on the table, so lubricating the entrance well, as well as the head of my pego, my rather big prick effected an entrance much more easily than it had the first time I tried to ravish her cunt. Her face was turned round toward me, and I could see tears of pain start to her eyes as I gradually pushed past the sphincter muscle; but then easing for a moment or two, I began slowly to move within the delicious sheath, which held my affair so tightly clasped within its folds and throbbed so convulsively upon my delighted instrument that I could not refrain from spending, making her actually scream with delight as the warm balsam of love seemed to penetrate her very vitals.

'How I burn, how deliciously warm! And it makes me spend more than ever. Oh! oh! frig me in front, dearest, don't let us lose an atom of such heavenly pleasure!'

It would weary my readers too much to repeat all our loving exclamations during this long and ecstatic bottom-fuck, but I will merely say that at the end of about half an hour, and after I had spent at least six times without withdrawing, we both actually fainted from excess of emotion, which finished our fun for that day, but it is needless to say that the performance was afterward repeatedly given, by special request of my loving Mary.

In conclusion I may say that if the last incident appears in any way incredible, or if my reader wishes himself to taste of this fresh source of excitement, a line to the author, undercover to the agent from whom this work was procured, will enable him to convince himself by means of practical proof beyond the power of the most incredulous to doubt.

Another extraordinary thing I ought to mention is that the fucking had such a salubrious effect upon my young patient that she eventually quite got the better of her spinal complaint, and was married at the age of twenty but although apparently well and strong, she never had any children.

A curious incident befell me soon after losing Mary. I had been very virtuous for a week or two, in order to recover my usual vigour after the unreasonable requirements that my late patient had exacted from me before she left the shelter of my roof. John Thomas was quite resuscitated by his rest, and I was already casting my eyes around for fresh food for my convent (being a strict bachelor with only an old housekeeper and a very ugly middle-aged woman as servant), when one evening in early spring, a little after dark, I was sitting in my easy chair in the surgery, in a state of revery, my brain revolving all the luscious scenes of my experience, my prick at the moment actually at full cock, and almost ready to go off as I thought of how I had tied Mary down on my couch and ravished her second maidenhead.

A desperate ring at the little bell and a heavy rat-a-tat-tat on the small knocker made me almost jump from my seat. The room was in darkness, but I opened the door quickly, and a female figure rushed in and, stumbling against that mystical sofa, sank upon it sobbing, as if her heart would break. 'I'm undone. Oh! Oh! Oh!!! Doctor. What shall I do, I can't go home!'

My first idea was to light my lamp; then drawing the bolt, I approached the weeping person on the sofa, who I saw at once had evidently been roughly handled, as her dress was torn and patched with dirt in places.

'Come, tell me what it is; who are you, let me see your face. Surely you can trust your doctor if no one else; you are not killed, and apparently only a bit troubled about something; allow me.'

Saying this, I raised her face to see who it was.

'Goodness gracious, it is you, Miss Lover? Now, tell me all; you can confide in me sooner than your own papa, for I know the rector is very straitlaced!'

It was indeed our clergyman's only daughter, a sweet young lady of about twenty whom I had always considered quite beyond the pale of my operations, and a paragon of purity itself.

'I'm undone,' she sobbed. 'Oh, dear doctor, what shall I do?' she said again as she wrung her hands and floods of briny tears coursed down her crimson cheeks.

At last I calmed her a little, and gave her a drop of cordial; then she began to tell me, sobbing all the while, how she was secretly engaged to young

Pomeroy, the squire's son, because his father would never sanction his son's marrying without money. 'You know, doctor, my poor pa has only his living to depend upon, although he is proud and thinks anyone in holy orders quite equal to the highest in the land. Well, this evening I met George in the lane at the back of your house, and he persuaded me to sit down in the little coppice in your paddock, so as to be out of hearing of anyone going down the lane. He wanted me to elope with him, and at last, when every argument failed to persuade me, said he would have me then, if he was hanged for it; how I have struggled you may see, but at last I fainted from mere exhaustion, and only came to myself to find I had been ruined, and that he had left me. I suppose he thought I was dead.'

She still went on sobbing about his brutality and the ruin he had brought upon her.

At last I persuaded her to allow me to make an examination, and found that he really had effected his purpose, the hymen being broken and bleeding, and her thighs stained with bloody semen.

'Let me advise, you, my dear young lady,' I said, rising from the interesting investigation which you may be sure renewed my previous cock-stand, 'let me advise you to go home as quietly as possible; I will call my housekeeper, who is discretion itself, and she will put you right, so that no one will notice anything unusual; then you shall have a lotion to soothe the lacerated parts, and come again and see me about five o'clock tomorrow afternoon. I will do even better than your father for you, and perhaps can see George and make him do what is proper. But take my advice, it is no use crying over spilt milk, and time and patience will bring all right in the end. At any rate I will promise to shield you from any ill effects of his brutality that might otherwise bring you to shame and disgrace.'

She left protesting her everlasting gratitude for all my kindness, and begged me if possible to see George in the morning. I tried to do so, but found he had not been home all night, and had evidently absconded, as he thought he had killed Miss Lover.

I awaited her coming at five o'clock in a state of excited expectation, and as I nervously walked about my little surgery, kept fumbling a very mysterious something in my pocket (not my prick, but my readers may find out what it was bye and bye), which would impart a magic influence to my fingers, so that when I repeated my examination and handled the lips of her cunt and her clitoris the effect would be so exciting that she would be ready to let me do anything to soothe her at once.

She arrived within a few minutes of the appointed time. How she blushed as I shook her hand and told her she looked as beautiful as an angel and that I would do everything in my power to shield her from harm or disgrace.

'Now, take off your hat, and allow me to inspect the damage again, my dear young lady,' I said, making her take a seat upon the couch.

'It's so delicate, but I suppose I must. Besides, you know all, and will keep my secret, won't you, doctor?' she said in a low voice, crimsoning again to the roots of her hair.

'Certainly. Have no fear of that. But you must remove your skirt, my dear young lady, or I cannot do what is necessary in your delicate case.'

She reluctantly complied; then I made her lie back-ward on the couch and open her legs as wide as poss-ible, as at the same time I screwed up the lower end of the sofa. Then, proceeding with my examination,

I fingered the lips of the vagina and passed my fingers quite up into her deliciously tight cunt, which was ornamented with a profusion of silky, dark brown hair, between which could be seen a pair of vermilion lips, pouting as if ready to be kissed or parted by a roving prick.

My touches were magical; the vagina spasmodically contracted on my fingers, and I could see she could scarcely restrain her feelings.

'My dear Miss Lover, I'm afraid you may have a baby after such an outrage,' I said, 'and the only remedy I can suggest is that another man should do the same to you at once, for one will then undo any mischief left behind by the other.'

'Doctor, doctor, how awful!' she sobbed. 'I would rather poison myself to hide my shame; it is impossible.'

'Not quite so hopeless as you may think, my dear young lady; this is the antidote, if you will let me insert it in your lovely body,' I said, at the same instant bringing the head of my prick to the lips of that lovely cunt of hers. Her position had prevented her from seeing what I was about.

This touch seemed electrical; she gave a deep sigh, and I was soon buried to the hilt in what I once more thought the most delightful grotto of love I had ever yet entered (but almost every fresh cunt is the same at first); so warm, so tight, such lascivious pressures on my prick, that I kept still for some minutes to enjoy that sweet sense of possession, when you first feel really sure that you are actually in a cunt you have been longing for. When I began to move, it at once stirred up all the hitherto latent fires of an unusually warm temperament. What mutual transports we enjoyed, swimming in a perfect sea of lubricity; she could never have enough, and I was fairly drained when at last she released me from her arms and shed tears of remorse over her newfound joy, which she told me she knew was so wicked to indulge in.

My readers may be sure my natural flow of eloquence did not desert me at such a crisis, and I can assure them that I made a thorough convert of this virtuous and highly religious young lady, who carried on one of the sweetest liaisons of my life for three years, till old Squire Pomeroy died, and his son George came back and married the rector's daughter.

In the foregoing incident I mentioned about fumbling something in my pocket as I walked about the room, and to enlighten my readers as to what that mysterious article was, I will relate a little incident which had then only recently occurred to me.

We had a wealthy horse-dealer named Parker in our village, whose son John got married to one of the prettiest girls in the place; well, a few days after the wedding, poor John, a regular country-bumpkin, came to me one morning in sad trouble. 'What be I to do now, Doctor, my wife Carry don't go to horse at all, zur?'

These were his exact words as he stood despondently wiping his forehead with a red cotton handkerchief.

I had often cured John of little venereal evils, especially after he had been to London on business. As he was a rare fellow to spend his money on the girls, so I could not help fairly laughing at his question.

However, he was serious, and informed me that Carry certainly had suffered him to take her maidenhead, but that there was no pleasure in it then or since like he had had with common women, and, in fact, his wife was as cold as ice, merely consenting to let him do it because he was her husband.

I thought the case over for a minute or two, and then told him I thought that if I made an examination I might slyly apply something to make her randy and ready enough to take his prick in future.

'I'm good for a tenner, zur, if you can just make her go to horse a bit, the stallion's up to his work, I know.' Saying which, he took his leave, promising to send her to me in the afternoon.

The fact of his being a horse-dealer had given me an idea about ginger, and also made my cock stand, so that I was glad to see him go, for fear he should observe it and refuse to give me the chance of making him a cuckold.

Carry had always been a prude, so that when she called in the afternoon, I was almost at a loss how to open the business.

After saying how pleased I was to see her and how well she looked, I went on: 'You must not mind me speaking to you, dear Mrs Parker, seriously upon a subject that is of the greatest possible consequence to the future happiness of both yourself and your husband. In fact, he has seen me upon the subject of your being so cold and unsympathetic in the act of love—the act of coition, I ought rather to say—which, unless enjoyed and fully entered into by both male and female, causes so many separations, divorces, etc. Besides, you would have no children. How would you like John to go after other girls because he has no pleasure with you? It is such a serious business, that you ought to let me make an examination, as I hope to be able to make both of you grateful to me for the rest of your lives.'

After all sorts of objections and difficulties, she at last seated herself on the throne of bliss, as I called it (my sofa), and allowed me to raise her clothes. I did everything with the greatest possible delicacy, telling her she had better cover up her eyes. Then I examined most minutely one of the most delicious little cunts I had ever looked into, a beautiful, pinky little slit, shaded by the softest brown hair, with a delightful, little pink orifice beneath it. That was where my gingered fingers first touched her; then they slowly opened the luscious lips of her love-gap, squeezed the clitoris, and gently rubbed a little inside, till I perceived very evident sighs of rapidly increasing excitement. You may be sure my cock was ready enough, so I gently introduced him to Venus's wrinkle, and John's big tosser had so effectually opened her, that I had no great difficulty in slipping in, as she was already spending and almost unconscious from excess of emotion. I spent too almost directly (in fact, I afterwards found I really made her first baby), and then, throwing my arms around her, I glued my lips to hers as I pushed on, and asked if she did not like it now.

'Could you, my darling, now refuse such bliss?' I exclaimed, as I spent for a second time. 'You will go home and enjoy it with your husband in future, won't you?'

She kissed me in her frantic state of lubricity, and shed tears of sorrow to think she was John's wife, instead of mine, but as this was out of the question, she made the best of a bad job and called in my professional assistance upon every possible occasion, telling me to charge for it well in my bill, as John really owed me so much for teaching her the real joys of fucking.

Next morning her husband burst into my surgery. 'Hi, hi! Ha, ha!! Doctor, yer made her go to horse to rights now, thars yer tenner, and that's only a quid of time. Ten times, zur help me God, she helped herself, when I couldn't quite come to time. When yer want a good fuck, try ginger-boys, she told me, what yer put on her, what a fool not to think of't myself. But it's the best lot I ever had for my rhino, Lunnon, or anywhere!'

It is really surprising how many married women actually pass through life without ever feeling the great pleasure of coition. I consider that medical advisers ought to catechize young married ladies on the subject, and that it is their duty to enlighten the fair but cold innocents to the joys they lose by simply submitting to the marriage rites as a necessity, and not entering into the spirit of the fun.

In the foregoing pages I have endeavoured to give my readers a brief outline of my intrigues and adventures as far as they could be entered upon in so limited a space, and I can only say that if they enjoyed as many opportunities in their wanderings as have fallen to my share, they ought to have as lively a recollection of them as myself; for pleasure, though the actual indulgence of it vanishes, yet leaves the recollection ever vivid in the minds of those who have partaken of her sweet and luscious cup.